MW00883765

DREAMWALKER

RED DRAGON ACADEMY
BOOK 1

RHYS BOWEN & C.M. BROYLES

All rights reserved. This book may not be duplicated in any way without the express written consent of the author, except in the form of excerpts or quotations for the purposes of review. The information contained herein is for the personal use of the reader and may not be incorporated in any commercial programs or other books, databases, or any other kind of software without the written consent of the publisher or author. Making copies of this book, or any portion of it, for any purpose other than your own, is a violation of United States copyright laws.

Copyright © 2014 Rhys Bowen and C.M. Broyles

ISBN-13: 978-1503102057

Printed in the United States of America

Red Dragon Press

This is a work of fiction. Names, characters, places, and other incidents are either products of the writer's imagination or are used fictitiously and are not to be construed as real. Any resemblance to actual events, locales, organizations, or persons, living or dead, is entirely coincidental.

CONTENTS

INTRODUCTION

Rhys Bowen and C.M Broyles are a mother-daughter writing team who both love fantasy. Rhys Bowen is a New York Times Bestselling author of two adult mystery series, winner of multiple awards. She formerly wrote bestselling young adult novels under the name Janet Quin-Harkin. C.M. Broyles has degrees in music and literature and has written background music for plays (winning an Arizona Tony award), a children's opera and numerous songs. This is her first venture into prose.

DEDICATION

To our number one fans: Sam, Lizzie, Meghan, T.J. and Mary Clare.

PROLOGUE

I've never been so cold in my life! It's freezing up in this tower. The cold from the massive stone walls bites into my back as I sit here hugging my knees to myself. The turret room is pitch-black except for a sliver of moonlight coming in through the slits in the wall. Raj would probably tell me their name and that that they are where archers shoot their arrows, but Raj isn't here. I wish he was. The windows are overgrown with vines and they cast creepy shadows like long tentacles on the round tower wall. I can make out the shape of other kids sleeping on the floor. They are lying as far away as possible from Pippa and me because they're afraid of us.

A bone-chilling howl comes from the forest. I know what animal made that howl and wish I didn't. So a Rancur is close by and that must mean that the Fallon Gwyn are with it. They've come for us. I huddle closer to Pippa. She seems to be sleeping, in spite of the cold. I prod her and whisper, "Are you asleep?" and she only grunts. A boy is whimpering and moaning in his sleep. How can they sleep at a time like this? There is no way I'd allow myself to fall asleep tonight, even if I wasn't afraid of dreaming. I can't stop thinking about tomorrow and what horrible thing is going to happen to us. No one will say exactly what it is, but I can tell it's pretty bad.

For once I wish this was a dream, but I know it's very real.

Was it really only a month ago that I was an ordinary seventh grader in California, surfing and going to the mall with friends? I had nothing more to worry about than getting my homework done. Then my mom died. That messed me up so badly I don't know if

I'll ever be OK again, but that wasn't when the danger started. The danger started when I first walked down that dark hallway and found myself in this world that I don't understand. Or maybe earlier. Maybe it started when I arrived at crazy Red Dragon Academy. No – even that wasn't right. The danger started in my own living room when I saw the two old ladies. The danger started when I climbed onto the back of the red dragon.

I RIDE A DRAGON

I was kneeling on the window seat, watching a seagull soaring down over the redwood trees until it melted into the fog over the ocean. It was normally my favorite view, but today I was only concentrating on the seagull and wishing I could fly with it. To soar effortlessly like that bird and fly far enough away that it didn't hurt anymore. But I had no idea how far away that would be.

"You haven't been listening to a word I was saying, have you?" My aunt's snooty English voice snapped me back to reality. "Really, Addison, we have no time to waste. We have to catch that plane to London and the house has to be emptied before we go. Now please come and help."

I had tried to be polite to Aunt Jean, because she was my mother's sister, after all. But I couldn't keep it up much longer. "How would you feel if it was your stuff that was being dumped into garbage bags?" I demanded. "This is my life we're throwing away. All this stuff means something to me. You might call it junk, but I like it."

Aunt Jean's expression got a little kinder. "I'm sorry. I understand that this is hard for you. It's hard for me too, you know. Your mother was my only sister. But daydreaming is not going to help and the cleaning service will be here shortly, so anything you want to save needs to be packed up right away. And we must be on that plane to London tonight." And she started off again, moving round the room like a wind-up toy, her high-heels clacking on the hardwood floor. She was still dressed in her black suit from the funeral. The *clack clack* sound of her high-heels made the house sound empty in a way it never had when my mom lived here: even back in the days when we hardly had any furniture.

I watched her grab things and stuff them into bags without even looking at them twice and I decided I hated her. She didn't even look like she was related to me. I was a surfer girl with freckles and sun-streaked blond hair pulled back in a ponytail. And my eyes were gray. She had dark hair and brown eyes and she looked like she had just come out of a business meeting. In fact she always looked like one of those people you see on TV, talking about banks and the economy. Just as I was thinking this, her iPhone rang and she started yelling into it as she went on throwing things into boxes.

I tuned her out and turned back to the window, watching the fog curl among the redwood trees and suddenly there they were – two women looking up at me, wearing long green capes, standing on either side of a large red dragon. For a moment I couldn't believe what I was seeing. But then the dragon shook its head impatiently and a great burst of flame came out of its nostrils setting some dried leaves crackling on fire. And one of the women called up to me, "Well, are you going to come down? We are waiting for you."

I looked back at Aunt Jean, but she was still talking into her phone and didn't seem to have heard anything. "What do you mean, they can't deliver by the fourth? Of course they can. You better get on to Tokyo right away. Oh, and have you rescheduled my meeting in Shanghai for the 10th?"

I opened the front door and went down the steps. I didn't really expect that the women and the dragon would still be there. It didn't make any sense that I would see a dragon in the real world of iPhones and corporate aunts, but there they were standing among the trees. Well, the women were standing among the trees, the dragon was almost as big as the trees! The women's faces were hidden under their hoods but I could see their eyes sparkling. Their hands rested on the dragon's neck, one on either side, one black hand and one white hand.

"Ah, there you are," one woman said. I couldn't tell which one was talking. "We've found you at last."

"What are you, part of some kind of Renaissance fair? Or are you shooting a movie?" I asked. "Cool looking dragon. He almost looks real."

"Of course he's real. Come on, he's getting impatient." And she patted the dragon's neck, making him toss his head and shoot out another puff of smoke.

"Whoa." I jumped back as I felt the real heat of that breath.

"You want me to ride that?" That dragon was huge, and it was looking at me with bright yellow eyes while smoke still curled out of its nostrils.

"Of course. That's why we're here. We've come for you. On you get."

"Hey, no way—" I began. Then a weird thing happened. One minute I was standing on the wet grass, the next I was sitting on the dragon's back. I have no idea how I got up there, but I could feel the hard smoothness of the scales and the warmth of its fire through my jeans. And the ground looked a long way down. "What if I fall off?" I called down to the women. I tried to find something to hold on to.

"If you are meant to ride him he won't let you fall," one of them said. I still couldn't tell which one was speaking. "Go on now. We'll be waiting."

Then suddenly the dragon was lumbering forward across the grass. It took off with that great beating of wings—the noise of it sounding like the flapping of paper, or of sails on the ships down in the harbor. I flung my arms around the dragon's snake-like neck. It was too fat to wrap my arms all the way around. I slipped one way and then another. I screamed as my hands couldn't find a hold. Then we were up in the air and the dragon's back leveled out. I felt the wind in my hair and all of a sudden I felt like I had been doing this all my life. We flew across the lawn, up over the roof of my house, almost hitting the tops of the redwood trees until we soared up over the hills. White fog was beneath us with the glint of the blue ocean. When the fog finally lifted, we were flying over high, green mountains and far below I could see sheep on the hillsides, moving like little white dots. The cold wind in my face made my eyes water. I was still scared, but it was exciting, too. Then the dragon banked to one side and we were heading towards the ocean. Blue water stretched beneath us and I saw seagulls glide beneath us and smelled the salty tang of the sea.

Then, without warning, the dragon plunged down into a steep dive. I was thrown forward and tried to cling on. The sharp scales dug into my cheeks and arms as I tried to wrap my arms around the dragon's enormous neck. We kept falling and falling. The sea rushed up to meet us. "Hey, stop! Pull up! Pull up!" I screamed.

But the dragon ignored me. One second we were above the waves, the next we hit the water. The impact pushed me away from the dragon, tumbling and twisting in the freezing water as I went down. I looked up to see bright sunlight streaming down through the blue sea. Suddenly, I was calm, enjoying the feeling of floating suspended in another world. A shadow passed over my head. It was so big that the world around me went black. I could hear a voice calling in a language that I didn't understand. The voice seemed to be saying, "Come Reeham Beth."

As the shadow passed I saw an impossibly big shape looming through the blue water on my right and another on my left. One was directly beneath me. They were circling me, almost close enough to touch, but not quite. And they began to sing, their strange mournful song echoing through the depths.

"Whales!" I tried to say. I was surrounded by whales. Then I remembered I had to breathe. I kicked for the surface, brushing against one of the huge creatures and then another until finally my head came out into the air just in time to see an enormous tail slap the ocean beside me. The force of that slap threw me sideways and I bumped my head ... I opened my eyes and realized I was sitting up and leaning against a cold hard surface.

"Please fasten your seatbelts and put your chairs into the upright position as we begin our descent into London Heathrow Airport," a crisp English voice said.

I looked around me with my heart thumping. Outside the window the plane was descending into dark gray clouds, bumping and shuddering a little. For a minute I wondered what was real, the airplane or the ocean. Then my eyes began to focus and I saw my aunt's face in the light of her laptop screen. I remembered. We were on an airplane. I really was on my way to London with Aunt Jean. So was the dragon only a dream? It had seemed so incredibly real. That's one thing you should know about me if you are going to understand this story at all. I sometimes have trouble telling dreams from reality. My mom always said I was a little bit psychic. I knew that dreams could have something special to tell me - a message. I wondered what this one meant. Whales ... and dragons. Whatever it meant I kind of wished that the dream had been real and I was flying away from Aunt Jean as fast as I could. As if she heard me thinking about her, my aunt looked up. She sighed and put away her laptop. "Get your things together, Addison. We'll be landing soon."

I MEET A REDHEAD

A t any other time I'd have been so excited to see London. I had heard all about the old castles and palaces and art galleries from my mom. But all I could see from the taxi were tall gray buildings. It was raining too and people were huddled under umbrellas.

It had been raining when we left California and I closed my eyes wishing to be back there. 'When I open my eyes I will see redwood trees,' I thought. 'One, two, three.' But when I opened them I was still in a London taxi sitting beside a strange English aunt. The only splash of color in the gray world was a tall red London bus. I watched it pass us and suddenly I realized:

"Hey, it's driving on the wrong side of the road. That's what looked so weird. "

"We would call it the correct side of the road," Aunt Jean said her in snooty voice. "Don't forget that we had rules of the road before America was even colonized."

"Well, excuse me," I wanted to say, but I didn't want to push it.

'It's like a mirror world,' I thought. 'Maybe everything is opposite here in England.' Aunt Jean was definitely the opposite of my mom, who was easy going and loved to laugh. To tell you the truth, I had never felt comfortable with Aunt Jean. She'd come to visit a couple of times when she was in California on business and she had always made me nervous, the way she stared at me with those dark eyes while she fired questions at me. Mom told me she was a super important business executive and she always seemed to be dressed for a business meeting. And her face was so perfectly made up that I was sure it would crack if she smiled. She didn't smile, so the make-up stayed perfect. When I was little I asked my mom if Aunt Jean was a robot, not a person. Now I'd spent three days in her company, I was sure of it. Even at her own sister's funeral Aunt Jean hadn't cried. She had only looked slightly annoyed, as if she was wasting time and couldn't wait to get back to England and back to work. But then I hadn't cried either. I had made myself stare out of the church window at the trees blowing in the wind as people around me hugged me and cried. And I'd tried not to think about what might happen to me now.

I spotted a group of kids walking in twos along the sidewalk, dressed in funny old-fashioned uniforms and I thought of books I had read. "Hey, Aunt Jean, are those kids orphans?"

Aunt Jean looked up from her texting. "Good heavens no. They are ordinary school children."

"Ordinary children dress like that?"

"Naturally. All children in England wear uniform to school. The better the school, the stricter the uniform. What did you wear to school at home?"

"Whatever I liked. Jeans in the winter and shorts in the summer."

Aunt Jean made a clicking sound with her tongue. "I knew my sister would be a disaster as a mother. Far too free and easy. No sense of discipline at all."

I tried to bite my tongue but I couldn't stop myself. "She was a great mother," I said. Well, actually, I yelled. My aunt gave me a look and I tried to control my voice. "She brought me up to think for myself, not act like a robot. And she was kind and funny and – and I miss her." The last words came out as a big gulp and I stared out of the window so that Aunt Jean couldn't see me cry.

Aunt Jean cleared her throat. "Of course you do. I miss her, too. It's just that…. Never mind. You'll be fine once you're settled somewhere." She patted my lap as if I was an unwelcome pet. "We'll have to get you into a good boarding school right away. It won't be easy after the school year has started, but my job requires me to travel all the time and I can't leave you in the flat on your own. I'll start making inquiries immediately. I am not without funds so you will be properly educated. We have to find a school that can give you special help. The American standards are very low compared to Britain's."

I went to say something about that, but Aunt Jean added, "Ah, here we are." The taxi pulled to the curb outside a big white apartment block and a uniformed doorman stepped out to hold a huge black umbrella for us. We rode up in a fancy elevator then walked down a long hallway. Aunt Jean opened the front door. She looked inside and then back out at me as if reconsidering whether letting me come in was such a good idea. "Careful," she said. "There are lots of valuable items in this flat."

I stepped inside. On the walls were paintings and old shields and masks. There were tall vases on the floor. Through one of the open doors I could see a wall lined with books. "Wow," I said. I was going to say that it looked creepy, but I decided I'd better be polite. "It looks like a museum in here."

"I collect rare artifacts from around the world," Aunt Jean said with a hint of pride in her voice, "so no horsing around." And she went through into a dark narrow bedroom and took off her coat.

I don't know what she thought I was going to do—start practicing my basketball shots? I peeked into one room with a sofa and bookshelves. Then another with more bookshelves, a big wooden desk and an armchair. And a kitchen. That was it. "Uh–where's my bedroom?" I asked as she came out of hers again.

"Follow me," Aunt Jean said. "You will sleep in my study for now; only make sure you don't touch anything."

So we went back into the room with the desk and the old books. I was about to ask if I was supposed to sleep on the desk or the floor. But Aunt Jean said, "Come and give me a hand with this," and I found that the armchair pulled out into a bed.

"I expect you must be hungry," Aunt Jean said. "It's time for supper."

"Supper? We only just had breakfast, didn't we?"

Aunt Jean actually smiled. "We've crossed several time zones and gained eight hours. It will take your body a day or two to adjust, I expect. I have to do it all the time and frankly I never get used to it."

She walked through to the kitchen and I followed. "I'm not sure what children eat," Aunt Jean said, "and I've been away for a while so we'll have to have what we can find." She opened a tin of pâté and some smelly cheeses with crackers. I didn't think she'd be likely to have any peanut butter and jelly lying around so I forced myself to take a few bites. Aunt Jean poured herself a glass of red wine and a glass of milk for me. The kitchen was spotless and looked as if it had never been cooked in. We sat in silence at a small table.

"Aunt Jean," I finally dared to ask, "is there nobody else I could go to? I mean I know you're super busy, so I thought that maybe there were some cousins who had kids or something?"

"I am your only living relative, Addison," she said snippily, "apart from an aged aunt in a retirement home. And I'm not thrilled about being stuck with you either, so we'll both have to make the best of it."

That night I lay on the narrow chair-bed, wearing my mom's T-shirt as a nightdress, curled up in a little ball, shivering uncontrollably. I couldn't believe that the rest of my life would be sleeping among someone else's books that I couldn't touch and never having a place to call my own. In the tiny apartment the silence was broken only by the loud ticking of the grandfather clock, the groaning and dripping of the radiator and an occasional car going by outside.

"How can I take it?" I wondered. Then I answered myself, "I'll have to take it because there is no choice." I threw off the quilt, knelt down by my suitcase and unwrapped a wooden photo frame—the one that had always stood on my bedside table at home. The photo was of me and my mom on the beach in the good old days, the days when it was just the two of us against the world, the days before she got sick. The days that were gone forever. The tears that I had been holding back through the funeral and the long journey finally started trickling down my cheeks and I crawled back into bed hugging that photo to me.

Almost immediately I was walking down a dark hallway. The walls and ceiling were oak paneled and the floor had squeaky floorboards and it smelled of chalk and drains and boiled cabbage. It was so dark that I couldn't see what lay at the far end in the darkness. I was just wondering where it led and whether I should go on when I saw something bright coming toward me. As it came closer I saw that it was a girl, about my age.

The girl had bright red hair and freckles and she was wearing a long grey cloak—right down to her ankles. When the girl got close to me she stopped and smiled. She had a friendly smile and I found myself smiling back.

11

"Hello," she said. "You're new, aren't you? I haven't seen you before. Are you coming to the school?"

"I think so," I said.

"See you there," the girl said. "Only watch out and don't act as if you know me."

"How come?"

"They'll think you're a Fareeth, of course."

She gave me a smile and was gone.

THE COMPUTER GOES CRAZY

I opened my eyes and found myself in Aunt Jean's study. "How totally weird," I muttered. Like I said, I had often had strange dreams, of fantastic places, of mountains and oceans where I had never been in real life, but since my mom died they seemed to be happening almost every night. It was still dark so I closed my eyes and drifted back to dreamless sleep.

When I woke up again the rain was still tapping on the window. The world outside looked cold and gray. When I had been in a sad mood at home, mom had said, "There is always something to be glad about" and made me come up with a list of ten things. Now I tried hard but couldn't think of one single thing.

Aunt Jean tapped on my door. "Hurry up and get dressed. We have a lot to do today. I have just heard that my company wants me in Venezuela by Monday so we'll have to find you a school and get you settled by then."

She came in to fold the bed back into an armchair and tucked my suitcase under the desk so that the room looked perfect once again.

After a very quiet breakfast in the tiny kitchen, at which appeared the only cereal in Aunt Jean's pantry was some kind of health food that looked as if it had been swept off the forest floor, we tried to get me ready to go and meet important people at important schools. It was not a big success. Aunt Jean kept making 'tsk tsk' noises as she went through my suitcase of clothes. I was pretty sure she just did it for show because she must have seen what I had in my closet at home.

"You appear to have no sensible clothes at all. You certainly can't visit a prestigious school wearing jeans. You'll only need one outfit for now as of course you'll be wearing uniform so I suppose Barkers will do for that. Hurry and eat some breakfast and then we'll go out."

I was marched to a department store in Kensington High Street and stood cringing with embarrassment while my aunt bossed the saleswoman around and chose a pleated gray skirt for me, a white blouse, black sweater and black jacket. She even chose black lace up shoes to go with them.

"Do I have to wear this?" I said as my aunt took out her wallet to pay for them. "I look like a forty-year-old midget. I look like a mini-you."

"Which would be admirable, since I am known for my impeccable taste in clothes," Aunt Jean said dryly.

"I'm not wearing it," I said. I had been polite long enough.

"You will do as you are told, Addison. I normally do not think black suitable for a child, but you are in mourning after all. Black is a sign of respect."

"My mom would think it was really dumb to make me wear black to show I miss her. She'd know I miss her and she'd want me to do anything I could to feel better. Like paint, or go swimming, or call my friends, or go to the Boardwalk ... none of which I can do here," I said to Aunt Jean's back as she walked to the register with the clothes, clearly not paying any attention to me.

Back at the apartment she made me change into the ugly black and grey clothes and sit reading while she booted up her computer.

"I am going to begin searching for boarding schools online, Addison, so I don't expect to be interrupted," she said. "You may watch the television or pick any book on the shelves as long as you are careful with it. I have all the classics."

I spent a few minutes flipping through the three channels she had on her television then turned it off in boredom. I tried the books, looking at all those dark leather covers, hoping to find something that looked interesting or familiar. I took out my iPod to listen to music while I read, but the battery was dead. I pulled out my charger but the weird English plug had three holes in the wrong places. Great. How was I going to charge the battery over here? I walked to a shelf full of leather-bound books obviously chosen to match the furniture. "Do you have any normal kid's books?" I called to Aunt Jean.

"Only English classics, Addison." She emphasized the word

English. "I'm sure I was reading these novels by your age."

I pulled the books out one by one until I found a title I recognized: "Alice's Adventures In Wonderland" and "Through the Looking Glass." At least I knew that one. My mom used to read it to me and I used to play at falling down rabbit holes. I sat on the sofa and started flipping through it. But the writing seemed kind of old fashioned and very British—just like Aunt Jean. I flipped through the pages, admiring the illustrations. Of course I was interested in anything to do with art. Painting and drawing were what I loved most—well, I would, wouldn't I, with a mother who was a well-known artist?

I half read and half stared out of the window at the London scene below, taking in the red double-decker buses and the policemen in helmets and noticing that even the smallest children wore uniforms. 'Still, even a uniform can't be any worse than what I'm wearing,' I thought and grinned to myself. At least I'd managed to find one thing to be glad about. While I read I toyed with my necklace, moving the small pendant back and forth on the cord. I had worn it all my life, for so long really that I almost forgot I had it on. I took it off and examined it in the light from the window. It was six-sided with a little jewel in each side. A tiny dragon was in the center.

Suddenly there was a burst of music from the computer. I looked up in time to see a lifelike picture of a red dragon pop up on the computer screen.

"What on earth?" Aunt Jean exclaimed and quickly deleted the page.

"Wait," I went to say, but Aunt Jean was already on the next website. "Ah, this may do," Aunt Jean said more to herself than me. "St. Philomena's Convent. Intense academic preparatory, especially for slow learners and those who have fallen behind in their studies. Rigid discipline. High expectations."

I held my breath while Aunt Jean dialed the phone number. "Oh, what a pity," she said as she put down the phone. "They only accept pupils at the beginning of the academic year and are quite full."

"Yes, what a pity," I said.

Aunt Jean looked at me to see if I was being rude but I met her with the blank stare I had become so good at during the last few days. At that moment the trumpet music blared out again from the computer, this time more loudly. We both jumped. The dragon was now flashing bright red on the computer screen.

"I must have turned my pop-up blocker off." Aunt Jean 'x'd it out again. "Honestly. I have such a problem with spam these days. There—it's off. Now, where were we? Let's try the next school on the list." The next phone call and the one after that produced the same results. None of the schools had any openings in the middle of the year.

"This really is too short-sighted of them," Aunt Jean said angrily. "After all, it's only October. At the very least they could make an exception for you because you are coming from America."

Trumpet music filled the room so loudly that I jumped up and held my ears.

"My goodness. This is ridiculous." Aunt Jean closed the pop-up only to have it open again immediately.

"Turn it off. Turn it off!" It was the first time I had ever seen Aunt Jean get flustered and I have to confess I was kind of enjoying that part. She found the volume control and muted it. Silence filled the room and we gave a sigh of relief. "A virus. It had to be a virus. I must call—" She turned back to the screen. On it was the blinking picture of the red dragon. Under the dragon in big letters were the words:

RED DRAGON ACADEMY

MIND HANDS HEART

CLICK HERE

"Red Dragon Academy. It's a school. Do you think that's a boarding school?" I asked. The screen changed. Now it read:

BOARDING SCHOOL FOR YOUNG LADIES AND GENTLEMEN

CLICK HERE

ATTACKED BY WALES

Aunt Jean clicked on the flashing letters and we both read.
Red Dragon Academy
Institution of Academic excellence founded on the
Seven Pillars of Wisdom with emphasis on discipline, culture
and good manners. Our aim is to produce young ladies and
gentlemen of refinement who can take their places in the
highest levels of society. International students welcome.
Places are currently available.

"What an extraordinary coincidence," Aunt Jean said, scrolling through the web pages. "I've never heard of this place before but it sounds as if it might be what we're looking for. Manners, discipline, culture, international students welcome. Absolutely ideal. I'm going to phone them right away, although I suppose it's too much to ask for that they have a place open now."

I held my breath as she dialed. Please let there be no place for me, I found myself praying. Let there be no place anywhere and make Aunt Jean send me back to California.

Aunt Jean was using her best 'I am an important businesswoman' voice on the phone with the school. "Yes, with the headmistress. No, her second-in-command will not do. Yes, I will hold on."

She glanced up and gave me an annoyed look.

Then I heard her saying, "Yes, for this school year. Unfortunate emergency. A death in the family and I can't possibly take care of her. My job takes me all over the world at a moment's notice so I was hoping you might make an exception and—what? You can? You will? Today? But that's marvelous. I can't thank you enough. Do you have a website we can check out? Thank you. We'll take the next train. What is the closest station? Conwy? Very good. We look forward to seeing you this afternoon."

She put the phone down with a triumphant gleam in her eye. "Go and brush your hair, Addison. And pack an overnight bag. We have a long journey ahead of us."

"This Red Dragon place? They have room for me?"

"They do and they are delighted to have a student from America, apparently. The headmistress sounded most brisk and efficient. Exactly what we're looking for."

"Not what I was looking for," I muttered under my breath, "but nobody asked me." Out loud I asked, "Do they have a good art program? You know that I like to paint and my mom said that…"

"I expect that art will be part of the curriculum. It usually is," Aunt Jean said impatiently. "Now for heaven's sake bring me your hair brush and let me attempt to put that unruly hair into braids. Oh, and bring the book you were reading. You'll need something to keep you occupied on the journey."

"Is it very far?" I asked as Aunt Jean jerked a brush through my hair. "Ow! I didn't think England was that big? My mom once said you could drive from North to South in one day."

"Compared to America it is small, I agree," Aunt Jean said, braiding my hair as efficiently as everything else she did, "but as it happens this school is not in England."

"It's not?" This was getting worse by the minute. Where was it—Siberia?

"Actually, it's in Wales," Aunt Jean said.

"Whales?" The word came out as a shriek. "In the ocean, you mean?"

Aunt Jean laughed a superior laugh that made me blush. "Wales is part of Great Britain but it's a separate country. The people speak another language called Welsh." She walked into the bedroom and started checking through the smallest of the suitcases laid neatly on the bed.

"But I can't speak Welsh." I followed her.

"Only the local Welsh people speak Welsh," Aunt Jean said impatiently. "You would not be required to learn that language. Besides, the school is part of the normal British educational system. Lessons will be conducted as they would at any other school in the UK. Come on. We need to catch that train."

Aunt Jean's iPhone and the phone in the apartment rang at the same time. "Make sure you have all your things," she barked as she ran to answer the phone and began texting on the cell at the same time.

"Yes? Gillian. I'm glad you called. Can you call and cancel my noon meeting?"

"You sound stressed out," I said as she and I pulled our suitcases out into the hall.

"I'm hoping for a promotion this year," my aunt said, walking so fast down the hall that I could barely keep up. "I can't drop the ball now." She put her smartphone up to her ear. "Gillian ..." she yelled into it, "– how long until that taxi's here? No, I need it here now. If anyone asks where I am—I'm working on the Johnson account." She put the phone away. "That's all I need now— my boss finding out that I'm taking time off for a child."

I MEET A KILLER HORSE

The train station was huge. It had twenty platforms, trains pulling in and out, loudspeakers squawking and people rushing every which way. It was kind of exciting and really confusing. Aunt Jean seemed to know exactly what she was doing, buying tickets from a vending machine and yelling at me to 'come on' as I waited too long at the electric turnstile and got caught behind it. I had to crawl underneath and then run to keep up. We hauled our cases on board and found seats facing each other by the windows. Aunt Jean didn't need the view. She pulled some papers out of her briefcase, put on her glasses, and started working away.

The train started with a lurch. I don't remember ever riding a train before. First we went through ugly parts of the city: tunnels with graffiti, row after row of houses, all exactly the same, and factories and sad back yards with laundry flapping in them. But soon the city ended and there were houses with bigger back yards and trees and fields with horses and cows in them and then we were in the middle of the countryside. The sun finally came out and I was surprised to see how green everything was. I thought that Santa Cruz was green but it was nothing compared to this. The train went very fast. It flew by villages straight out of story books with quaint old houses and churches with high towers. Trees went by so quickly that they turned into a green blur. Cars drove alongside us on the wrong side of the road and waited at train crossings for us to pass. Two girls about my age were riding ponies along a country lane.

'I wouldn't mind learning to ride a horse,' I thought. My mind drifted to the school. How strange it was to be going to a boarding school in a country I never even heard of until yesterday. And I found myself thinking about Whales and Wales. How completely weird that I would have had that dream about being in the middle of Whales, and now I was going to the middle of Wales. Maybe that was the message in the dream that I was looking for. The dream had told me to come—or at least someone called Beth something to come.

And if the dream about Wales turned out to be true, then maybe the friendly girl with the red hair and the grey cloak was named Beth and would be waiting for me at the school.

"Aunt Jean," I asked tentatively, "do you believe in dreams? I mean, do you think that dreams can come true?"

Aunt Jean shook her head. "I have always thought that one should face up to reality."

"Well, my mom believed in them."

"Addison, your mother was always a hopeless dreamer." Aunt Jean and I were never going see eye to eye on my mother so I tried again.

"No, I meant, do you think you can actually dream things that are going to happen? Because I had this dream about whales—the ones that swim in the ocean, I mean, and now I find that I'm going to school in Wales. And we didn't know that until this morning, did we? And I dreamed that I was riding a red dragon, and now we're going to Red Dragon Academy. Don't you think that's weird?"

Aunt Jean managed a smile. "Then let's hope it is a good omen and you'll be happy there."

"And there was this girl I saw in my dream last night," I went on, encouraged that she was actually talking to me like a human being. "She asked me if I was coming to her school."

"Really? You do have vivid dreams, don't you? But I suppose it was to be expected. Your mother obviously filled your head with fantasy."

"Don't you dream?" I asked.

Aunt Jean shook her head firmly. "Hardly ever. If I do it's one of those tiresome nightmares about trying to pack my bags and missing my flight—which is understandable, I suppose as I'm always rushing—" She broke off as phone rang yet again. "They can?" I heard her say. "Splendid. That is good news. Then we can have the whole thing settled on Tuesday."

She nodded to me with satisfaction. "At least that's one thing less to worry about. Now what were we saying?"

"We were talking about dreams, and how I dreamed about whales, and then I met a girl in my dream and she asked if I was coming to her school. She was nice. I hope I really meet her."

Aunt Jean rolled her eyes. "Addison, you are reading far too much into this. I understand people dream about being chased by wild beasts or monsters, but it certainly doesn't happen to them. It's about time you learned to face reality and grow up. Read your book and let me get on with my work."

I took out Alice in Wonderland and Through the Looking Glass, but the swaying of the train made it hard to focus on the small print and I started to feel sick. Instead I flipped through it, idly looking at the bizarre, old-fashioned pictures full of mythical beasts.

The train made a strange rhythm along the track and swayed slightly as it went. I guess that jet lag caught up with me because I must have fallen asleep.

One minute I was looking at those green fields. Then the green fields turned into a forest. I was walking through the trees. Sunlight fell through the leaves. The ground was soft under my feet and all around was complete silence. Even though everything was so beautiful, I sensed a great tension. It was too silent. I was being watched. Ahead of me I heard a noise in the bushes—a large animal moving around. I started to back away, but then a branch moved and I saw that the animal was only a big white horse, head down and eating grass. I couldn't see any rider. Maybe the horse had wandered off and someone was looking for it.

I moved toward it quietly, my footsteps making no sound on the moist earth. Its coat was sleek and so dazzlingly white that it almost hurt to look at it.

"Oh, you beautiful thing," I whispered.

Suddenly somebody grabbed my arm and pulled me backward.

"Don't touch it. Can't you see it's a Nightmare?" a voice hissed in my ear.

At the sound the horse looked up from its grazing. Its face was like a skull and through the empty eye sockets and the nostrils there came fire. It turned and started toward me….

I ARRIVE AT THE INSANE ASYLUM

I must have yelled in my sleep because suddenly I was being shaken. "Wake up, Addison. We'll be arriving soon." I opened my eyes, my heart still thumping. I sat for a moment wondering where I was and why I was being shaken around. Then I remembered we were on a train. I had no idea how long I had been asleep but the crick in my neck told me it had to be quite a while. I looked out of the window and started with surprise. I was looking at sparkling water.

"I didn't know it would be near the ocean," I said.

"North Wales is on the Irish Sea." Aunt Jean shook her head. "Didn't they teach you any geography at your school?"

"We learned about North America and South America and the continents," I said, "but we never studied England much. It was just part of Europe."

"Don't let the local people hear you calling this place England," Aunt Jean said. "They are very proud of their country and their heritage."

"So we're already in Wales?"

"Yes, ever since Chester."

"When do we get off?" I asked, standing up and pressing my nose to the window.

"That's more like it," Aunt Jean said. "Much more cheerful. I'm glad you are now prepared to make the best of things. So much easier."

She took down the overnight bags from the rack above our heads. "We should be coming into Conwy soon. If you keep watching you'll see the castle."

Almost as she said this the railway line rattled across a bridge over a river mouth. Lots of small boats were bobbing on sparkling water. And then I looked up and gasped.

"It's a real castle," I yelled. "Just like the knights and King Arthur and Cinderella. I didn't know there were still real castles outside of the movies."

"Plenty of them," Aunt Jean said. She looked satisfied as if she had provided the castle herself. "These castles in Wales are some of the oldest and finest. I'm sure you'll be taken to visit Conwy Castle. The school is only five miles out of the town."

I kept staring at it as the train slowed to a crawl past the tall gray stone walls. It had towers and a drawbridge, just like the toy castle I'd had when I was a little girl. I half expected to see a knight come riding out of it. As the train came to a stop, people in the carriage stood up and started getting their bags down from the racks above the seats.

"Come along." Aunt Jean fought her way along the crowded aisle and down onto the platform. My suitcase caught on my seat and by the time I made it out of the train there was a crowd in front of me. I tried not to lose sight of my aunt's black overcoat in the sea of people and luggage. I passed between two women carrying shopping baskets.

"Mae hi'n brav heddi, ond ydy hi?" one was saying and the other replied.

"Ydy."

So this was the different language Aunt Jean had told me about. I dragged my bag though the crowd and sprinted to catch up with Aunt Jean. Outside the station Aunt Jean looked around for a taxi, while I was still listening to people speaking Welsh. Clouds had rushed in to cover the blue sky and as we stood there it started to rain. A taxi pulled up beside us. A little old man hopped out, wearing a faded tweed jacket and with an old tweed cap on his head.

"We wish to go to a school called Red Dragon Academy," Aunt Jean said in her most snooty voice.

"What was the name again?" He cocked his head to one side, like a bird.

"Red Dragon Academy. It is in the direction of Llanwryst." (She stumbled over the Welsh pronunciation.) "Do you know it?"

The taxi driver's face lit up in a grin. "The old loony bin?" he asked.

"Loony bin?" Aunt Jean sounded horrified.

"Used to be the insane asylum, didn't it?" He had a lilting voice. "Stood empty for years because nobody wanted it. I did hear that they'd made it into a school recently."

"Then please take us there," Aunt Jean said firmly.

The town of Conwy looked as if it belonged in Disneyland—narrow streets and houses straight out of Beauty and the Beast. The cab driver took off, driving through those narrow streets as if they were a freeway, not seeming to notice the near misses with parked cars, phone booths and people until we passed through an archway in the old town wall. The road didn't get any wider but we were in green countryside now. On one side of us was a wide river and on the other fields and white cottages. As the road began to climb I saw green hills and beyond the hills were real mountains that reminded me of home. Sheep stood in fields and the sound of bleating came in through the window. The road climbed into dense stretches of forest then came out to give glimpses of the river again. Then the road became even narrower with a low stone wall on either side. We turned off the main road and went winding up a valley so green that the color seemed unnatural to me. As we got closer to the mountain at the end of the valley, the forest formed a canopy over our heads and it became dark and gloomy. It had also started to rain and drips pattered onto the roof of the cab. The narrow road ended in ancient wrought iron gates.

"This is it, I believe," he said. "Do you want to get out here, or shall I drive you in?"

"Drive us in of course," Aunt Jean snapped. "Do you expect us to walk in the rain?"

The cab driver got out reluctantly to open the massive wrought iron gates in a high brick wall with broken glass on top of it. Beyond the wall the gravel driveway was lined with a high hedge on either side. We drove slowly up the drive until it wound around and suddenly a large building loomed up ahead of us, among tall dark pine trees. It was another castle, not square and friendly like a toy castle this time, but long and rambling, with turrets and towers, wings going off in different directions, sometimes three stories high, sometimes four or five. In the front part, now facing us there were two tall square towers and a massive front door. It was built of rough gray stone and the windows were set back in little arches at intervals along the wall. Ivy climbed up one side of the wall and spilled over the top of the tower. It didn't look like a place that people had lived in for a hundred years. As I stared at it in horror, I noticed the bars on the windows.

RED DRAGON ACADEMY

"This looks awful," I burst out. "It's like a prison or a horror movie. Look, there are bars on the windows." Suddenly I felt as if I might cry any minute. "Please, Aunt Jean, please don't leave me here."

"I must admit it doesn't look too inviting." Even Aunt Jean sounded doubtful. "But now that we're here, at least we'll have a look around. People have done wonders with modernizing old buildings in Britain, you know."

"They haven't taken the bars off the windows," I muttered.

"That's true," Aunt Jean said, "but plenty of the finest old schools are in buildings that look like this from the outside. It's part of the British tradition." Then she looked at my face and put a tentative hand on my shoulder. "I only want to do the best for you, Addison. I wouldn't send you to any school that was not up to par in any way."

She told the cab driver to wait, which calmed me down a bit— at least we still had our way out of here. Our feet scrunched on the wet gravel. Aunt Jean pulled her heels out of the muddy gravel and clacked up some well-worn stone steps, then knocked on a huge oak front door. I heard the sound echoing inside. For a minute or so we stood there waiting. Then we heard a voice calling and turned around and saw a lady motioning to us.

"Over here. You're knocking on the wrong door. We never use that old front entrance any more. It's too difficult to open and close." She hurried up to us, carrying an umbrella.

"I'm Miss Neves's secretary, Gwyneth," the woman said. She was young and kind of plump with dark hair cut very short. "And you must be Miss Walker. And this is our new pupil?"

She looked at me and smiled.

"This is my niece, Addison. She has just arrived from California."

"I'm pleased to meet you, Addison. California?" she said as she ushered us to the open door, holding the umbrella over us. "Oh my goodness. I hear it's beautiful there."

I nodded, not trusting my voice to say anything.

"Are you from Hollywood, then?" Gwyneth asked, giving me a smile. "Know any big movie stars? Ever met Brad Pitt?"

"No." I smiled. "We lived in the mountains near Santa Cruz. Nowhere near Hollywood."

"Well, we've got our share of mountains right here," Gwyneth said, "so you'll feel right at home, won't you? Come on, then. Miss Neves will be in her office."

We followed her to one of the towers, where a small door had been cut in the wall. Inside was a hallway with a high wood-paneled ceiling and wood-paneled walls. To our right a stone staircase spiraled up out of sight. It smelled old and cold, a damp and musty sort of smell.

Gwyneth started to lead us down the hall. Our footsteps echoed loudly from the stone floor. Before we could reach the office a woman came out.

"Ah," she said. "I thought I heard footsteps. I am Miss Neves (she pronounced it Nev-ess), headmistress of this fine school, and you must be Miss Walker."

She extended her hand to Aunt Jean.

"And I take it this is your niece?"

I couldn't help staring at her open-mouthed. She looked exactly like an older version of Aunt Jean—same dark business suit, same hairstyle perfectly in place, although Miss Neves's hair was iron gray, and the same plain, high-heeled shoes.

"Say 'Good Afternoon' to Miss Neves, Addison," Aunt Jean hissed. "Remember your manners."

"Good manners are the backbone of our education," Miss Neves said. "We expect politeness at all times to each other, to the teachers and to the employees. When Addison leaves this school, she will be able to mix in any level of society in the world. I guarantee it."

She held out her hand to me. "Good afternoon, Addison."

I took her hand, then almost snatched mine away in surprise. As

I'd shaken Miss Neves's hand, I had felt a strange tingling sensation.

GOODBYE, AUNT JEAN

Miss Neves studied me for a long moment before she said, "Welcome, Addison. I believe that you have come to the right place. Do come into my office."

She ushered us into a room that looked exactly like Aunt Jean's study. It was lined with books and not a thing was out of place. In the center was a large polished desk with some photographs of school activities on it.

"You will want to know about our academic program," the headmistress said as she motioned us to sit on a leather couch. "It is rigorous, demanding. Our aim is to find the strengths and gifts of all our students and to develop them to the highest level. If Addison chooses to come here, our first step will be to test her to find out what abilities may lie hidden."

I stared around the room and toyed with my necklace as Miss Neves and Aunt Jean talked about academics. I was sure that nobody would care much what I wanted anyway. Miss Neves seemed a carbon copy of Aunt Jean. Same dark suit, white blouse. They even both had similar pins on their right lapel, although Aunt Jean's was a silver Celtic knot and Miss Neves was ... 'That's strange,' I thought, suddenly focusing on Miss Neves's pin. It looked just like my necklace! As well as six jewels on the sides and the dragon in the middle, it had the words 'Heart Mind and Body' written on it. I lifted my necklace up and looked at it closely trying to see if there was tiny writing on my necklace that said the same thing. When I glanced up I saw that Miss Neves was staring at me.

"Miss Neves, your pin is exactly like—"

"The Red Dragon, symbol of Wales, of course," Miss Neves cut in. She turned back to Aunt Jean.

"I rather fear that you will find her standard is below that of most girls her age who come here," Aunt Jean said. "She was sent to an extremely easy-going sort of school in California and her mother didn't value education the way I do."

"She did." I wasn't going to let her put down my mother. "She cared about the things that matter and…." I broke off when I saw Aunt Jean giving me a warning glare.

"Tell me about your mother, Addison." The headmistress looked at me with cool gray eyes.

"My mother was an artist," I said. "She's sold paintings all over the world. I'd like to be an artist too some day."

"We have a well-equipped art room in the school. We encourage study of all the arts—music, painting, dance. They are all important. One cannot grow up to be a cultured being without them. Even our boys have to take dancing lessons, however much they complain. And our girls have to take carpentry." She glanced at Aunt Jean. "Our students have no time to be bored. We keep them challenged and ready for whatever life may bring them. We send them out to be leaders in whatever field they choose, in whatever place their destiny sends them."

She stood up. "You will want a tour of the school, of course. Follow me."

Aunt Jean stood up too and I hesitated. Was this when I should make a scene? If I didn't take charge of this I would be left here at this nightmare school. Aunt Jean's iPhone rang and she glanced at a moment before shoving it back in her purse.

"I am afraid I really don't think I have time for a tour," she said apologetically. "The cab is waiting. I have to get back to London and this all sounds absolutely excellent. It is exactly the sort of place I was seeking for Addison. Now the question is, when can she start?"

"Do you wish her to start immediately?" Miss Neves asked.

"If that were possible."

"Why not? Her uniform and supplies can be ordered from our outfitters in Conwy," Miss Neves said. "They can probably have the basic items delivered tomorrow. My secretary will give you a list of everything she needs. And she will explain the fee schedule." Aunt Jean seemed eager to go but Miss Neves motioned for her to wait. "I do have a few more questions. Are you her legal guardian?"

"Yes – since her mother … since my sister's death I am her legal guardian."

"And can we expect any other family that might visit. Is there a father?"

My attention was fixed suddenly on Aunt Jean because I had been wondering that all my life. I'd asked my mom about him over and over but she refused to say anything. I can't tell you how many times I'd fantasized that he'd show up one day and want to get to know me.

"No, there is no other family. I don't believe that my sister had any contact with the birth parents at all."

"Birth parents? What are you talking about?" I suddenly felt as if I was Alice, falling down that rabbit hole.

Aunt Jean was staring at me in horror. "Oh no – she never told you? I thought we agreed you were old enough."

"Told me what?" My brain was fighting to understand what she was saying.

Aunt Jean shook her head. "I urged my sister to tell you the truth while she had the chance. But now I suppose it is up to me." She cleared her throat as if she was about to make a speech. "The truth is that you were adopted."

The room was silent while I let this sink in. "Did she know who my real parents were?"

"I have no idea, Addison. You know what your mother was like—impulsive. She showed up on the doorstep one day with a baby. All she'd say was that she had adopted you and weren't you the most beautiful baby ever."

I had to smile at that. I was so like my mom, only focusing on the things that mattered.

"So that was in England? I was adopted in England?"

Aunt Jean nodded. Then she seemed to remember that Miss Neves was in the room with us. "I'm sorry, Headmistress. I didn't expect it to be such a shock. I can't believe her mother hadn't told her."

"I'm sorry, too." Miss Neves's voice was kind. "I hope you will consider this your new home and us as your new family, Addison."

I still couldn't make myself speak and there was no way I wanted a place with bars on the windows to be my new home. Aunt Jean's phone was ringing again. "Oh, excuse me. It's work." She got up jerkily and walked to the corner of the room speaking quickly into the receiver. "Yes – the Johnson account. I'm out of

London at the moment."

"It's better to know, I suppose," I said because I could feel Miss Neves watching me.

"It is always better to know the truth," Miss Neves agreed.

Aunt Jean put away her phone and held out her hand to Miss Neves. "Thank you, Headmistress. I leave her in your capable hands. Most satisfactory. If I hurry, I may be able to catch a train back to London tonight." She turned to me and put a hand on my shoulder. "Goodbye, Addison. Please be a credit to your mother and to me. I'm sure you'll be very happy here. If you need anything I will leave my secretary's number with the office."

"Wait." I ran after her into the hall. "You can't leave me here without even seeing the place," I whispered to her. "What if it's awful? Where are the kids, for one thing? Have you seen a single student? What if they're kept in the dungeons and fed on bread and water."

"I think you'll find that the food is one thing our students never complain about," Miss Neves said with a laugh from inside the office.

How had she heard what I said, when she was still standing by her desk?

I stepped into the doorway to look at her.

"Actually I'd say that most of our students are very happy here. I think this is the right place for you."

"Just give it a try, Addison," Aunt Jean said. "And if it's really not to your liking, then—then we can make other plans. But at this moment, I'm afraid that…' Her voice trailed off. She patted my shoulder again. "I really have to go."

I thought about crying or screaming, saying I would not stay here no matter what – she couldn't make me; but something about Miss Neves made me curious. I wanted to see what this place looked like. Maybe I was stupid, like the people in horror movies who walk down into the basement while you yell at the screen, "No! Don't do it." But whether or not it was a mistake, I didn't say a word.

Aunt Jean's footsteps echoed on the stone floor as she left. She didn't look back.

I TOUR THE LOONY BIN

M iss Neves was staring at me with a strange expression on her face. "You seem to have a busy aunt," she said. "Well, let's get you settled in," she said walking to the door. "Follow me."

She set off at a fast pace down the long, dark hallway. "You are too late for lessons today but I'll show you where you'll be sleeping and then you can join the rest of our happy family for supper."

I wanted to say that not many happy families lived in crumbling old castles with bars on the windows. I'd had some bad dreams in my life, but this was a real nightmare. I thought about the dream on the train and wondered if it had been warning me. If it had, there wasn't much I could do about it. It seemed I was stuck here whether I liked it or not.

Miss Neves came to a small white door, which she unlocked with a key. Inside was an old metal staircase that spiraled up as far as I could see. "Come along. No dilly dallying," the headmistress said and started up the stairs. I wondered how old she was. She looked like an old woman with the creases in her forehead and her gray hair and yet she almost flew up the stairs as if they were no effort at all. The stairs went up and up, round and round until I felt really dizzy. I was totally out of breath when we reached the top, but not Miss Neves. "Some healthy walks in our local mountains will do you good," she said. "And the riding lessons will be good for you too."

"Riding? You have horses?"

"Naturally. Riding is an essential skill. Absolutely essential."

That got my interest. I pictured myself riding like those two girls I had seen from the train. At the top of the stairs Miss Neves unlocked another white door. We stepped out into the largest room I had ever seen. Golden chandeliers hung from the ceiling. The walls were painted with ribbons and cupids and flowers. Huge Grecian columns reached from the floor all the way to the arched ceiling. The ceiling was painted blue with constellations of stars sprinkled across it. But the chandeliers had cobwebs strung across them, the paint was peeling in places on the ceiling. It was like a scene from Sleeping Beauty after the hundred years of enchantment. It must have been a ballroom long ago, I decided. Did loony bins go in for balls?

"Of course it was a ballroom once," Miss Neves said at the very moment I was thinking the words. "We still hold our dancing classes in here today. It gives just the right feel, don't you think?" Miss Neves's voice echoed in the vast space.

As she spoke, I was staring up at the constellations on the ceiling. I didn't recognize any of them, and stargazing was something I had often done with my mother on their balcony at home. Some of them I almost recognized. That one was almost like the Big Dipper but—

"Come along. This way," Miss Neves said. She crossed the room and put a key into a small locked door in the right hand wall.

As I ran to catch up with her I suddenly realized what was weird. The big dipper was backward. I stopped and looked up. Yes, it was true. The rest of the constellations were backward, too.

"What's the matter?" Miss Neves asked.

"The constellations are painted backward," I said.

"Are they? I suppose it seems that way," Miss Neves said. The door opened into a narrow corridor that disappeared into darkness. This corridor was carpeted with a cheap hospital carpet and smelled of disinfectant. It made me think of what the cab driver had said.

"Miss Neves," I asked, "did this school used to be a loony ... um, I mean an insane asylum?"

"This castle has a long and rich history," Miss Neves said without slacking her pace. "It was owned by a noble family long ago. It was used for a while in the nineteenth century to care for mentally ill individuals. Those in charge at that time cared more for security than convenience. Which is why," she smiled, opening the last door on the right of the corridor to reveal another metal staircase, "we had to come up to go down again. This way." And she led me down stairs that emerged into a square courtyard. In the middle of the courtyard was a large fountain and water spurted from the mouths of various mythical creatures. On top of the fountain was a dragon. It looked interesting but I hardly had time to take it in before I had to run to catch up with Miss Neves again, through a garden and beside a high stone wall. Roses spilled over archways along the path and the path was covered with rose petals. The air smelled like rain and roses. In front of us was another big stone wing of building just like the one we had just left.

'I can't believe how big this castle is!' I thought.

"Yes, it will seem confusing to start with," Miss Neves said, "but you'll soon get the hang of it. Most of the rooms you will use are in this wing." She entered the second building through what looked like a large windowed closet crowded with muddy boot and coats. The room opened into a long light hallway. As we walked down it I could hear the clang of pots and pans and smell delicious smells coming from what I guessed must be the kitchen. I could hear people laughing and talking in the rooms that we passed. A group of kids my age were standing in the hallway. They were all dressed in green skirts or pants and matching jackets with a badge on the pocket showing a red dragon. They all said," Good afternoon, Miss Neves," politely and stopped to let her pass. Miss Neves nodded to them and marched on. I lost track of the corridors we passed and staircases we climbed until Miss Neves opened a final door and we stepped out into the open air.

The wind almost took my breath away. I saw we were on a narrow walkway on part of the roof. Down below I could see that courtyard with the fountain—a long way down below.

"Whoa," I said. "This is really high up. Where are we going?"

"Follow me and don't fall," Miss Neves said.

I WISH I WAS INVISIBLE

"The first year's dormitory is on the fifth floor of the Great Tower," Miss Neves said, looking back over her shoulder. "Unfortunately the inside stairs are currently being repaired, so this is the only way to reach your rooms for the time being. I don't need to remind you to be careful at all times up here. It is a long way down."

I swallowed nervously. It was an awfully long way down and the wall that ran along the side of the walkway was not that high. The rain had made the stone walkway slippery. I was sure a school in America would not be allowed to have anything so dangerous.

"First years?" I said to take my mind off the narrow walkway. "I started seventh grade this year."

"Our first year students are either twelve or thirteen. About the equivalent of your junior high school, I believe. "

'Great,' I thought. 'I was going to be top of the school next year and now I get to be a first grader again!'

Ahead of us loomed a large stone tower, much higher than the rest of the building. I held my breath as Miss Neves opened an arched wooden door in the rough stone wall. I wasn't sure what to expect. Stone tower rooms with bars on the windows and locked doors? But the corridor we came out in was surprisingly normal. The walls were painted white and a green carpet and bright green doors made the hall feel cheerful and homey.

Suddenly a door on our left opened and a tall thin girl leaped out. "What are you doing up here?" she demanded. She had a thin, weaselly face with little darting eyes. Her expression changed immediately when she saw Miss Neves. "Oh hello, Headmistress," she said quickly clasping her hands meekly in front of her. "I thought it might be some first formers sneaking up here to get out of chores."

"Hello, Fern. I've brought you another new student. This is Addison. Addison, this is Fern, your dormitory monitor. Fern, we're going to put Addison in room 7 with the two newest girls. "

"Yes, Miss Neves," said Fern, and then added, "This is the fourth new student we've had since school began. I don't know how I'm expected to study and show them all around. If I could maybe miss my classes tomorrow ..."

"I quite understand, Fern," Miss Neves said, looking at her calmly. "And I wouldn't dream of making you miss your classes. Phillipa has finished her testing now and Addison still has to complete hers. I will take it upon myself to make Addison acquainted with our life here."

"But I really wouldn't mind...." Fern began.

"Thank you, Fern. I will show Addison her room now. Please resume your studies." Miss Neves walked off in front of me with the hint of a smile on her face.

"Ah. Here we are." Miss Neves opened a door farther down the hall. I gave a sigh of relief to see that the room looked comfortable and pleasant. It had a bunk bed against one wall, a single bed with a beautiful down comforter against the other, a built in closet and chest of drawers against the back wall. It was painted a light buttery yellow and was carpeted in a sort of sandier yellow. On the wall was a picture of Welsh mountains and out of the window was a view of the real thing.

I ran over to the window. The clouds had cleared, except for one small white cloud that clung to the top of the highest mountain. The sky glowed beyond the peaks. Already my fingers were itching for my paints.

"It makes a good picture, framed like that in the window, doesn't it?" Miss Neves said.

I looked up quickly, but Miss Neves's expression hadn't changed. "You may put your clothes in these drawers," she said. "I know you only have an overnight bag with you, but the outfitter should be able to send up most of what you need tomorrow. In the meantime I believe a uniform might be hanging in the wardrobe." She opened the door and nodded. "Yes. I see it's here."

I stared at the green skirt and blazer that hung there.

"Whose uniform is that?"

"Yours, obviously," Miss Neves said.

"How do you know it's my size?" I went to the closet and looked at it.

"I'm sure it will fit you perfectly," Miss Neves said calmly. She closed the closet door again. "When the rest of your things arrive from the outfitter, you will mark every item of clothing with your name and room number."

"Okay."

Miss Neves shook her head. "You don't say 'okay.' You say 'Yes, Miss Neves,' or 'Yes, Headmistress.' Respect at all times, Addison."

I almost said "Okay" again but I swallowed it quickly and nodded. I'm normally better at standing up for myself, even with adults—but you try being shown around a castle half way across the world and see what it does to your attitude!

"You will be sharing this room with two girls who are also new at the school this term. Philippa Masters-Johnson is from Kent, and Celeste du Bois is from Paris. I hope you three will become good friends. One needs friends in this world to survive."

A distant bell rang. "That will be the supper bell. We keep to a strict schedule here. A copy of the schedule and the school rules will be sent up to your dorm room after supper. Study it by morning. Take off your overcoat, leave your bag and come along."

We set out again at the same quick pace, retracing the way we had come. I tried to memorize all the twists and turns, worried that I would never be able to find my way back. As we walked I heard the sound of feet, drumming on stone floors, echoing back from stone walls. They sounded like an approaching army, louder and louder—thump, thump, thump. I looked around nervously, as students of all sizes, some of them older than me, came pushing and shoving past, pouring in through a door marked Dining Hall.

"The food must be extra good tonight if you're all in such a hurry," Miss Neves said, her strong voice carrying over the noise of the feet. Instantly the students froze as they noticed her, then walked quietly through the door, heads down. 'Like robots all in uniform,' I thought.

Miss Neves put her hand on my shoulder and steered me into a large dark-paneled hall. Tall arched windows along the far wall let in the last of the setting sunlight and painted everything with a rosy glow. The ceiling was arched and wood paneled too, almost lost in the gloom, and there were polished dark wood tables set in rows across the room. About a hundred boys and girls were scrambling to sit down. The sound of benches being pulled out over the stone floor echoed, horribly loud. Along the right-hand wall was a high table, at which teachers, all wearing black gowns over their normal clothes, were now taking their places. They looked old and strict and scary. Not a friendly face among them. My heart was beating so fast that I found it hard to breathe.

If this is one of my dreams, it would be a good time to wake up, I told myself. I even pinched myself but it didn't do any good.

Miss Neves pushed me forward to the front of the room. "Attention, everybody," she said, clapping her hands, and there was instant silence. "I have an announcement. We have yet another new girl come to join us. This is Addison Walker, just arrived from California. She will be entering our first year class. I want you to make her feel welcome."

I could see a hundred pairs of eyes all looking at me. I looked down at my new black lace-up shoes and wished the ground would swallow me up.

I PUT MY FOOT IN MY MOUTH

"Can someone please find a place for Addison?" Miss Neves asked. "One of the first year tables?"

"She can sit 'ere." I looked up and saw a skinny boy waving his hand.

"Thank you, Sam. Most kind of you." Miss Neves pointed at the far table. "Off you go then."

I crossed the stone floor, my new shoes tap tapping loudly. I passed a group of girls with glossy, styled hair who were attempting to make even the school uniform look fashionable. As I came by they whispered to each other and pointed at me. Then they dissolved into giggles.

I felt my cheeks burning as I slipped onto the bench beside the skinny boy. He had a small, pointed face, a cheeky smile and lots of unruly curly hair. In fact he reminded me of an elf, or maybe a pixie.

"'ello!" he said.

"Hi." I returned the smile.

The girl sitting across from me had auburn hair and a rather superior expression. She held out her hand to me like a movie star or a queen. "I'm Pippa. How do you do?"

I wasn't sure how to answer her. "Uh – hi." I took her hand awkwardly and shook it. "Nice to meet you."

The skinny boy stuck out his hand to me. "And it is a great pleasure to make your acquaintance, your 'ighness." He gave a good imitation of Pippa's voice. "I am known at the palace as Samuel." He shook my hand exactly as Pippa had. "But you can call me Sam." He added in his normal London cockney accent.

"Well, I must say," Pippa said.

"Must you?" Sam chuckled and turned back to me. "So you're from America? That's bloody brilliant! I've always wanted to go there. Have you been to Disneyland?" I took a breath to answer but he went on, "Sorry, I've forgot your name already." Let me guess – don't tell me – what are American girls called—Taylor?"

I shook my head.

"Miley? Brittney? Can't fink of any others at the moment."

I smiled. "It's Addison but please call me Addy. Only my aunt calls me Addison."

"Addison," he said slowly. "No movie stars named Addison." He sounded disappointed. "In fact I don't think I've ever met someone called that. Is it a dead normal name for a California girl then?"

"Dead normal? Oh – no, it's not exactly usual. My mom liked unusual things. I don't know where she got it from."

"Well, she's sent you to the right place then," the boy on her other side chimed in. "We're as unusual as they come. In fact we're all complete nutters here." At first glance he didn't look very unusual to me. He had neatly combed dark hair and looked very preppy in the school blazer and green tie. But as I looked again I noticed that his eyes were a clear light gray which seemed odd in his obviously Indian face. He grinned at me to let me know he was teasing.

"Hi – I'm Raj by the way. And you're from California? Wow. Did you live close to Lawrence Livermore Lab? Have you been to the Stanford Particle Accelerator?"

"The what?"

"The Particle Accelerator. It's this long tube that scientists shoot protons down…."

"I have no idea what you're talking about," I said.

"Don't mind him, he's a science nut," Sam said. "He can't help being weird. He's quite harmless, on the whole."

"I 'ave been to the United States many times with my mother," the girl seated across the table next to Pippa said, speaking over Sam. "I am Celeste. My mother is the famous opera singer Elise du Bois. Perhaps you have 'eard of her?"

"Sorry, I don't know anything about opera," I said.

"Who does?" Sam said. "So go on, tell us about California. Were you at school with movie stars or their kids then?"

"No," I laughed. "Why does everyone think California is full of movie stars? I live about three hundred miles away from the nearest movie star. And I went to just a normal school."

"A normal boarding school like RDA?" Pippa asked.

"RDA?" I felt my stomach grumbling as wonderful smells were coming out of the kitchen.

"Red Dragon Academy."

"This is supposed to be normal?" I couldn't help laughing. "A creepy haunted castle with bars on the windows? That's normal here?"

"Believe me, I've been to worse than this," Pippa said. "In my last school we slept in dormitories of twelve and the food was disgusting. Rice pudding every day. Red Dragon Academy seems all right so far—a little strange, but all right."

I shook my head. "My school was so totally different."

"In what way?" Pippa asked in her superior fashion.

"Well, for one thing it was on a normal city street, in a regular building. I called all my teachers by their first names. I got to wear whatever clothes I wanted and no one cared too much about manners."

"No one here cares about manners much," Sam said.

"And only one hallway of the castle is reputed to be haunted." Raj added.

As we talked, plates of sausages and mashed potatoes and big bowls of green beans were being placed in the center of the table in front of us by older boys and girls wearing aprons. The good smell of fried onions rose from the platters. Sam grabbed the serving spoon immediately and began piling food on his plate.

"Zey let you wear whatever you wish?" Celeste asked looking pointedly at my awful outfit.

"This is not my choice, trust me," I said hurriedly. "My aunt made me wear it because my mom just died."

An awkward silence fell. How dumb of me to say that. I wanted to take back the words as soon as I said them.

WHAT THE HECK ARE BANGERS AND MASH?

The kids around me were looking down uncomfortably, not sure what to say. All except Raj. "Sorry about your mum," Raj said. "That's too bad. My mother died a few years ago, so I know what you're going through."

I nodded, and swallowed back the lump in my throat.

"Help yourself. Bangers and mash. Lovely grub," Sam said.

I served myself some food to avoid looking at anyone. "So my Aunt Jean bought me these awful clothes. She's the one who chose this place so that I could learn proper English manners and stuff like that."

"Don't worry; no one here will make you mind your manners. Except maybe her," Sam said with his mouth full pointing a fork full of food at Pippa.

"Some of us were raised to think that good manners are important," Pippa said in a very superior voice.

"Sorry about that," Sam said cheerfully. "Can't do nuffink about the way we was brought up, can we? You can't help it that you was raised bone idle and spoiled rotten…."

"How dare you!" Pippa snapped.

Sam grinned. "She says her name is Pippa but we've decided it's really Pepper, on account of her hot temper."

The other kids chuckled. Pippa's face had flushed bright red. "My parents would be horrified if they realized they had sent me to a school with gutter snipes like you," she said. "I'm used to being with a different class of people."

"Well, pardon me for breathing" Sam said with a good-natured grin. "Anyhow, I don't think your high falluting manners matter too much here."

I thought about this. "But my aunt thought this school was all about good manners. The ad on the computer said the school's goal was to produce 'young ladies and gentlemen of refinement,'" I quoted, trying to mimic my aunt's voice. "It sounded awful. How did you end up here?"

"It was either 'ere or the young offenders program," Sam said cheerfully.

"Young offenders?" I asked cautiously. "You mean like juvenile hall? What did you do?"

"Probably murdered his grandmother," Pippa said.

"Didn't do nuffink at all. At least, not much. Always innocent until proven guilty." He gave me a wink.

Pippa turned to me. "I wouldn't believe a word he says if I were you. I'm new like you, actually. I just arrived a week ago."

"And how is it?"

"It seems all right so far. I'm allowed to ride every day."

"Ride horses you mean?"

"What else? Broomsticks?" Pippa looked at me as if I was stupid. "And the food's not at all bad."

"Not bad? It's bloody brilliant," Sam said. "You can eat as much as you want to. Come on. Tuck in." He put an extra sausage on my plate.

Celeste looked at the pile of food on my plate and made a face. She helped herself to a tiny portion of green beans and potatoes.

"Are you feeling okay?" I asked, trying to make conversation.

"I find ze food 'ere quite disgusting," she said in her strong French accent. "It is full of grease! I shall put on weight."

I sneaked a look at her. She was tall and very slim, with hooded eyes, a beaky nose and dark hair tied back with a green bow.

"If you got much skinnier you'd slip down the plug hole," Sam said and got a general laugh.

"I shall not like it here," she said. "You are very rude."

"Only teasin'," Sam said. "Everyone gets teased at school which you'll learn soon enough. She's never been to school before," he added to me. "Can you believe it?"

"I 'ad a tutor," Celeste said. "My mother travels around the world singing, so my tutor came with us. But my mother thought I should improve my English skills. Someone sent her a brochure about this school, and that it was known for teaching English to foreign students. I did not want to come and do not think I shall like it."

"What did you call this food?" I asked Raj. Between Sam's cockney accent and Celeste's French one I was having trouble following the conversation.

"Bangers and mash." Raj pointed at her plate. "What do you call it?"

"Uh – sausages and mashed potatoes. I thought they spoke English in England."

"Well – you're in Wales at the moment so maybe they should be ... uh ..." He shook his head. "Nope – we haven't learned the Welsh words for 'Bangers and Mash.' I'll have to ask Gwylum. He's the only one who speaks Welsh. Hey, Gwylum," he yelled down the table. A dark-haired boy with a round, worried-looking face looked up. Just then Miss Neves walked by the table and gave Raj a look that made him start eating with an innocent look on his face. I watched Miss Neves walk by, sure that Raj was going to get into trouble.

"Hey, don't look so worried," Raj said as soon as she'd passed by. "Miss Neves isn't that bad. Her bark is worse than her bite."

We both looked up to see Miss Neves, now at the far end of the dining room, looking directly at us.

Raj lowered his voice. "Actually she's pretty scary if you ask me. She always seems to know what you're talking about."

"She must have good hearing. She overheard what I whispered to my aunt today."

"Oh, so you've been living with your aunt, have you?"

"No. She's my only relative so she came to get me from California, right after my mother's funeral. It's all kind of a blur at the moment and I'm not sure which is worse, being with my aunt or being here."

"It's not too bad here. You'll get used to it. I expect being this far away from home is a challenge."

"You can say that again."

"I expect being away from home is a challenge," Raj repeated.

"No, I meant—" I started to laugh. "It's an expression."

"Oh, I get it." Raj laughed too.

"Did you have no one to look after you at home? Is that why you're here?" I felt a little awkward bringing the subject up.

"My grandmother took care of me and my dad, but my father thought I needed a place with more challenges, especially in science. They offered me a science scholarship to come here.

That's why I thought you might have seen the particle accelerator. This is supposed to be a top science school but I haven't found anyone yet who is a real science nut like me. And the way they teach science is really weird—I mean instead of teaching things they make you find out for yourself. There's an awful lot of explosions in that lab, I can tell you. Bloody dangerous if you ask me – but fun."

I attacked my large plate of bangers and mash. It was delicious and it was followed by hot apple tart and a vanilla sauce.

"Let me guess," I said to Sam. "This is called hammers and mush?"

"Apple Tart and custard," he said between the bites he was shoveling in his mouth as fast as he could. I didn't blame him. I finished every last bite and would have licked the bowl like he did if I hadn't noticed Pippa staring at me.

I looked around as I ate. An older boy of maybe sixteen or seventeen was sitting at the head of our table. The fashionable group of girls giggled and whispered together at the other end. You might ask me how I know they were the fashionable ones if they all had uniforms on – but trust me, if you're a girl you know! Across from us a boy with dark skin was turned around in his seat, speaking earnestly to an older girl at the next table who had red hair and freckles. Sam, Celeste, Raj and Pippa were laughing and talking to each other and I had trouble following their accents. It's like a little United Nations, I thought, and everyone has come here for such a different reason. Weird.

The days of traveling suddenly caught up with me all at once. I felt as if I could sleep for a million years. If only I could just crawl up to my room and sleep.

Suddenly I remembered my dream about the girl in the grey cloak. I looked around the room.

"What are you looking for?" Raj asked.

"A girl I might know," I said. "Tell me, do some kids wear grey robes?"

"Grey robes? Not here. It must be another school ... robes? That sounds like something from another century. Our uniform is green, green, and more green, as you can see. It's really hard when we play football. We blend in with the grass." He laughed.

I kept glancing around the hall and by the end of the meal I was sure that the girl I had met in the dream did not go to this school. I felt ridiculously disappointed.

I MAKE SOME FRIENDS?

A nother bell rang and a boy who looked much older than twelve or thirteen stepped onto the stage. "Right, you lot," he shouted in a deep man's voice, "here are your assignments. Rooms 2 through 4 are in charge of dining hall cleanup, rooms 5 through 7 will be washing dishes, rooms 8 through 10 have breakfast duty and should report to Mrs. Williams at 6:30 tomorrow. Okay, don't just sit there. Get moving."

"That's us. We 'ave to wash the dishes," groaned Celeste and I got up from the table with the others. She had to raise her voice above the noise in the dining hall. Students were leaving through the large double doors talking and laughing.

"I thought a big school like this would have a cleaning staff," I said, surprised.

"They have a staff. There's Mrs. Williams, the cook and several helpers, but Miss Neves thinks it's important for us to learn through manual work," Raj said. "'Chores build your Heart, Mind and Body,'" he intoned, mimicking Miss Neves's voice, "'and save loads of money for my retirement in the south of France.'"

"How true, Mr. Puri," said a voice behind us and we all jumped. Miss Neves was standing there. "Wasn't your room in charge of washing dishes, girls? She turned to look at the three of us and we hurried off to the kitchen.

"I can't believe we have to wash the dishes!" said Pippa angrily as we joined the row of girls and boys at stainless steel sinks and put on yellow rubber gloves. She had to yell to be heard over the sound of running water and all the people talking and yelling around us. We were in a long narrow room between the dining hall and the kitchen. Sinks ran the length of the room. Dirty dishes were piled on the right side of the room. Celeste and I scraped dishes and passed them to Pippa who dunked them in hot soapy water and gave them a quick wipe before sending them on to the next sink to be scrubbed more thoroughly. The dishes were passed from student to student through soapy water, clean water and finally dried and put away in large cupboards at the end of the narrow room by the older students. The process went surprisingly quickly with all of us working all together.

"It is disgusting," Celeste complained. "My family pays money for me to come here to learn, not to be a servant. And I shall ruin my nails."

"I think I might run away," Pippa said dramatically.

"Run away?" I looked up in surprise.

Pippa shrugged. "I do it all the time. This is my fifth school. They send me to these awful schools and suddenly I can't take it any longer and I run away."

"Wow. If you run away can I go with you?" I had never thought about running away before. I had been too much in shock. But it suddenly seemed like a good idea.

"Where would you go if you ran away?"

I shrugged. I was about to say "back to California," but I realized before the words came out that there was no way I'd get there. I didn't have the money for one thing and Aunt Jean was my legal guardian. She had taken my passport with her when she went. I tried to think of a good answer. "We could camp out in the woods or something."

Pippa gave me a cold stare. "I always go home. One of these days they will run out of awful boarding schools and they'll be forced to let me stay home."

"Can't you go to a regular school if you hate boarding schools?" I asked. "Can't you tell your parents you'd rather be at home?"

"Of course. But in my family the children have always been sent away to school. It's been a tradition for hundreds of years."

"Maybe I will run away, too," Celeste said. "But I would merely 'op on the next plane to find my mother. I certainly find it most disagreeable here. Do you know that they do not allow me any makeup? And Miss Neves took away my Prada shoes."

I caught Pippa's eye as she passed me a plate to be washed, and we exchanged a grin.

"I'd have my face scrubbed if I was caught wearing lipstick at home," Pippa said. "Wouldn't you, Addy?"

"My mom would have just said that I looked silly pretending to be grown up and I should enjoy being a kid," I answered. "And what are Prada shoes?"

"You have not heard of the designer, Prada?" Celeste sounded shocked. "He is one of zee most famous designers in the world. My mother was a model once. I only wear clothes from the most famous designers."

"How old are you, Celeste?" I asked.

"I am thirteen. I only must be in class wiz the twelve year olds because I do not write English so well. It is most annoying."

"Well, I'm sorry you find us annoying," Pippa said sarcastically and slapped a plate down into the water so that the spray splashed Celeste. "We'll try to act more maturely in future, right, Addy?"

"Right." I grinned back at Pippa realizing that I might have found a friend even with her kind of strange English manners.

By the time we were finished another bell rang in the castle. "Half an hour until lights out." Pippa explained as we walked out of the dining room doors. She looked up and down the hallway, clearly unsure of which way to go. "I'll never get the hang of this place," she said.

"I have a superb sense of direction," Celeste said over her shoulder as she took the lead. "I have had much practice walking around so many cities by myself. This way."

I had forgotten that they were new to the school like me. In spite of Celeste's confidence we had to stop several times and consult each other before we finally made it back to our dorm. I was so tired that my feet didn't want to obey me. Jet lag was definitely catching up with me.

I MEET THE CAT-EYED MAN

"That's our common room," said Pippa as we passed a large corner room on the fifth floor. I glanced in. A fire burned cheerfully in a large stone fireplace in the corner and students were gathered around the tables or sitting on the floor by the fire talking.

"It's where we do our prep and go to just read and relax. We can make hot cocoa and there are biscuits."

At that moment the older girl called Fern who had spoken to Miss Neves and me earlier came out the common room.

"No point in going in there now. It's almost lights out," she said as if she enjoyed giving us the bad news. Then she frowned at me. "So you're the new one," she said. "I'm your dorm monitor and I expect you to behave yourself. Lights out is nine o'clock sharp. Go on then, off to bed."

She stood scowling at us as we walked down the corridor.

"Watch out for Fern," Pippa whispered as she closed our bedroom door behind us. "She's absolutely poisonous—and awful sneak and a tattletale. Luckily she's also very lazy so she doesn't bother to check on us as often as she should."

"She didn't look very friendly," I agreed. "Where do I sleep?"

"I've been sleeping on the top bunk," Pippa said, "and Celeste has had the bed over there, as you can tell by that oversized down comforter."

I looked at it with envy. It looked so luxurious and warm and the room was already cold. "Were we supposed to bring our own comforters?" I asked.

"No, we were not," Pippa said. "It clearly said that bedding was supplied. I don't know how you are getting away with it, Celeste."

Celeste shrugged her shoulders and grinned. "I suppose my parents must have paid extra because they are so rich," she said. "The comforter just arrived one morning, just after I was thinking I should write to Mama because I was too cold at night. Mama is so wonderful. She always seems to know exactly what I want."

Pippa shot her a disgusted look. "Anyway, that means you get the bottom bunk, Addy. Is that all right with you?"

"As long as you don't sleepwalk and put your foot in my face," I said.

Pippa was already throwing her clothes off and pulling on thick flannel pajamas. I started to change, too. Pippa looked at my oversized T-shirt in horror. "You'll need something warmer than that. You'll freeze."

"Maybe they'll send up some warmer pjs when the rest of my stuff arrives in the morning," I said. "For tonight there is nothing I can do."

"Keep your socks on for one thing," Pippa said. "Maybe even your cardigan."

"Definitely the sweater," I agreed. "That's all it is good for, sleeping in. Isn't it the ugliest thing you've ever seen?"

"Mais no," Celeste said. "In France it is fashionable to wear black, even for children."

"You've achieved a miracle already, Addy," Pippa said, as she slid under her covers. "Celeste thinks you're fashionable." She gave a giggle. Then she pulled out a little book from under her pillow and started writing in it, with as little of her head out of the covers as she could manage.

"What are you writing?" I asked.

"My diary." Pippa almost shoved it under the covers as she answered.

"Don't worry, I'm not about to peek," I said as I climbed into my own bed. It felt icy cold. A freezing draft was coming in from the window.

"Don't they have central heating in here?" I asked.

"They do but it gets turned off at night. Supposed to be healthier," Pippa said with a snort. "As if freezing to death is healthy for anyone?"

I pulled the covers over my head and scrunched into a tight little ball. "Oh my god, I'm freezing!" I moaned.

"I have many warm nightgowns I can lend you but you are not a size 0 as I am. Nightgowns are the only clothes of my own zey let me wear in this 'orrible school." Celeste sat on her own bed and brushed out her long hair all the time reciting a long list of complaints about the things that the school wouldn't let her do. Pippa occasionally looked up from her journal to answer. I sort of half listened without really taking in their words. It was hard enough to understand an English accent but a French one was way harder. My brain seemed to have developed a complete fuzz. The bell rang again and Pippa quickly shoved the book under the covers. The door banged open and Fern poked her head inside. "Lights out you lot." Fern flipped the switch. "No more talking, Celeste."

I lay there feeling cold and dumb. So much had happened to me in one day it was hard to take it all in. It almost didn't feel real. I'm in a foreign country, I told myself, in a boarding school, sharing a room with two strange girls. My only relative in the world couldn't wait to get rid of me. And then the thought that I had pushed to the back of my mind crept to the surface. The enormous, most scary thought of all. I had been adopted. Even my own mother was no longer really mine. I belonged to no one. Wait – that wasn't right. I belonged to someone, somewhere, didn't I? Someone who had given me away. Someone who didn't want me either. A tiny bit of hope crept into my mind—that maybe somehow I could trace my real mother and she'd be glad to see me again, but I shut that thought out instantly. I didn't want a new mother; I wanted my mom and she was dead.

I squeezed my eyes tight shut, trying to make sleep come. I could already hear Pippa snoring. I tried to picture my home in California—the breezes blowing in from the ocean, my mom's long blond hair blowing out behind her as she walked, the distant sound of the waves, the smell of the redwood trees. Then I could feel that soft breeze in my face and I thought I heard my mom's voice, saying gently, "It's going to be okay."

The breeze became stiffer and colder. I had a strange sensation that I was flying and realized I was riding the red dragon again. I could feel the scales digging into my thighs and hear the crackling beating of its wings sounding like someone flapping paper. Higher and higher we went, riding on air currents like the hawks and vultures do at home. The air became crisp and cold and before me were mountains tipped with snow. The central peak was glistening in the sun and as we came closer I could see that it wasn't a snow-covered mountain at all, it was a crystal pyramid, from which the sun was reflected with dazzling brightness.

I stared at it, fascinated, but at the same time I knew absolutely certainly that I didn't want to go any closer. "No,' I yelled. "Not there." I pulled at the dragon's neck, trying to make it turn away. Suddenly a great beam of white light shot up from the pyramid. We were frozen into the middle of it. I heard the dragon's fire crackle out just as if water had been poured on a campfire, and it started to plunge downward. Faster and faster we went until I couldn't breathe. I closed my eyes waiting for the moment when I crashed into the glass pyramid.

Then suddenly I was inside, standing barefoot on a cold marble floor. It was cold and so bright it hurt my eyes. At one end of a huge room was a throne, and on the throne was a figure. He was very tall and very thin. He was dressed in silvery white robes that shimmered as if they were glowing with their own light. A silver crown was on his head. He had a long pale face with a thin sharp nose and pointed chin. Wisps of pale white hair hung around his cheeks. His eyes were closed.

At his feet lay a small animal of some kind. A lizard? Then it sighed in its sleep and smoke came from its nostrils. And I realized that it was a small white dragon.

"I shouldn't be here." The thought screamed through my head. I looked around to see how I could get out without the man on the throne waking up and seeing me.

Just as I was tiptoeing across the floor he spoke. "Who are you?" he asked and his voice was soft and silky and icy at the same time. "Turn to face me."

I turned. I couldn't help myself.

"How did you come here?" he asked.

"I'm sorry. I didn't mean to be here at all, it just happened. We got caught in a beam of light and just sort of fell."

"We?"

"I was riding this dragon."

He stood up. He was extremely tall, taller than any basketball player I had ever seen. He started to come toward me, his long shimmering white cape dragging on the floor behind him. I wanted to run, but my legs wouldn't move.

"I'll ask you again: who are you? Look at me!" The last words were an icy command.

I looked. The man had bright green eyes, like a cat's. They sparkled with green fire and when I stared at him suddenly I was trapped. I felt a brilliant beam of light shoot from the man's eyes, boring into my own eyes, and past them into my brain, into my mind. I'm not going to tell him who I am, I repeated over and over. The pain was unbearable. I felt as if my head was going to explode, as if I was going to shatter into a million little pieces. "I won't," I tried to shout but it came out as a yell of despair ….

CREEPY CAT-EYED MAN, PART TWO

Then someone was shaking me. "No,' I shouted. "Leave me alone. Let go of me."

"Wake up, Addy. You're having a nightmare."

I opened my eyes to see Pippa standing over me in the dim light, a worried look on her face.

"You were moaning horribly," she said.

"I hope you do not intend to do this too often, or we shall get no sleep," Celeste muttered from under her down comforter.

"Oh, come on, Celeste," I heard Pippa whisper. "Her mother just died and she's just come to a new country. No wonder she's having bad dreams."

At that moment our door was flung open and Fern stood there, wearing a long flannel nightgown.

"What's going on in here?" she demanded. "Who's making all this noise?"

"Addy had a nightmare," Pippa said, giving her a cold stare. "It's all right. We can take care of her."

"Then quiet down and go to sleep," Fern said. "You're much too old to have nightmares. I never dream myself."

"That's because you need a brain and imagination to dream," Pippa muttered as Fern closed the door behind her. "And clearly she has neither."

I was still shivering. Pippa sat on the edge of her bed. "Do you want to tell me your dream? I make up funny endings for my nightmares and laugh them off. Or ... was it about your mum? Sorry. That probably wasn't a very tactful thing to say."

"No, it wasn't my mother. It was a horrible man and he looked at me and..." I tried to picture the dream. "No, it's gone. That's funny. I normally remember my dreams."

"Now, please, let us get back to sleep," Celeste said. "I was having a delightful dream about shopping with my mother at

Galleries Lafayette."

"I have nightmares at all my new schools," Pippa said with the air of someone who had done this a hundred times. "You'll feel better in the morning."

"Thanks, Pippa," I mumbled, but I didn't dare go back to sleep. I lay awake, forcing my eyes to stay open, staring at the bottom of Pippa's bunk above me. Why had that dream been so scary? Why couldn't I remember it? I was so tired that my whole body was aching, but I knew one thing… I didn't want that dream again.

I lay there, trying not to sleep, staring into the darkness. I heard the hoot of an owl and I thought I saw something flapping past my window. We had owls at home—they were nothing to be scared of. And I shouldn't be scared of a silly dream.

"Dreams can't hurt me," I muttered over and over. "They are just my brain freewheeling when I'm not using it. Just my imagination."

Pippa and Celeste were breathing heavily again now and the sound was rhythmic and comforting. I felt my eyes closing in spite of myself and suddenly I was back in that palace. I knew instantly where I was, even though this time I was standing in a small side room. Through a big arched doorway I could see a long gallery and beyond the doorway I heard voices.

"You summoned me, Lord Grymur?" a man's thin voice asked. I could hear it trembling with fear.

"Who was she, Regulator?" I recognized that smooth, silky, terrifying voice instantly and shrank back behind the drapes that hung in the doorway.

"She, my lord?"

"I have just been visited, in my own palace, by a young girl. She was apparently riding a dragon. A red dragon, Regulator. She flew, unhindered, undetected until my thought-beam caught her. So I want to know how anybody, let alone a child, could still have the power to conjure a dragon, and have been brazen enough to defy me in this way. Is she one of yours?"

"Mine, my lord?"

I looked around desperately. The drape in front of me was the only way out.

"Did she escape from the school?"

"No, Lord Grymur, I assure you, we have no child at the school with that sort of power. I would have informed you immediately if such a one had been discovered."

"Then it is true. There are still Fareeth hiding out undetected."

"I promise you, Lord Grymur, that there are not. If any Fareeth have survived, they are poor, wretched creatures who lurk in remote places, waiting for death. And there are no Fareeth children. You know that. The hounds of the Fallon Gwyn would sniff them out at birth and destroy them. And your Watchers are vigilant in every settlement, making sure none of the old powers are reborn."

I couldn't resist peeking out, even though my mind was yelling at me that it was a dumb move. The tall king-like guy was standing over another man, also dressed in white, who knelt at his feet, groveling.

"Nevertheless she was here, Regulator. She spoke to me. And when I tried to question her, she was able to depart from me. She broke away, Regulator. She left my presence. What have you got to say to that?" He was shrieking now.

"I suppose there is a chance she could have been a Dreamwalker." The man cowered as he said the words and bowed his head, as if waiting for a blow.

"No." Lord Grymur's face was twisted with rage. "That's not possible. There are no more Dreamwalkers! She would have been detected by now, unless a Watcher has failed me."

"Watchers never fail you, Master. How could they?"

"Then tell me how a Dreamwalker could have survived to come here, to my palace, to Caer-Eira itself, and to challenge me in front of my own throne?"

"I can't give you an answer, Master. I am as perplexed as you are."

"You had better be, Regulator. If I were you, I would be quaking in my boots at this moment. It has been valuable to me to allow you to keep your small power. That can change. And I understand a Watcher's position has just become vacant up in a settlement on the high moors. Very bleak and cold up there, so I'm told. Very dreary."

The Regulator cowered even lower. "Master, I beg you. I'll do anything…"

Lord Grymur grabbed the Regulator by his shirt and lifted him from the ground so that his face was only inches away from his own. "Then find her, Regulator. Scour every settlement. Send out the Rancurs and the Fallon Gwyn, only find her and bring her to me so that I may destroy her! What's that?" He dropped the man. "Someone is here. She is here. I sense her presence." His eyes began to scan the room. I looked around desperately for an escape. It was only a matter of seconds before he found me.

"Wake up, wake up!" I told myself. "Time to go, now!" But I had no red dragon this time. I tried to picture my new dorm room and Pippa and Celeste. Then there was the sound of singing. I looked around to see where it was coming from.

I GET TOTALLY LOST

I opened my eyes and saw Celeste standing in front of the mirror, doing vocal exercises in a beautiful high soprano voice. "Shut up, Celeste," Pippa's voice growled from under the covers.

Gray dawn light shone in through the window. It was freezing cold in the room. The heat from the little radiator under the window didn't warm the room at all.

"I 'ave to do my warm-ups every morning. I promised my music teacher."

I sat up. "I wish warm-ups really warmed you up. It's freezing in here."

"Hand those up, would you?" Pippa pointed to some clothes draped over the radiator. I handed them up and the bunk bed shook as Pippa twisted and turned under the covers and then emerged fully clothed.

"Oh, so that's how it's done, is it?" I grinned, then shivered as I took down my new uniform from the closet and jumped back into bed. "But aren't we supposed to take a shower or something?"

"Supposed to, yes. And Fern's supposed to check on us, but as I said, she's awfully lazy, thank heavens."

"But we need to shower sometime, don't we? My hair's a total mess."

"You can take one now if you want to," Pippa said. "Rather you than me. It's icy in there in the mornings."

"I usually take my shower at night," Celeste said, "but we were too late last night."

"And I take mine after riding. I don't like smelling all horsey. I'd try to slip up during the day and take one if I were you. It's warmer then."

"Only make sure you avoid the terrible Fern," Celeste added.

I tried to wriggle into my clothes under the covers then lay there, enjoying one last minute of warmth. Celeste went back to her doing singing exercises. "I want my Pra-a-da shoes," she began to sing instead of mee, mee, mee." I want my Pra-a-da shoes." Pippa glanced down at me as she brushed her hair and rolled her eyes.

"I have to practice you know. A good singer never stops singing. My mother does her vocal practice every day. I wish to be like her." And she went back to walking around going, "Mi, mi, mi, mi, mi, mi, mi. Mu, mu, mu, mu, mu, mu, mu. I wish I were feeling warmer…"

A bell echoed somewhere down below.

"Breakfast in ten minutes. Come on, hurry up," Pippa said and yanked the covers off me. I rushed to finish buttoning my shirt then followed the others down the hall to the girls' bathroom, where other first formers were already washing and brushing their teeth. I looked at my reflection in the mirror. It was almost as if a stranger was looking back at me—a stranger in a green skirt, white shirt, green tie and a green sweater. For a second it almost looked as if my eyes had turned green to match everything else. Bright green, like a cat's.

"Weird," I muttered as a second bell rang. There was an immediate stampede down the hallway. I wiped away the toothpaste quickly and ran to keep up. I had no idea how to find the dining hall but I followed everyone else, across the freezing causeway and down staircases into the dining hall in which we had eaten the night before.

The dining hall looked more cheerful in the morning than it had at dinnertime. I had somehow lost Pippa and Celeste in the stampede and was glad to spot some familiar faces as I found my place and sat down. Breakfast was milky tea with sugar, scrambled eggs and toast with either a bitter orange jelly Pippa called marmalade or a black paste that was the saltiest thing that I had ever eaten in my life.

"What on earth is this? It tastes disgusting."

"It's Marmite. It's brilliant," Sam said. "You've spread it too thickly."

I tried another slice, spread thinner but it still made me pucker my lips. "Yuck," I said. "It looks like motor oil and tastes worse."

"Maybe you have to be born British to like Marmite," Pippa said.

"But I was born British and I still don't like it."

"Born over here, were you?" Sam asked.

I nodded. " I moved to California when I was a baby." I didn't want to say out loud the word 'adopted.' It was still too painful. So I left it at that and settled for a few bites of plain toast. I was too nervous to eat much anyway.

"Come on, hurry up," Pippa said. "We'll be late for class if we don't hurry. I've got to grab gloves. I left them up in the common room." She rushed off. I joined the crush surging out of the dining hall.

Everyone seemed to know where they were going. I was swept along in the tide of students until they all headed in different directions. I looked around for a teacher to ask where I was supposed to go but there were none in sight. No sign of any other first formers either. I knew I had to find a stairway and go upstairs, but there weren't any. At last I heard the sound of pots and pans clanging and walked toward it hoping to find someone. I opened a door I hadn't been through before and found myself in a huge cavernous kitchen. A plump woman with wispy hair pulled back in a bun was sitting at a large kitchen table, her feet propped up on the chair next to her, drinking from a ceramic mug.

"Hello, love," she said as she looked up and saw me. "Are you lost? It's your first day, isn't it?"

"Yes, I don't know where I'm supposed to be." My voice must have sounded a bit shaky. It was nice to hear someone speak to me in such a kind tone.

"The first formers are all gardening right now. That's them out there." She pointed. Through the kitchen window, I could see students bending over the raised beds in the kitchen gardens outside. "No one will mind if you miss gardening your first day. Have a cup of tea and calm yourself a bit. You look like you're about to jump out of your skin. No one here is going to eat you, you know." She smiled. "I'm Mrs. Williams."

"The cook?"

"The same." Mrs. Williams spoke in the same singsong accent that I had heard at the station. Without asking she poured me a large mug of strong tea and added sugar and milk. "That'll fix you up. Been cooking here for twelve years now. Seen a lot of jumpy first formers. And what is your name, love?"

"I'm Addy." I sipped tea in silence for a minute. "Do you know all the students here then, Mrs. Williams?"

"Most of them. I know all the first years because my boy is one of them. That's my Gwylum right there." She pointed at a plump boy with a round face and dark hair digging in the garden. I could see the resemblance instantly. Mrs. Williams smiled fondly looking at him. "Grown up in this school he has. And now he's old enough to be a proper student here. It's wonderful that he'll be getting such a good education, isn't it? But that's enough about us. Tell me where you're from, Addy. Your accent sounds quite different from the other students. From a different place, are you? Have you come from the city?"

"You mean London? No, I'm from America. From the United States."

Mrs. Williams frowned, then shook her head. " No – you won't catch me in the city. Much better that you are here. Safer. Anyway." She leaned forward and patted my hand. "What's wrong then, my lovey – why did you come to my door trembling as if someone was going to eat you?"

I felt safe and warm in the big kitchen and found myself telling Miss Williams how strange it felt to come to a new place and how lost I felt in the old castle.

"I know just how you feel," Mrs. Williams sympathized. "I felt the same way when I came here. All alone and lost." She patted my hand comfortingly. "But cheer up now. It's always brightest before the dusk."

"Wait, don't you mean…" I stopped myself. Perhaps she had translated wrongly because she spoke Welsh as her first language. She might be strange, but at least she was friendly and I certainly needed friends at this moment. The tea and the conversation had cheered me up and I was feeling much happier when Mrs. Williams said, "Here they come then. You'd better have someone show you the way to your next class. It's up on the fourth floor and that's a bit tricky to get to." I watched the students taking their boots off in the glassed-in closet. I heard talking and laughter as they poured into the corridor. "Gwylum," called Mrs. Williams, walking out into the hall as the boy came in from outside.

"Yes, mum?" he asked coming over to us. "Do you need something?"

"Take Addy here up to maths would you, love. It's her first day and she's already got lost once."

"All right, Mum." Gwylum said cheerfully in the same sort of singsong accent. He looked at me with a shy smile and then blushed.

"Have a good day, Addy," Mrs. Williams called after us. "Study hard, Gwylum, bach. And Addy, you come and see me if you need a chat."

"Thanks. I will," I said gratefully as Mrs. Williams disappeared back into the kitchen.

NOT A GOOD FIRST IMPRESSION AT MATH

"Come on then, Abby. Hurry up," Gwylum said. "Mr. Thomas doesn't like it if we're late."

"Sure." I followed him along a corridor filled with students hurrying to class. "Uh ... it's Addy not Abby."

Gwylum blushed again. "Sorry."

"Don't worry about it. Everyone does it the first time they meet me. And I don't remember your name either. Was it William?"

"It's Gwylum. That's Welsh for William so you're sort of right."

"William Williams – that's kind of cool."

"Silly really, isn't it? When you think about it. But that's the way it's often done here in Wales." He pushed open a door and started to climb a winding staircase.

"Were you born here?" I asked.

"That's right. Born and brought up here in the school."

"So do you speak Welsh?" I asked.

"Yes, I do. But not in school, of course. Just to my mum in the evenings."

Gwylum didn't say any more and I was too wiped out from climbing all those stairs to ask any more questions.

"Here we are." Gwylum said as we came to the fourth floor. "In you go." He gave the same shy smile and hurried into the classroom.

I was pretty relieved to see it was a perfectly normal classroom. It had rows of desks that all faced the teacher's desk at the front of the room. Mr. Thomas didn't look too scary either. He was not too old with long wavy light brown hair and a worried expression. I saw Pippa and Celeste at the front of the room but the desks around them were all taken. I slid into an empty seat at the back, trying to be as inconspicuous as possible. A group of girls came in talking and laughing loudly. I recognized them as the ones who had laughed at my clothes the night before. They stopped talking when they noticed me.

"That's Angela's seat," a girl with long dark hair said, looking down her nose at me as if I was a worm.

A tall blond girl came right up to me and leaned over the desk. She held out her hand and smiled at me even though the smile didn't quite reach her eyes. "I'm Angela," she said pulling her hand away just before I could take it. "You're new so I won't hold it against you this time. But that's my seat."

I felt myself going red as I scrambled to my feet. "I didn't know we had assigned seats. Where am I supposed to sit?"

"Anywhere but here obviously," the dark haired girl said, looking at Angela. As I moved down the aisle, one of the girls stuck out her foot. I tripped and went flying forwards, fighting hard not to go sprawling on my face. Mr. Thomas looked up in surprise.

"My. I've never had a student before so keen to get to maths class that she comes running in," he said, but he smiled. "You must be Miss Walker. I've been told you were joining us. Welcome. I am Mr. Thomas. Can we find a seat for Miss Walker?"

"Over 'ere," Sam called, patting the chair beside him.

My cheeks were still burning with embarrassment and I went to join Sam over by the window. Mr. Thomas started talking in that singsong Welsh voice and I stared out of the window, trying to wish the whole classroom and the whole school away. As I looked out at the green countryside below something in it made me think of the dream I had had the night before... not a dream, a nightmare ... and a man with green eyes ... and he had tried to ...

"Addison ... Miss Walker." I came back to reality. Mr. Thomas was talking to me and once again everyone was staring at me. "Can you do this sum, Addison?"

"Sorry?" My mind was still on that dream.

"Can you do this sum for us?"

"Some what?"

The whole class laughed. "I expect they don't even learn to add in American schools," Angela said from the back of the room pretending to whisper but making sure everyone could hear her. Then I looked at the whiteboard at the front of the class. $46745.35 + x = 89994.67$ was written on the board. A simple algebra problem that we'd done years ago.

"Oh – that's easy," I started to say when Miss Neves walked

into the room. She was frowning in my direction. Oh God, what had I done now?

"Addison, I have been looking all over for you. You were meant to see me right after breakfast. Did Fern not tell you?"

"No, she didn't," I said.

"I saw Fern tell her, Miss Neves," the dark haired girl said smugly, "during breakfast." She smiled at the Headmistress and looked so innocent that I wanted to throw up.

"What the..." I stared at her and started to argue with her but before I could get the sentence out Miss Neves interrupted.

"Thank you, Penelope. Well, I've found you now, Addison. We need to find out what level you have reached before I know which classes you should be in. Let's go, Addison. I'm sorry for the disruption, Mr. Thomas."

"Not at all, Headmistress." Mr. Thomas gave me a smile. He seemed nice enough. "Hope to see you soon, Addison."

As I followed Miss Neves through the classroom a boy said, "Ooh, the testing. She's off to the dungeon."

"Half the kids who go down there never come back," another boy said, grinning at me meanly as I walked past him.

"Good riddance," Angela muttered to the girl next to her.

"Shut up," Pippa snapped, swiveling around in her seat. "Good luck, Addy."

"Yes, good luck," Mr. Thomas called after me.

Why did I need good luck? And what was that about a dungeon? This was turning out to be the worst school day of my life and it was still only nine o'clock.

I GET SENT TO THE DUNGEON

Miss Neves led me back down the stairs toward the dining hall. She stopped before a heavy oak door and opened it with a large old-fashioned key.

"Please watch your step," she said as she stepped through to a spiral stairway. "The light is not very good, I'm afraid and the steps are broken in places."

Then she started to go down. And down. I followed her feeling the wall cold and damp as I touched it. I had thought that boy was joking when he said 'dungeon.' Now I wasn't so sure. This couldn't be for real, could it?

"No one will disturb us in here," Miss Neves said as she pushed open another thick oak door with studs in it and ushered me into a small room. Her words echoed from the vaulted ceiling. The walls and floor were made of rough stone. There was only one tiny slit of a window high in the wall and a lamp on a rough table only threw a narrow circle of light. I looked around me. "Is this really a dungeon?" I asked, trying not to sound too scared.

Miss Neves chuckled. "A dungeon? We're not exactly that primitive, Addison. This room is ideal because it has no distractions. Now please take a seat."

I sat at the one table in the room. Ideal for what? My heart was beating so loudly that I was sure Miss Neves would hear it.

"Our students come from many different backgrounds and from all over the world," Miss Neves said nicely enough. "We find it a good idea to test their abilities before placing them in their classes. I have no doubt that you will be placed in the same classes as most of your peers. But these tests will help determine if there are any subjects with which you require special attention from one of the teachers. Also we need to discover if you have any special gifts that this school can foster. Every afternoon we give an hour to private lessons in the field of your choice. For example, your classmate Mr. Puri is working with Mr. Thomas on advanced chemistry. Your roommate Phillipa is working to become a show jumper – that is horseback riding – and Celeste is taking voice lessons from Miss Tiery along with English grammar and diction. Let us see where your special talents lie."

She placed a pencil and a testing booklet about 20 pages thick in front of me. "You have two hours to complete this booklet. I will return then." She got up and closed the door with a horridly final thud, leaving me alone in the room. I pulled my chair closer to the table and the sound echoed from the stone walls.

"It's okay. You can do this," I said out loud and my words echoed back at me. I tried not to think of where I was. "I'm perfectly safe in a school," I said. "They wouldn't leave me anywhere dangerous." Then I remembered the walkway to our dorm with the three-story drop. Okay, so maybe they don't care about danger in Wales. What on earth was the test going to be like? I stared at the cover of the booklet, decorated with a Red Dragon. The way it was drawn made it look almost familiar—like the one I rode. Somehow that was comforting. Underneath was written, "There is a bookcase against the wall. You may find it helpful to use the books."

I turned around and saw a bookcase I hadn't noticed before. Then I cautiously turned the first page. I almost cried with relief. It was full of regular math problems. Math was one of my best subjects. I'd show them what I could do. I worked quickly through the math pages. I couldn't do the last couple of problems because they were concepts I had never seen before and I started to worry again. Could the other kids do this stuff? Were they going to think I was stupid? Then I turned the page to find a section on social studies. Now I really felt stupid. I didn't know much about world history, especially not British history and especially NOTHING about Welsh history.

I got up and walked over to the bookshelf. A big fat volume on Welsh history caught my eye and I took it down. I looked at the first question. "What animal represents the national symbol of Wales?" I started to page through the book hoping that the answer would be in the first chapter. Then a piece of paper fluttered to the floor. I picked it up and my heart started beating fast again.

1. The Red Dragon
2. To save the Welsh kingdom

3. To repel the British invaders

4. The Legend of King Arthur

I carried the paper and the book back to the table and checked the questions again.

"Oh my god! It's the answers," I said out loud. "I have the answers in my hand." For an incredible moment I considered Miss Neves's face when every bonus answer was right. That would show them that an American girl wasn't as ignorant as they thought. But then I heard my mom's voice. "Being yourself is always enough. Don't change who you are to please anyone."

I crumpled up the piece of paper and wrote, "I never learned any Welsh history."

The next section was English. First a section on grammar that was easy enough and then a paragraph on one of the following topics:

Absolute power corrupts absolutely.

Is solitary confinement the best punishment?

Our duty is to make the best use of our talents.

What would you do if you found yourself locked in a confined space?

I sat staring around me. It was totally silent down here and now I wasn't concentrating on the test I realized again that I had been shut in a dungeon. I got up and went across to the door. There was no handle, just a big iron ring. I pulled on it and the door didn't open. I tried pushing it and the door didn't budge. I turned it... and nothing. Now I could really feel my heart racing. I had been locked in a dungeon. Had that boy been joking when he said half the students never came back?

This school was too weird for me. I was sure that even my strange Aunt Jean would not want me to go to a school where they locked students in a dungeon for hours. I was getting out of here now. I'd find a way out of this dungeon, go down to the nearest town and telephone Aunt Jean. Luckily I had my binder with me and her office phone number in it. All I had to do was to see if I could get out of the dungeon.

I tried the door again, rattled it, twisted the handle, but it wouldn't move. The only other way out was the window. It was high in the arch of the stone wall and was only a tiny narrow opening. Was it big enough for me to crawl through if I could get up there? I stood on the table, but I wasn't high enough. I put the chair on the table and stood on that. Then I could just about reach it, but there was no way I could haul myself through. That's when I thought of the books. You may find the books helpful, the booklet had said. Totally right. I climbed down and began stacking the biggest, heaviest books on the seat on my chair. Then I climbed carefully to the top of the pile. The window was barred, but the bars looked old and rusty. I pushed hard and felt the bars fall away with a clang. I managed to stick my head through the narrow window and felt rain on my face. I saw that the window was only a foot above the ground. That was good. I dropped my binder ahead of me then I started to pull myself through. Boy, it was a tight squeeze and at one point I thought I might be stuck there until someone found me. But the thought of Miss Neves coming to see my legs hanging out of the window made me pull and wriggle harder and harder until I popped free like a cork from a bottle.

I jumped to my feet, looking around to see if anyone could see me. I was in a deserted courtyard with blank walls rising above me. It was raining so hard that I was soaked right away, but I wasn't going to risk finding my coat. I was clearly at the back of the building and I also wasn't going to risk walking around to the front and going out through the front gate. There had to be another way out. On the other side of the courtyard there was an arch and beyond it were trees. I sprinted across the courtyard, out through the arch and then across a lawn to the trees. It seemed like the forest went all the way up a hill. There had to be some place I could climb over a fence or get out up here. Then I'd find the road and a village.

Rain sounded loudly on the trees above and dripped down my neck as I slipped on a carpet of fallen leaves. After a while I got a strange feeling that I was being followed. I spun around but nobody was there. I shivered. My shirt was soaking wet now and the wind blowing down from the mountains was cold. This didn't seem like such a great idea any more. But I couldn't go back. I didn't want to go back. If I refused to go back, Aunt Jean would have to find me another school.

How big were the school grounds, anyway? They seemed to go on forever. A mist had come down, hiding the way ahead and making the trees look like unreal ghosts, looming out of the swirling mist. I sensed something too—a watchfulness, almost as if the forest itself was aware that I was there. "Don't be ridiculous," I told myself. Too many creepy things had happened to me recently, but it was no reason to be hysterical. I was in an ordinary British forest. Were there bears in British forests?

A flash of red made me jump until I realized that it was a red squirrel darting across the path. Well, something had made this path, so it must lead somewhere. I started to walk faster. Then I saw a flash of red ahead of me again. This time I jumped and let out a little scream. Something red was moving fast ahead and for a moment it looked like my red dragon, its wing billowing out behind it as it moved through the trees.

I RUN INTO TROUBLE

I peered again as the mist swirled, parted, and then closed in again. Wasn't that a dragon's red wing? Was that a wisp of smoke I saw?

I stopped, not wanting to meet whatever it was. Were there such things as dragons in Wales? Did they perhaps patrol school grounds? You can see how freaked out I was by everything that had happened to me, if this was the way I was thinking.

'Like Aunt Jean said, I have too much imagination,' I thought with a grin. 'I've got red dragons on the brain.'

And I started out to my left where I thought the road through the valley should be. Suddenly I saw the swirl of red ahead of me again and something stepped out in front of me, between two giant oak trees. I swallowed back a scream and then felt really dumb because it was only an old woman, dressed in a red cloak that fell to the ground with a hood that hid much of her face. But I could see her eyes. They were extremely bright—so bright green that they almost glowed.

"You won't get out that way," she said in a voice that sounded surprisingly young. "The way you are going only leads to the top of the mountains."

"I wasn't…" I stammered, because her piercing eyes were staring at me.

"Yes, you were. You wouldn't be the first student to try to run away. What's so bad about it anyway?"

I wondered if she was an old teacher and I'd get in trouble, but at this point I didn't care. "It's not my kind of school. It's too…well, old and weird. I'm used to schools that are light and modern and open and let you do what you like."

"Dear me," she said. "I'm afraid you have to learn that we can't always do what we like. Sometimes we have to do what is best for us."

"Being locked in a dungeon isn't good for anybody," I said. "I don't belong here."

"Oh, I think you will find that you do," she said. "If you decide to give it another try, that is. Up to you, of course. But if you're looking for the road, you have to take that path. It leads straight down."

And she pointed to a path I hadn't noticed before.

"Thanks," I turned to say, but she was gone.

I stared at the spot where she had been, watching for a glimpse of her red cloak or the sound of her feet moving through the dry leaves. But the forest had gone quiet again, apart from the patter of rain. I thought I'd better get out of there before she called the school to report me. I didn't wait a minute longer but set off downhill to my left, at a run. I stumbled a couple of times and slithered on mud, but then I was climbing up steps over a tall brick wall and down the other side and there was the road ahead of me.

I wasn't sure which direction to take. If I went to my left the road might bring me close to the front of the school and I might be seen. And I had no way of knowing if there would be any towns to my right, or the road might just peter out on a mountain. I heard the sound of a car approaching and tried to decide whether to thumb a ride. But my mom had always warned me about taking rides from strangers, and besides, the car might take me straight back to school. So I hid in the bushes and watched it go past. It was a delivery van and it was traveling fast. Best Bakery in Bangor was painted on its side.

That decided me. If a van was making deliveries to my right, there had to be some kind of business there—a pub or a café at least. I started walking. The rain was coming down harder now I was out in the open and I felt cold and miserable, and scared, too. What if Aunt Jean wouldn't take me away from this school? What if I was punished for trying to run away and locked up in a dungeon again? I squeezed my eyes shut to force back tears.

'Don't give up so easily,' I told myself. 'At home you always fought for things.' I started to run and soon I saw smoke curling up between trees. Then there was one gray stone cottage, then another. I came into the main street of a little village. There were a few shops and a café and a pub. I looked around for a phone then remembered I had no English money with me—or rather Welsh money. Was it the same? It didn't matter much because I had none of either.

Two women came toward me, speaking in Welsh. One of them looked at me.

"My but you're soaking, my dear. Where's your coat?" one of them said, switching to a lilting English.

"You'd better get inside before you catch your death of cold," the other added.

"I'm looking for a phone," I said. "I have to make an urgent call."

"Use the one in the tearoom," one of the women said. "She won't mind, I'm sure." She pointed at the café across the street. Light was streaming out and it looked warm and friendly. I only wished I had the money for a cup of hot tea and a cake. I pushed open the door. Inside felt warm and smelled of fresh baking. People were chatting at several tables. A woman looked up from behind the counter and came out, drying her hands on her apron.

"Can I help you, love?" she said.

"I need to make a phone call," I said. "But I'm afraid I don't have any money. Could I possibly use your phone and I'll repay you, I promise."

"Of course you can, if it's urgent," she said.

"Don't worry, Mrs. Richards, I'll pay for her telephone call," a voice said from a corner.

"I was waiting for her anyway."

And I looked right at the face of Miss Neves.

I MEET AN OLD FLOWER-LADY

"Congratulations, Addison," she said in her deep, smooth voice. "You made it. Quite ingenious."

I was still staring at her with my mouth open.

"What do you mean, congratulations?" I asked. "Were you expecting me to come here?"

"Of course. You followed the directions, didn't you? You used the books. Most useful things, books."

I was still staring at her as if I couldn't quite believe it. Directions? Was the test really to see if I could escape from the dungeon? If so, it was very different from the kind of tests given at my old school.

She motioned to a chair. "Sit down, dear. You're shivering. A cup of tea and some of your excellent scones for Miss Walker, if you don't mind, Mrs. Richards."

I sat. A cup of tea was placed in front of me. Then a plate of warm scones with cream and jam. I ate and drank while Miss Neves said nothing.

"We'd better get you back to school and change those wet clothes before you catch a nasty chill," she said. "We'll have Gwylum's mother dry and press your clothes for you, and you won't need to go to the dining hall tonight as you'll be dining with me."

"With you?" I stammered out.

"Oh yes. I always invite a new student to dine with me at the end of their first day. It's important for me to get to know you well. As I said, this is a day of testing. I'm looking for talents, both known and unknown to you, Miss Walker. I see you've enjoyed your scones. Now I suggest we get in my car and go back to school—unless you still need to make that telephone call, that is?"

I shook my head. I didn't think I could telephone Aunt Jean

with Miss Neves standing there. What would I tell her with Miss Neves listening to every word? So I followed her out to her car and soon we were back at school.

"How are you feeling?" Miss Neves asked. "Up to more testing? Because Miss Rorrim is expecting you." She obviously saw my face because she went on. "Not in the same place this time. In a perfectly normal classroom. Go and change and then take your uniform to Mrs. Williams. I'll meet you there."

I did what she said, but my head was still whirling with strange thoughts. How had she known I'd come to the village and to that teashop? How had she known I'd try to escape? Had there really been instructions on how to get out in that little booklet? I changed into my awful black skirt and sweater, then I found Mrs. Williams in the kitchen.

"The headmistress said you'd be coming here for your lunch," she said and put a bowl of stew and some crusty bread on a table for me.

"I think she said she wanted me to go back for more testing," I said, looking at the soup. It smelled really good.

"Nonsense. She'd want you to eat first," Mrs. Williams said. Even though I'd just had scones I sat down and started to eat. It wasn't until I'd finished that Miss Neves showed up again. "Good. You've had lunch," she said. "Come along. We mustn't keep Miss Rorrim waiting." And she led me to a small classroom at the end of a second floor corridor.

"Wait here for Miss Rorrim," she said, opening the door for me. "Have a good afternoon, won't you. And don't forget I'm expecting you for dinner tonight at six, Addison."

As she was about to leave a voice said, "Here I am, Headmistress. All ready to administer this afternoon's tests." She stepped into the room and smiled at me. "Good afternoon, Addison."

I tried not to stare at her, because she was one of the most peculiar people I had ever seen. The words "a flowery person" came into my head. She wore a sky blue dress covered with yellow cornflowers. Her body was large, soft and curved where Miss Neves was thin, bony and angular so that the two of them together reminded me of the old nursery rhyme "Jack Sprat could eat no fat, his wife could eat no lean." Over the blue dress was thrown a green cloak with ribboned pink roses. Her gray hair, which was braided into cornrows, had real roses tucked into the braids. Her brown face was furrowed into permanent laugh lines. On first glance it looked like the flowers were not merely placed in her hair but growing out of her braids like so many gray ropy vines. She was weighted down with a large canvas bag full of what I was delighted to see were tubes of paint. And she carried a stack of large books.

"I'll leave you to it then," Miss Neves said and closed the door behind me.

"I am pleased to meet you, Addy," Miss Rorrim said softly, putting the bag and the books down on the table and stepping forward to take my hand in her own.

My hand tingled as if a bolt of electricity had run through it. I jumped, knocking the stacks of books all over the table.

"I'm sorry," I muttered, trying to pile them up again.

Miss Rorrim smiled. "Now... I hear you are a painter. I've seen some of your mother's art so I am sure you have a talent we can work with. Can you paint with acrylics on canvas? Or do you prefer watercolors?"

"Acrylics, please," I said, still staring at her as she set up two easels and put a canvas on each.

"I think I'll join you," she said. "I can't bear to watch anyone paint if I'm not doing it, too. Is that the way with you?"

"What do you want me to paint?" I asked.

"Whatever comes to mind."

"I can paint much better from nature," I confessed. "It is kind of hard to paint in this bare room."

"Yes, but it is inside you that I want to see. What kind of landscape is in there?" Miss Rorrim tapped my chest with her paintbrush. "That is my job to find out. Let me see you do a painting entirely from your imagination. Clear your mind. Don't decide on what you are going to paint. Just let it come alive on the canvas."

I tried to do what she said. Slowly a picture began to appear in my thoughts. A green hill (no surprise, everything I'd seen since coming to Wales had been green), a tall gnarled oak with leaves changing to yellow and red, and under the oak a sleek horse just like the one in my dream but with a shiny black coat. Its face was turned away towards the edge of the picture, as if it waited expectantly for its owner.

"Well done." I jumped at the sound of Miss Rorrim's voice

over her shoulder. "You have drawn the mare very clearly."

"Yes, it must have been because of my dream," I said. "On the train I dreamed about a beautiful white horse just like this. But then my dream turned into a nightmare."

"How so?" Miss Rorrim's gaze was suddenly intense.

"When the horse turned to look at me, its head looked like a skeleton, fire came out of its eyes. Like something out of horror movie!"

"A nightmare? A Nightmare indeed." Miss Rorrim was suddenly agitated. "I must see Miss Neves about this at once." She stopped, remembering something. "But before I go I have one last assignment. No – not painting," she said as I returned to my easel. "A descriptive essay. Describe the object that is most precious to you. The one thing that above all you would not want to lose. Describe it in such detail that the reader can see it just as clearly as you can. This will be your last assignment."

"A Nightmare ... oh my." She bustled out of the room. I moved to a desk and sat down with pen and paper and described the one photograph I had brought with me. It was the photo with my mother at the beach on our perfect day. I was better at painting than writing but as I pictured that scene it was as if I was there again. I could smell the salt water and feel the sandy wind on my face. And my mom smiling and her hair blowing out in the wind.

I was startled when Miss Neves entered the room. "That will do for now, Addison. I expect you are thoroughly exhausted. If you hurry, you'll make it for the last of tea. Then go outside and get some good fresh air. Since you have no prep you could even take a nap before you join me for dinner."

"Yes, Miss Neves," I said meekly. 'I'm turning into one of them!' I thought as I stood up, stretching after sitting for so long. "A clone. Yes, Miss Neves. No, Miss Neves." I looked back and saw my painting still there on the easel. 'Well,' I thought, 'it's not so bad if I can have art classes. Miss Rorrim seems nice. If a little crazy.'

Then I looked at the picture Miss Rorrim had painted beside me. It was exactly the same scene.

'There is something definitely weird about this place,' I thought. 'Maybe Pippa can tell me what's going on here.'

As I came out of the dark hallway I was surprised to find sunlight streaming in through the windows and white clouds racing across a blue sky. I remembered what Miss Neves had said about the last of tea. What was all this great fascination with drinking tea all the time? It seemed hardly worthwhile finding my way to the dining hall for a drink. Besides I didn't want the kids to see me dressed in this uncool black outfit again. I followed the sunlight out into the main courtyard. Lessons had obviously ended for the day and kids were playing soccer or Frisbee, or just walking together talking and laughing. I looked at them with longing. Would I make real friends here? Did I want to stick around long enough to make real friends? And if Aunt Jean found me another school, would it be any better than this?

I FIND A HAUNTED HALLWAY

A large fountain was splashing noisily in the center of the courtyard. I sat on its edge and ran my fingers through the water. The fountain had a stone dragon in its center. Water was rushing from its mouth as if it were breathing liquid fire. Statues of fairytale creatures surrounded the fountain. A knight was on my left and a unicorn on my right. I could make out a lion right across from me although part of its mane was missing. 'Probably chipped off by flying Frisbees,' I thought as one just missed me.

"Sorry," a boy called.

The fountain looked vaguely familiar and I tried to remember where I had seen it before.

Then I saw Pippa coming toward me, dressed in her riding outfit, carrying her crash helmet and her crop.

"Brilliant ride today," she called to me, her face glowing with joy—quite different from the snooty, cold expression she wore most of the time. "How did your testing go?"

"It wasn't too bad," I called back. "I survived the dungeon."

"This place is something else, isn't it?" Pippa said, coming to sit beside me. "I've never been to a school like it and trust me, I've been to plenty of schools. The lessons are never the same two days in a row, for one thing, and as for some of the teachers—definitely strange. But as long as they let me ride, I might just stick this one out."

"And they let me paint," I said.

The big clock on the front tower struck five. Pippa looked up. "Oh rats. I'm probably too late for tea and I'm starving."

"Starving? Is there food as well as tea?"

Pippa burst out laughing. "Are you serious? Tea is the best meal of the day. Bread and jam and cakes. At home there are scones and cream and crumpets…" A wistful look came over her face again. "I should go and shower and get out these smelly clothes," she said abruptly, "Unless you want our whole room to smell of horse." Then she hurried toward our dorm tower before I had the chance to ask her all the things I wanted to know—about escaping from the dungeon and how Miss Neves knew where I'd go and the old woman with the red cloak, and Miss Rorrim….

At quarter to six I started down to the courtyard again. I wanted to allow plenty of time so that I wasn't late for my supper with the headmistress. I was showered and my uniform had come back, all clean and pressed, so I was as neat and clean as I could make myself. Entering the building opposite, I took what I thought was the correct staircase but it came out to a hallway I had never seen before. Now I was conscious of time getting short and I could picture Miss Neves's look of disapproval when I showed up late. I started to run. I needed to go to the right, surely? But all passage ways seemed to branch off to the left.

Suddenly I stopped. Ahead of me stretched a long dark passageway, its walls and ceiling paneled in dark oak. It smelled old and musty. At the end of it I thought I saw something shimmering—some kind of light. As I started toward it I heard footsteps coming along the hall behind me.

"I wouldn't go down there if I were you," a voice called out.

I stopped and turned around. It was Angela and her clique of girls.

"You're not supposed to be in this part of the building," Angela said in her superior voice. "You could get in trouble for being here. That's the haunted hallway."

"Then what are you doing here?" I asked defiantly. I suspected they were having another laugh at my expense.

"None of your business," Penelope said, and they giggled.

"I'm trying to find Miss Neves's room. I have to have supper with her," I said, not too hopeful that they'd point me in the right direction.

"You should have turned left at the top of the stairs," Angela said. "You really are clueless. I learned my way around this place in ten minutes, but then I live in a house almost as large as this. I suppose you live in the Little House on the Prairie."

"Little House on the Prairie?" I gave her a patronizing smile. "For your information the prairies are about two thousand miles from California, which is mostly mountains and desert. But I guess geography isn't your strong subject."

Since she couldn't find an answer for that one I added, "As if it matters how big and important your house is. For all you know my family could be Hollywood movie stars."

Angela glared at me, then turned to glare at some of the rest of her group who were giggling behind their hands.

"Good one," I heard one of them mutter.

"Come on, you lot. Let's see if Barry is in the prefect's study yet," Angela said and stalked off in a different direction with her nose in the air.

I looked back down the long dark hallway. It couldn't really be haunted, could it? They must just be messing with me. The silvery shimmering thing at the far end was unnerving. Did I see a figure moving down there? I didn't believe in ghosts but I wasn't about to wait and test my luck. Besides, Miss Neves was waiting. I turned left and followed the twists and turns through the ballroom, down the stairs and soon found my way down to the big hallway through which I had first entered the school. I stood outside Miss Neves's door and took a deep breath. Having supper with the headmistress was not exactly something I was looking forward to. I guessed this was yet another form of test—probably to see how terrible my manners were. I was sure I'd do something awful, like spill soup down my front, or drop peas onto the tablecloth.

I was about to knock when I heard voices inside the room.

"But she completed the picture." This sounded like Miss Rorrim. "She got it all right, including the mare. Not many of them pick up on that, do they? And then she told me about the Nightmare. Described it perfectly."

"Interesting." The deeper voice had to be the headmistress herself.

"So what are we going to do?"

"Nothing at the moment. Watch and wait. It would be foolish to reveal anything at this stage. She could be a spy, you know."

"Oh, surely not."

"It wouldn't be the first time he's sent a spy into our midst, would it? And I sense we have one among us now—don't you?"

"I have to admit I feel—a certain uneasiness, but not this child, surely. You can't believe that HE sent her? That she is anything to do with the Fallon Gwyn? I won't believe it."

"Then let's hope you're right, Rorrim."

I heard footsteps coming toward the door. I leaped back and acted as if I was just coming down the hallway. When the door opened, Miss Neves herself looked out.

"Ah, Addison. I was just wondering what had happened to you. Did you get lost again? Come on in. Supper is waiting."

She ushered me inside. Dishes full of food were laid on a white-clothed table but there was nobody else in the room. I looked around to see where Miss Rorrim could have gone, but there was not another door in the smooth stone walls.

She must have been talking on a speakerphone, I decided, but I couldn't see a phone anywhere either. And there was something else strange about the room....

"Do take a seat," Miss Neves said. "You have been through a rough few days, I'd imagine."

She waved at a chair opposite her as she sat down. "A rough few months actually," I said.

Miss Neves nodded. She looked at me as if she understood. "Indeed. Probably the hardest thing you will ever have to do is to watch a loved-one die. I know it won't help much with the pain now, but trust me when I say that it will make you a stronger person. If you have come through this, you will be up to any task ahead."

I wondered for a moment if Miss Neves was about to give me another challenge, but I looked up to see that the headmistress was smiling kindly. I also noticed for the first time that Miss Neves wasn't dressed like she had been. Her iron gray hair was not up in a severe bun, but hung down behind her shoulders and she was wearing a soft green dress.

I realized then what was different about the room. Yesterday the walls had been lined with bookcases and there had been a large impressive oak desk stacked with papers. Today there was not a bookcase in sight.

"Let's get down to the important business of the evening, shall we?" the headmistress said. "The food, I mean. I gather that Mrs. Williams has prepared a spread for us. Don't let it get cold."

She removed the covers, one by one. A roast chicken. Crispy roast potatoes. Green peas. Herby stuffing and rich brown gravy. It all smelled wonderful. Miss Neves carved a drumstick and slices of breast for me and told me to help myself to the rest. I was so hungry by then that I forgot to worry about manners.

As we ate, Miss Neves asked me questions about my home. She seemed so genuinely interested that I found myself talking freely, telling her about my mother, my life in California and even blurting out what a shock it had been to find I was adopted.

"So my birth mother could be anywhere," I said.

"Indeed." Miss Neves nodded. "But I hope you will look upon us as your family for the time being. If your real mother is destined to find you again, she will."

"Do you really think that?" I asked.

"Oh yes. I am a complete believer that we are summoned to fulfill our destiny."

Miss Neves took my empty plate and placed it on one side. "You have saved some room for pudding, I hope," she said. "Mrs. Williams makes a particularly good trifle." She spooned a large helping of a dessert topped with cream onto my plate. It had various layers—melting sponge cake, fruits, jam, custard and, on top, a layer of cream. It was totally the most delicious thing that I had ever eaten.

"So tell me about your dreams, Addison," the headmistress said.

"My dreams?" I looked up sharply. "What do you mean," I asked cautiously. "Do you mean what I dream at night or what I want for my future?"

"Both, but let's start with the former. I always find dreams most interesting, don't you? They reveal a lot about personality. Do you have any particular recurring dreams?"

"I dream that I'm flying," I said. I was about to say "on a red dragon" when I remembered the nightmare I had last night. Had Fern told Miss Neves that I had woken everyone up shouting in my sleep? I blushed with embarrassment. "But that's about it," I added. "Nothing special."

"And as to your dreams for the future?"

I looked down at my plate. "I don't know anymore. I thought once that I'd grow up and study to be an artist like my mom and live in California, but now I have no idea where I'm going. It's like nothing's safe anymore."

"I think you'll find that you are in the right place and that you'll like it here when you get used to us," Miss Neves said and gave me a friendly smile. "Now do you have any questions you'd like to ask me?"

A thousand questions whizzed through my mind but I said, "Miss Neves, some of the girls said there is a haunted hallway. Is that true? Are there ghosts in the castle?"

"Some students swear they have seen figures wandering in that hallway and then vanishing," Miss Neves said seriously. "It is, after all, a very old building. But I think that such apparitions can be explained by tricks of the light and an overly vivid imagination. However, just to be on the safe side, I have placed that part of the building out of bounds for the lower forms. We don't want anyone having nightmares, do we?"

And she looked at me in a way that I couldn't quite understand.

I MEET SAM AND ALMOST GET ARRESTED

I looked around. I was standing in a narrow street with row houses on either side of me. Garbage blew down the street in a cold wind. At the end of the street several tough-looking boys leaned against a mailbox, their hands in their pockets against the cold. The door nearest me opened and Sam walked down the steps quickly. He looked different out of his school uniform. His shabby coat looked a size too small and his eyes had a tough, hunted look. He stopped when he saw me.

"I know you," he said puzzled. "But you shouldn't be here." He came down the street toward me.

The door opened again and a heavy woman walked out, sat on the top of the steps and lit a cigarette. She had on baggy sweatpants and an oversized faded T-shirt. When she saw Sam standing there with me, a string of swear words flew in our direction.

"Get off to school then, you lazy, no-good kid or I'll have Child Services out here asking about you again," she bellowed.

"Give us a quid for me dinner, then, Auntie and I'll be off like a good little boy," Sam wheedled.

"You'll get out of here right now if you know what's good for you," she yelled, standing up and throwing her cigarette stub into the scraggly bushes by the house. "Or shall I call Norman? Norman!" she called loudly.

"I'm off. I'm off!" said Sam grudgingly and turned toward me.

"Come on, let's go. You don't want to meet my foster dad."

"So that's not really your aunt then?" I asked as we walked away from the woman who was still swearing and muttering to herself.

"That old cow. Not likely. Just the latest foster mum. Not much different from the last nine. All smiles when Child Services hands over the checks, then scrimp on the grub, buy secondhand clothes and it's not a bad living for her and her live-in."

"That's terrible," I said indignantly. "Why don't you run away?"

"Why do you think I'm on my tenth go?" Sam snorted. "Seriously, it's not so bad now I can get around a bit on my own. I look a bit younger than twelve for one thing."

Sam's face suddenly resembled that of a helpless seven-year-old. His gray eyes swam with tears. "Please miss. I've lost me fare home and me mum is going to wallop me if I'm late." His face resumed its normal expression. "Then people give me money. I'm quite good at it."

"Does it ever get you into trouble?" I asked, feeling that somehow I knew the answer.

"Sometimes. But it beats going hungry. I'm quite good at it." He drew a handful of pound coins from his pocket.

"I don't think this is right," I said suddenly.

"You try starving and see how you feel then," Sam said.

I shook my head. "No, I meant we shouldn't be here. I'm not in London." I looked up and down the street. Police cars were pulling up on either side of us.

"Time to go!" Sam shouted. "See you back at school." A giant eagle swooped down out of nowhere and landed right in front of us. In a second Sam was on its back and he and the eagle were up over the roof of the nearest house. Policemen were getting out of the cars and coming toward me.

"This isn't right!" I yelled. "I haven't done anything wrong. I'm not even supposed to be in London. I'm somewhere else ... at ... school," I said sitting up as my eyes opened. Light was streaming in the window of her dorm room. "What?" said Pippa sleepily.

"Nothing – go back to sleep." I said, lying back down. What a strange dream.

I CHEAT BY ACCIDENT

After breakfast I stayed close to Pippa and Celeste. I really didn't want to get lost again and I expected them to make their way to the mudroom to get ready for gardening. Instead they collected books from lockers and started upstairs.

"Where are we going?" I asked. "Don't we have gardening first period?"

Pippa looked back over her shoulder at me. "That was yesterday. Today it's Welsh history and culture. It changes. Nothing's ever the same in this school. I still haven't got everything straight."

'Me neither," Celeste complained. "It is too stupid 'ere. I just hope my mother finishes her world tour soon so that I can go back to France and my tutor."

I broke into a trot to keep up with them. There was a sinking feeling in my stomach about a Welsh lesson. I had seen that test yesterday and hadn't known a single answer. Another chance for Angela and her friends to have a good laugh at my expense. And sure enough, as we entered the classroom, there was Angela, whispering with Penelope. They glanced up in my direction and grinned. "So you didn't get swallowed up by the haunted hallway yesterday," Penelope said. "Pity."

"Why would anyone be scared of a haunted hallway?" Pippa gave Angela a cold stare. She turned to me. "Now if you really want to see ghosts you should come to my house. The BBC came to us to do a special on 'Ghosts from the 16th century.' They took some brilliant photos that look like ghosts but I don't think they found any of the real ones. There's a young woman in a nightgown who haunts the long gallery and there's even a headless horseman in the stables. I don't know why anyone would be afraid of a hallway." She said disdainfully, raising her voice to make sure Angela could hear.

At that moment a young woman came into the room. She had a nice looking face and her long dark hair fell over her shoulders. She was wearing a long skirt with several trailing scarves that looked as if they were hand knitted.

"Bore da, plentyn," she said.

"Bore da, Mrs. Lloyd Price," everyone but the three of us replied.

"Sorry, I'm late, everyone. There were some things I had to discuss with Miss Neves." She looked around the room and spotted me.

"Oh, I see we have another newcomer," she said. "And your name is?"

"Addy Walker," I mumbled.

"Have you been in Wales long, Miss Walker? Have you had Welsh history before?"

"No, sorry. I just got here from California."

"Well now, that's a long way, isn't it?" Mrs. Lloyd-Price said in her musical voice. "And I don't suppose you've had any chance to even hear Welsh spoken over there. No matter. You'll soon pick it up." She gave me a copy of the Welsh history book that the other students had. "Now, where were we?"

"We were reading about Llewellyn the Great and his dog," someone muttered. "Page 56."

"Ah yes, the famous Gellert. We must take a field trip to Beddgellert soon to see his grave. Can anybody tell me what Beddgellert means in Welsh?"

Gwylum's hand shot up.

"Other than Gwylum?" Mrs. Lloyd-Price looked around hopefully. "Oh, very well. Tell us, Gwylum."

"It means Gellert's grave," he said.

"Well, duh," said a voice at the back of the class and Gwylum sat down again, red faced.

"I'm surprised that nobody else could answer that," Mrs. Lloyd-Price said. "Perhaps we had better revise our basics, especially since we have had several students join us recently who have no knowledge of Wales at all. So let's turn back to chapter 1, The Myths of Wales. Welsh myths are an important part of our history."

The class was silent as we read the first chapter.

"Let's start with the symbol of Wales. We see it on the flag.

What is it?'

"The red dragon," several voices called out.

"And can anybody tell us the legend of the red dragon?"

Hands shot up. "It defeated the white dragon," Raj said. "And now it lies deep in a cave somewhere in the mountains, waiting for the day when it will be summoned to defend Wales again."

"Very good," Mrs. Lloyd-Price said, "and the motto of Wales is?"

"Cymru am byth," the class shouted in unison. It sounded like "Come ree ham bith."

I let out a squeal that made everyone turn to me. "It was what they called in my dream. Then I am meant to be here."

Suddenly I realized that I had yelled out loud and everyone was staring at me as if I was crazy. I turned bright red. "I've heard that before," I stammered. "– Uh, it's a good motto." Shut up, I told myself.

"It is indeed. It means Wales Forever." Mrs. Lloyd-Price looked at me with interest. "Now let's repeat the motto of Wales…"

I went through the rest of the class with my mind racing. I had been told I was coming to Wales in my dream. First the red dragon taking me on its back until I was surrounded by whales, and they had called out the Welsh motto to me. What a weird feeling. Someone had called me here… for what reason?

My hand went up to my neck and touched the necklace I was still wearing. Who had given me a necklace with the school's crest on it when I was a baby? My fingers felt hot as they touched the metal hexagon. Somebody had cared about me enough as a baby to have given me that pretty little necklace. I hadn't just been abandoned. It made me feel much better. Confused – but better.

After Welsh it was math class again. I was making my way to the seat over in the window next to Sam when I heard Miss Neves's voice—loud and commanding as always.

"Sorry, Mr. Thomas," she said, "but I've come for Addison. I'm afraid she won't be in this class after all."

"She didn't even know what a sum was," Angela muttered to her friends and they giggled.

"Only one student has ever scored higher in math on the entrance test and that was Mr. Puri," Miss Neves went on smoothly. "So I'm afraid this class would not be making the best use of her abilities. I'll be coaching Miss Walker and Mr. Puri myself. Come with me, Addison. Mr. Puri is waiting in my study."

I felt horribly self-conscious for a different reason now as I followed Miss Neves out of the classroom and down to her study. Raj looked up and grinned as I came in.

"I was so glad when Miss Neves said you'd be coming, too," he said. "It's boring studying alone. But not nearly as boring as sitting in a class with clueless people."

"We all have different talents, Mr. Puri," Miss Neves said, frowning at him. "And learning patience is a necessary skill for all of us."

Miss Neves put down a sheet of paper on two small desks that were now in the middle of her room.

"I'm sorry but I've been called away to speak with a prospective parent," she said. "I've left you a problem to work through. Please work on your own. I don't want a collaborative effort. I want to see exactly how you handle a tough assignment."

I sat and picked up her sheet of paper. At the top of it was a tough word problem. All about the number of people it would take to harvest crops in a field so many yards wide and so many yards long... I sighed, picked up my pen and started to work. It was certainly tough but logical and I worked my way steadily through it. I had just finished when Miss Neves came back in.

"Pass me your papers please," she said. We handed her the papers.

Miss Neves looked at them. "This is most interesting," she said at last. "I thought I told you to work alone."

She turned the papers to face us. The two pages were identical with the same numbers on the same lines and the same answers at the end.

WHO IS COPYING WHO?

I went white. "I didn't copy, Miss Neves. I didn't look at his paper once, I promise." I glared at Raj. Why would he copy from me? He was glaring at me, too.

"And I didn't either," Raj said. "I was concentrating so hard I didn't even have time to look up."

"Neither did I."

Miss Neves nodded solemnly. "Very interesting," she said. "Then one can only conclude that you young people think remarkably alike. Let us proceed to today's lesson."

"That was weird, wasn't it?" Raj whispered as we left Miss Neves's study. "I mean, it looked as if the page had been put in a copy machine. How could that be?"

"You must have copied it," I accused. "I won't give you away, but you have to admit it to me. There's no way that could happen by chance."

Raj laughed. "That problem was so easy. Why would I need to copy from you? You're the new girl. Maybe you cheated on your placement test."

We glared at each other for another moment. Then I backed down. Did I really want to make an enemy of one of the only people who had been nice to me?

"Sorry – you're right. I guess it was just a weird coincidence. I'm glad she believed us. My old math teacher would have gone ballistic and called my ... oh ... I guess our minds work alike," I finished.

"I suppose so." Raj didn't sound convinced. He glanced at me and I could tell he was still wondering whether I had copied his work or not.

The rest of the morning was occupied with ordinary lessons like English and geography, which were taught pretty much as they had been at home. We were just finishing lunch, which was a thick lamb stew, followed by something called roly-poly pudding when Miss Neves came to get me again. "My assistant tells me that your supplies have arrived from the outfitter," she said. "Please pick them up from the front hall, take them to your room and put them away. I have told Miss Rorrim that you will be a little late for your art class."

I did as I was told and hung up a new green sweater, blazer, white shirts. There were also sweatpants and a sweatshirt, PE outfit and even riding breeches and helmet. I handled the latter cautiously, visions of falling off horses appearing in my brain. Then I put away the underclothes and socks in a drawer. I noticed they were all labeled with my name. It seemed funny that these things now represented my whole life. There was nothing left of the former Addy. Suddenly I remembered that I was missing art and I ran all the way to the art studio. Like everything else in this crazy castle, it wasn't simple to find and I was frustrated and out of breath by the time I opened the door to what I hoped was the correct room.

I stepped inside and gasped. On the far side of a bright room was a large window with a view of green fields going all the way down to the ocean. Leaning against the wall were canvasses of all different sizes. Dotted around the room were several easels with half-done paintings on them. And in the middle of the room sat Miss Rorrim, working at a painting that took my breath away.

She was painting me standing by the ocean with my mom. It was our last beautiful day together. It was a perfect copy of the photo I had carried with me from America. "How did you get my photo?" I demanded. Someone had gone through my things!

Miss Rorrim looked up now. "Photo?" She smiled.

"It's the picture of me and my mom," I glared at her. "The one from my photo."

"Oh no, dear," Miss Rorrim said. "This isn't any photo. I was just painting what I felt. A happy scene. And this was what came to mind. Nobody in particular, you know."

I continued to stare, first at Miss Rorrim and then at the painting. She had to have seen the photo, even though it was in my drawer. Did teachers go through the students' personal things? Miss Rorrim had resumed painting, her usual serene expression on her face.

"Set up an easel and stool where the light is good," she said.

"Help yourself to paint and canvas and paint what you want to. It can be still life if you like, or the view from the window or something from your imagination. Today I just want to observe your brush techniques."

I did as commanded and started to paint, but my head was in such turmoil that I found it hard to do anything and my brush strokes were jerky and awkward.

Miss Rorrim came to stand behind me and put a hand on my shoulder. "You are tense and upset," she said. "You don't have to be. You are among friends here. I am not here to judge you but to nurture a talent you already possess. Paint from your heart, Addy, not to impress me or anybody else."

I closed my eyes and took a deep breath. I tried to paint the view from my window at home but I couldn't stop looking across at Miss Rorrim's painting. It had to be a copy of my photo. She had even captured the funny smile mom always made when having her photo taken—sort of half embarrassed, half hamming it up.

It wasn't much of a painting lesson. Miss Rorrim didn't correct my brush strokes or teach me a new technique. She just kept encouraging me to paint from my heart. When the lesson came to an end, I lingered in the doorway, looking back at her picture. It almost looked as if my mom was smiling directly at me, sharing a secret joke with me. I really wanted to ask for that picture, so I could have that memory in front of me every day.

"I think I'll hang this painting up on the wall over here," Miss Rorrim said, as if reading my thoughts. "I'm rather pleased with it and it cheers up the room, don't you think?"

And she put it in the middle of the side wall, with the two figures smiling down on me. It was the weirdest thing that had happened so far since I arrived at this weird place.

Looking into my mom's smiling happy face brought tears to my eyes. Then, strangely, I felt better. It had to be a sign that my mom was somehow close to me here and that things were going to be okay. I cleaned my brushes then closed the door to the art room almost reverently.

SOMEONE TRIES TO KILL ME WITH A HORSE

The class schedule that had arrived with my supplies told me that the final lesson of the afternoon was riding. I changed into the new riding outfit, put on the padded helmet, and felt totally stupid as I went to find the stables. It took me a while to find the way out of the garden and then around the back of the dorm block. As I finally approached the stables I ran into Angela, whispering with her friends. They looked up with blank expressions as I approached.

"You're late," Angela said deadpan. "Mr. Thomas has already taken the beginners down to the paddock."

"Pippa said she'd help me the first time," I said.

"Pippa? She's already gone, too." Penelope said, staring at me coldly.

"Okay. Which way is the paddock?" I asked, not even sure what a paddock was.

"It's down that path," Penelope said. When I started off they all burst out laughing.

"You're not going to be much use down there without a horse," one of them called after me.

I blushed bright red. "Where am I supposed to find a horse?"

"It's called a stable, dimwit." They all grinned at each other and then went back to looking serious.

"You're supposed to go to a stall, select a horse, put on the saddle and bridle you find hanging there and then mount it," Angela said. "Don't you know anything?"

"I've never ridden a horse before. I don't know how to do any of that stuff."

"You come from the American west and you don't ride a horse?" Penelope dug Angela in the side. "What exactly can you do?"

"Things you can't. Surf, swim, ski, paint. Plenty of things. I just never had a chance to ride. So which horse am I supposed to take?" I tried to sound more confident than I felt.

"Tell you what. I've got Sultan already saddled. Since you're already so late, you can take him if you like," Angela said. "I really don't need any riding practice. I hunt when I'm at home. I could ride by the time I was two."

I watched her go over to a stall and lead out a huge black horse.

"Here you go," she said.

I stared in horror at the horse. It snorted and it looked as if fire came out of its nostrils.

"Isn't that horse rather big?" I asked. "I am a beginner."

"Old Sultan? He's as gentle as a lamb," Angela said. "And everyone knows that big horses are easier to ride than ponies. Their gait is smoother. Ponies bump you up and down like a sack of potatoes. Come on, up you go."

She showed me how to put my foot into the left stirrup and then face backward to swing myself into the saddle. I did this. The ground seemed awfully far below and Sultan danced irritably.

"Collect your reins," Angela instructed. "That's right. Go on then. Off you go."

She slapped Sultan on the rump. He set off, trotting down the leafy path. I bumped up and down in the saddle. There seemed to be nothing to hold onto. I felt myself going over to one side.

"Slow down, please," I yelled. I tugged on the reins and to my delight the horse stopped. "Okay, you can walk again," I said. Sultan didn't budge. I dug in my heels as I thought I'd seen riders doing, but still the horse didn't move.

Then I heard a shout behind me. "Addy, what you are doing? I told you to wait for me." Pippa, riding a beautiful chestnut horse, came galloping down the path toward me.

Sultan turned his head to look, then uttered a loud neigh and took off at a gallop, almost throwing me off.

"Whoa," I shouted as I fought to stay in the saddle and branches flew past us. But the horse didn't stop. As Pippa tried to draw level to grab my reins, Sultan obviously thought it was a race. He increased his speed. I could hear his hooves drumming on the leafy carpet beneath us. We were going so fast that everything was a blur. Dark fir trees stretched out on either side. I kept hoping that the paddock would come into sight but the forest went on and on.

"Pull on the reins," Pippa shouted. "You have to get control of his head."

It was easier said than done. Sultan had his neck stretched out and was galloping so smoothly that I was no longer bumped up and down. If I hadn't been so scared, it would have been exciting. Suddenly it came to me that I had done this many times before. It felt just as if I was riding the dragon. I could feel the horse's warm flanks through my riding breeches. Then we swung around a bend and there before us was a gate across the path. There was no time to try and stop. Sultan collected himself, then took the gate in a mighty leap.

ANGELA GETS POOPED

For a second I was conscious of flying, of feeling almost as if I was part of the horse and together we were this fabulous flying creature. Then we landed on the other side. Sultan cantered to a halt and turned to wait for Pippa. Pippa reined in her own horse on the other side of the gate, a look of wonder and amazement on her face.

"You've been fooling me," she shouted. "You do know how to ride."

"No, honestly, I've never done it before," I shouted back.

"But you took that gate perfectly. Your seat was absolutely right," Pippa said. "And you landed just right, too."

"It was the horse," I said. "He knew how to jump and land."

Pippa leaned out of her saddle and opened the gate for me to come back through. "Do you realize how long it takes for someone to learn how to jump over a little log?" she asked. "People fall off for ages until they get it. And even I would think twice about taking that gate."

"Just lucky, I guess," I said. "And a good horse." I didn't want to say, "I ride a big dragon almost every night in my dreams."

"I'll say." Pippa was now staring at my mount. "Who on earth said you could ride Sultan?"

"Angela gave him to me. She said he was safe and gentle."

"Angela? I might have known." Pippa glared. "Sultan is reserved for advanced riders. He's a hunter."

"Then she played a trick on me?"

"An awful trick. You might have got seriously hurt if he'd flung you off. You might even have got killed. And I told you to wait for me."

"Angela told me you'd gone on ahead and I should hurry to catch up," I said, feeling dumb and angry now.

"That girl needs teaching a lesson," Pippa snapped. "I'm going to tell her a thing or two."

"Pippa, be careful. You don't want to get her mad at you. People like that can make your life miserable."

"She's got to learn that we are not going to take her nasty little jokes lying down," Pippa said. "Come on. We're going back to Mr. Thomas to tell him that you don't need to be in the beginner's class. You already know how to ride."

We rode back side by side along the leafy path. When we got back to the stables, Pippa slid down from her horse and stomped over to Angela and her friends.

"That was a horrid mean trick you played on Addy," she said.

Angela and her friends were grinning. "Oh dear. Did she fall off?"

"No, she didn't. It turns out she is an absolutely brilliant rider. She kept it a secret from all of us, but she just jumped that gate across the forest path. You know, the one with five bars?"

"You're kidding?" For a moment Angela stared at me.

"Lucky for you," Pippa said. "She might have been seriously hurt. So I'm warning you now. You do anything else to us and you'll be sorry."

"Oooh, I am so scared," Angela said. "What exactly do you plan to do, shrimp?" She stepped forward menacingly. "Touch me and you'll be in big trouble."

"You're the one who will be in big trouble when I report this to Miss Neves."

"And you think she's going to listen to you? You just got here. Come to think of it, why don't you just run away again? You are the one who runs away, aren't you? Although I don't know why you bother. It's quite clear that they don't want you at home." And she gave a loud fake laugh.

"You take that back." Pippa's face was bright red now.

"Ooh, that hit a nerve, didn't it? So they only send you to boarding school to get rid of you, do they? I'm not surprised."

Without warning Pippa let out a roar of rage and pushed Angela hard. Angela lost her balance and sat down in a large pile of horse manure.

For a second everyone just froze, then Pippa smiled widely. "Ooops."

"You little…" Angela screamed. "Look what you've done. You've ruined my riding clothes. You're going to pay for this."

I grabbed Pippa's arm and led her away.

"That felt good," Pippa said, giving me a shaky grin.

Against Pippa's protests, I was put in the beginner class on a gentle old mare and had a boring hour of walking round and round the paddock. The old mare refused to pick up the pace, no matter what I did and only broke into a bumpy trot when we turned for home. At least I was glad that I did better than Raj who fell twice on the way back. I was behind him in the line of horses and even though I felt sorry for him, it was hard not to laugh as he slipped further and further sideways on the horse and finally slid to the ground. I was glad I had no problem staying on my horse, even if I couldn't seem to control it very well. I was also glad that being in the beginner class meant that I was far away from Angela. Angela was sure to get her revenge on Pippa somehow and I didn't want to be there when it happened.

IN THE FLOWER-LADY'S TOWER

I had never been so exhausted in my life, not even after a day's surfing. Too many new experiences, I guess. I dragged myself to bed that night and it seemed that I had just closed my eyes when I opened them and it was morning. I was just trying to get up the courage to jump out of my nice warm bed when Miss Rorrim's voice rang out: "First formers please report to my study for a special lesson after breakfast today." Both Pippa and Celeste sat up in bed and looked up to find the source of the voice.

"I didn't know they had an intercom in here," Pippa said, puzzled.

"Isn't it Saturday?" I said. "Do we have classes on Saturdays? That stinks."

"Not normally," Pippa said. "But you never know in this crazy place."

"I wonder what our special lesson will be?" I said. "I hope it's not more Welsh."

Celeste shrugged. "I do not know. Zis is ze first time I 'ave 'eard of Miss Rorrim giving special lessons. Quelle dommage. I was hoping we would 'ave the morning free. It's too bad that they make us work on Saturday."

We got dressed and followed the stampede down to breakfast. I was starting to get used to being part of a big noisy crowd and felt almost cheerful as we sat down to a huge Saturday breakfast of bacon, eggs, fried bread and hot sweet tea. Angela and her posse were talking loudly about their plans to walk down to the nearest shops in search of candy and fun.

"I guess they haven't heard the announcement yet," I whispered to Pippa. "Well, I won't be sad if they don't make it to class."

As we were stacking our dishes beside the sink, Pippa asked Celeste, "Have you been to Miss Rorrim's office? Do you know where it is?"

"In one of ze towers, I zink – but I am not sure. We 'ad better ask someone."

We looked around at the older students who were hurrying off laughing and talking. I didn't see anyone I recognized.

"You go ahead," I whispered to Pippa. "You ask someone. I don't know anybody."

But Pippa shook her head. "I don't know them either – except for Fern and I wouldn't talk to her if you paid me a million pounds. You ask them." She pushed Celeste forward. Just then I spotted Gwylum leaning against an open door, talking to his mother in the kitchen.

"Gwylum," I called. "Do you know how to get to Miss Rorrim's study?"

Gwylum looked up shyly. "I'm on my way there, too," he said. "I'll take you, if you like. It's up at the top of one of the towers. You wait till you see it. It's really cool."

"Good morning, Mrs. Williams." I waved to the cook as we passed and was rewarded with a broad smile.

"Doing all right now then, are you? That's good, isn't it? And making nice friends, too.

Go on then, Gwylum," his mother said. "Don't keep Miss Rorrim waiting."

Gwylum led us at a brisk pace across the courtyard with the fountain in it, past the rose bower, out of an ancient looking gate, crumbling and overgrown with ivy, and down an oak-lined path.

"Wow," I said to Pippa. "I'm glad we've got a guide. We'd never have found this on our own."

"You won't believe it when you see it," Gwylum called over his shoulder. "It's quite different."

The path twisted and turned until the trees parted to reveal an ancient-looking tower. I would not have been surprised to see Rapunzel leaning out of the top window and letting her hair down! Gwylum led us into the tower through an arched oak door that creaked when he opened it. It had been dark under the oaks and my eyes took a while to adjust to the light of the tower. Instead of the dark I had been expecting, the tower was bright and sunny. Plants in stone planters grew on every side of the circular room and even up the twisting staircase. As my eyes adjusted I saw that the light came from translucent blocks set into the stone. They were set in a pattern that I couldn't quite make out.

The center of the area was taken up with a tree of a type I had never seen before. Its pale green trunk was slender but must have been strong because it reached all the way up to the top of the tower, at least sixty feet above us. Its branches were the same pale green and its leaves were changing color, glowing like little orange and yellow stars. Its green twisted roots grew into a ten-foot planter filled with rich dark earth.

"Cool," I muttered, taking in the rich smell of growing things. Somehow it reminded me of home and the smell of the redwood forest around our house.

We followed Gwylum up the stone staircase that twisted around the inside of the tower, going around and around until I felt quite dizzy. In fact I lost count of how many times the staircase twisted around before it reached the top and we came to the door of Miss Rorrim's study. "Miss Rorrim must be in super good shape for an old lady," I gasped as we reached the top out of breath.

Pippa stepped forward and knocked on the door. It swung open and we stopped in the doorway staring. I had never seen a room like this one before.

SEVEN IMPOSSIBLE THINGS BEFORE BREAKFAST

I t was not a large room, but old-looking with a vaulted ceiling and a tall arched window like the ones in the dining hall. The window had crisscross bars across it and looked out onto a gloomy pine and oak forest. It smelled old, too, but in a green sort of way, like a visit to a hothouse. Plants hung in pots from the ceiling and sprouted from every surface of the room except the very center of the desk, which was piled with books. Even an old black chalkboard hung on the wall behind her desk had a vine with yellow blooms growing up one side of it. Bookshelves at the back of the study were piled with untidy stacks of books and papers. Raj and Sam were already sitting in the two wingback chairs that faced the desk arguing loudly about some sports teams that I had never heard of.

"Of course Arsenal is going to beat the Spurs," Sam was saying. "Goes without sayin'."

"Rubbish. They don't have Gonzales any longer, do they?"

Sam looked up as we came in. "Grab a pew if you can find one that the plants haven't taken over. And watch out where you sit. I swear this plant next to me has put out new tendrils since I sat here. I think it wants me for breakfast."

We laughed. I pushed past a leafy fern and perched myself on the broad window seat with Pippa while Celeste found a place on the floor next to the dark-skinned boy that I had seen across the dining table but not really spoken to yet. He had neat close-cropped hair, and a serious expression as if he was perpetually worried. He looked up at me curiously. 'I bet he thinks I'm an idiot like the rest of the school does.'

"Hi, I'm Addy," I said, forcing myself to smile at him. "I just got here."

To my surprise he rose to his feet and bowed. "And I am

107

Kobi," he said extending his hand formally to me and shaking mine heartily. "How do you do? I was wondering when you would arrive here. I was expecting you."

"You were expecting me?" I asked, puzzled.

He nodded solemnly. "Of course. But now you are here and I am delighted to meet you. Did I understand that you have come from America?"

"Yes, from California."

"Then you have come from as far away as I. I am from Ghana, where my father—" We stopped talking instantly as Miss Rorrim entered the study, her multicolored robes flowing out behind her. She looked around us and beamed.

"Good morning, First Years. I am delighted to see so many of you. Oh yes, really, really delighted." She walked behind the desk and stood, framed by the plants with the presence of a stage performer. "We have a very talented group here though perhaps you have not shared your talents with each other. Addison, I've seen that you will be a promising artist. Celeste, as you will hear, has a beautiful soprano voice. Raj is quite the scientist, and Philippa, I believe you have an amazing talent with horses, as well as being very athletic."

She stared at Pippa with such a knowing look that Pippa shifted uncomfortably on the window ledge.

"I'm looking forward to finding out what gifts the rest of you have," Miss Rorrim said. "Now, let us begin. You six have answered the summons," she began in her soft musical voice. "Wonderful. Splendid." Then she noticed Gwylum still standing in the doorway. "Thank you, Gwylum dear. You can go now. They're all here."

"Yes, Miss Rorrim, it's just ..." He stopped.

"Yes?"

"Well I know I'm not exactly new but I am in the first form this year and your announcement did say all first year students."

"What announcement?" Miss Rorrim looked puzzled.

"The one over the loudspeaker this morning. I heard it in the kitchen when I was helping mum with breakfast."

Miss Rorrim looked shocked and then she smiled in delight. "Oh, Gwylum. What a surprise. How lovely. Of course you are welcome. Come in." Gwylum shyly came in and leaned against a bookcase in the back corner.

"You seven have been summoned," she began again, in a rather flustered fashion this time, "to begin your Lessons. Do you accept?"

"Do you mean we don't have to do Lessons if we don't want to?" Sam asked with his cheeky smile.

"No, of course not, Sam," said Miss Rorrim seriously, "not in any class. Teachers can only teach. It is up to you to learn. Do you accept?"

We nodded our heads, unsure of what we were agreeing to.

"Well then." She smiled. "Here is your first lesson." She stepped up to the chalkboard behind her desk and in graceful flowing script she wrote the words 'Seven impossible things before breakfast.'

"This is your task. The rest is up to you." And before we could ask her a single question she walked to the door with a smile and left the room.

WE SCRATCH OUR HEADS

We sat in silence for a few minutes, wondering what would happen next.

"What kind of bloody stupid thing is that?" Sam demanded. "We came all the way over here to read one sentence on a chalkboard?"

We looked at each other, as it was clear that the others were as clueless as I was.

"Are we supposed to stay here and write an essay or something?" I asked.

"We don't have no pens or notebooks," Sam said. "And she hasn't put out any for us."

"Should we wait to see if she will come back?" Raj asked.

"She will not come back, I am sure," Kobi said in his solemn way.

"I suppose we should go back to the common room then," Raj said. "Or try to catch up with her and ask her." But there was no sign of Miss Rorrim who seemed to have disappeared very quickly.

"Really this is the strangest school I've ever been to," said Pippa, tossing her head angrily. "You never know what you are going to find. Some mornings you come to class and find perfectly normal teachers doing maths and geography, sometimes it's bullies in white cloaks and sometimes it's loony old ladies asking us to do seven impossible things before breakfast. I don't think I shall stay much longer."

"I heard your mum talking to Miss Neves the day you came," said Sam. "She said you had been kicked out of every posh school in Britain on account of your temper!" He grinned at her. "So I guess you're stuck here in this loony bin with the rest of us."

Pippa's grey eyes flashed. "And what would you know about posh schools?" she shot back at him.

"Uh oh – there's that famous Pepper temper," said Sam, not

the least bit put out. "Posh Pippa Plagues Poor Pauper with Peppery Prose."

Pippa glared at Sam then stalked ahead of him down the stairs and out of the tower. Once outside she seemed as if she was going off on her own. Raj got out his notebook and pretended to write earnestly. "Sam has left Pepper speechless. First impossible thing before breakfast." Everyone laughed. Pippa turned back to us and managed to grin, too.

"So where do we begin?" Kobi asked. "I surmise this is to be a group assignment of some sort but I have to confess to much puzzlement."

"Well, I am not standing out here in the cold while we discuss it," Celeste said.

"I agree," Sam said. "There's a fire in the library, isn't there? And it should be pretty empty on a Saturday morning. Let's start there."

It was drizzling now, and a soft gray haze lay over the campus as we walked back.

"Look at all this mud. My shoes will be ruined!" Celeste broke the silence.

"Oh no, my lady. If only I'd brought my cloak, I'd have laid it down in the puddle for you," Sam said, making us all laugh.

"Didn't Miss Neves confiscate your famous Prada shoes? I thought we weren't allowed to wear non-uniform things?" I said.

"I couldn't bear to wear those ugly school shoes." Celeste moaned as her heel sunk into a spot of soft mud on the side of the path. "My feet longed for Prada. I was thinking about my lovely shoes when I was practicing my singing this morning, and then there they were in my closet. So I suppose Miss Neves felt my longing and returned the shoes to me."

"Better you than me. Your feet look freezing."

"I still can't think what Miss Rorrim wants us to do," Pippa said. "Are we going to waste our whole day trying to figure out what's going through some crazy lady's head?"

"Maybe she wants us to discover seven things that were considered impossible until a new discovery was made," Raj said. "I'm sure sending radio waves and flying in a plane were once considered impossible."

"There are seven of us." Pippa looked around. "Maybe we should each work on a different discovery."

"What if she wants us to work on things that are still impossible?" Sam chimed in with his usual cheeky smile. "And she wants us to come up with the discovery?"

"That's silly." Pippa gave Sam her usual withering look. "If grown up scientists can't come up with answers, how can we?"

"Just a thought," Sam said easily.

"All right, Sam, we'll assign you defying gravity," Raj said, giving him a friendly shove. "And Pippa, you can work on travel at the speed of light. You should have that done by the end of the morning."

"Oh ha ha, very funny," Pippa said. "Really this whole thing is stupid."

"Maybe it's a quote from something," I said as we entered the main castle building and made our way up the stairs. "I'm sure I've read it somewhere."

"It sounds a little familiar to me, too," Pippa agreed.

"I hope we get some ideas at the library," Raj said. "It's a good thing we've just had breakfast. If we want to eat tomorrow we had better get working."

"You don't think she really means it, do you?" Kobi asked. "We don't get any breakfast tomorrow if we don't come up with the answer today?"

BACK IN THE HAUNTED HALLWAY

Finally we came to the double doors that opened out into the library. The library was a huge room filled with polished wood tables at which a few older students were working with books piled around them. More books than I had ever seen in one place lined the walls around the whole room from the twenty-foot ceiling to the floor. There were ladders on tracks to reach the books at the top of the stacks. A comforting fire burned in a great stone fireplace and a couple of kids were sitting reading in armchairs beside the fire. The whole room was delightfully warm. Raj motioned us over to a deserted corner and we sank down onto one of the thick sheepskin rugs that were scattered on the polished wood floor.

"I think it is in our best interest to work together to complete this assignment," Kobi said earnestly. "Let us commence to develop a strategy."

"Does he always talk like that?" I whispered to Celeste. "Did he memorize the dictionary or something?"

"'Is father is an African chief," whispered Celeste.

"An African chief? Do they still have those?" I looked across at Kobi who heard me.

"My father," Kobi said slowly, "received his doctorate from Oxford University. He is currently the CFO of a major Nigerian oil company and, yes, he is the chief of an upland people in the North of Ghana. I imagine that all Americans are not cowboys and Indians, neither are all Africans hut dwellers. Now may we proceed with this task please?"

"Oh ... I didn't mean ... sorry ..." I blushed, feeling hot with embarrassment.

"Apology accepted. Now to commence. Does anyone know to what Miss Rorrim was referring? What do you imagine the seven impossible things to be?"

"Let's look and see if there is a book on Impossible Things. We could check the library database on the computer," Raj suggested.

"I still think she wants us to do seven impossible things," Sam said.

"Okay, then go and jump out of the window and see if you can fly," Pippa snapped, frustrated.

Celeste sighed. "How can you do something if it's impossible? It makes no sense."

"I'm game to try something impossible," Raj said. "I wouldn't mind learning to fly, although aerodynamically I have to admit that my weight would make it impossible unless I were to grow some rather large wings ..."

"Oh, do be serious," said Kobi impatiently. "Some of us must stay and search the library, others must search the grounds and others the school. Perhaps we will find a clue."

"What kind of clue?" Sam asked.

"We won't know until we find it," Kobi said.

I was still trying to think. "I know I've come across that saying somewhere, or something very like it recently, but I can't think where. In a book, maybe?"

Sam indicated the floor-to-ceiling books. "Go ahead, start reading."

"I don't think I could even read all the titles by tomorrow before breakfast," I admitted. "Could we Google it?"

"There's no internet except in the secretary's office," Raj said.

"Oh my god. Talk about the stone age," I said, making the others laugh again.

"We could spend all day here and still not find anything," Pippa said impatiently. "Why don't we search the school first? I'm sure Miss Rorrim wouldn't have given us this assignment if it was impossible."

"Maybe it's one of the impossible things before breakfast," Celeste said, shrugging in a bored manner.

"Maybe Miss Rorrim has left us clues like in a treasure hunt," Pippa said. "We'll meet back in the library in an hour with our suggestions. Addy, you don't know your way too well yet. Do you think you could check the front entrance and Miss Neves's office?"

"Okay, I guess," I said, and set off down a corridor in what I hoped was the direction of the front of the school. I knew the library was on the fourth floor and I had to cross the courtyard to

Miss Neves's office at ground level. 'I have to find the stairs down,' I thought. I was pretty sure where they were, but I was lost within three turns and decided to go back to the library and look in the library database instead while the others roamed the buildings.

But finding my way back wasn't that easy. Was this door the one that led back to the library? The door I tried opened onto an unused room with strange figures covered in dustsheets. They looked kind of scary, like ghosts even in the dusty morning light and I found my heart was thumping. I made myself tiptoe over and lift up a dustsheet. Underneath was what looked like a store mannequin dressed in long green robes.

'Okay – hopefully these are for a play or a sewing class,' I thought, 'and not former students who have been turned into mannequins.' I think I've watched too many old episodes of the Twilight Zone.

I went back out into the hallway and started opening every door that I could find. 'Where is everybody?' I wondered. The school seemed totally silent and asleep.

I found a broom closet and a couple of antique-looking bathrooms. Finally, turning down a long dark corridor with no windows on either side, I caught a glimpse of something moving at the end of it. "Hello," I called hurrying forward. "Hey, wait up a second."

I ran forward. As I reached the end of the corridor, there was nobody else in it. All at once I realized what I was looking at and had to laugh. I had made the exact same mistake as two nights ago and ended up in the haunted hallway. At the end of the corridor was a large mirror with an ornate golden frame around it. The moving object I had seen in the mirror had been me. 'I bet that's how the rumor of the haunted hallway started,' I thought, looking at my reflection. 'People actually saw themselves moving and thought it was a ghost. In fact I bet that…'

I stopped in mid-sentence and stared into the mirror. Someone was hurrying up behind me: a girl in a gray cloak with bright red hair!

THROUGH THE LOOKING GLASS

I spun around but the corridor behind me was empty. I looked back at the mirror and there was the girl again. She was close enough to recognize. It was the girl from my dream.

'Okay – let's be logical here. Maybe it's not a mirror,' I told myself. 'Maybe it's some kind of window. Am I seeing into a different corridor?' And I reached out to touch the glass. I felt as if a bolt of electricity shot through me. The world around me flashed and crackled with bright green light. I closed my eyes and when I opened them the light was gone. I could see the girl in the gray cloak walking away from me. I turned back to the mirror but it was gone. In its place was a large portrait of a horrible-looking man with a long, thin face and bright green eyes. His face was very white and he was wearing some kind of white fur around his neck and a tall silvery crown on his head. He reminded me of someone but I couldn't think who. Above the portrait in large black letters were the words "ONE MIND, ONE WORK, ONE GOAL." I looked back down the corridor but there was no sign of the girl with the bright red hair.

"Wait!" I called and started to run down the passage after the girl. As I turned the corner the girl was walking away, but spun to face me. For a moment she looked frightened and defiant. Then she recognized me.

"You!" she exclaimed. "I knew you would come! Are you in the new batch?"

"I just got here a couple of days ago," I said. Suddenly I had the feeling that I had known this girl for a long time.

"I looked for you at dinner," I said. "Are you in a different class? Our class is hunting all over the school looking for 'Seven Impossible Things before Breakfast.'"

"Oh, you are wicked." The girl laughed, putting her hand up to her mouth, her face lighting up in horrified glee. "I can see why you're here. But don't let the teachers hear you say the S-word. We can't even say it in math, just write it down." She grinned. "I think I'll like you, wicked girl. Do you have a name?"

"I'm Addy."

"That's a strange name, Addy. What kind of plant is that?"

"Plant? It's short for Addison and I don't know where that came from. Just a name my mom liked, I guess."

The girl looked at me strangely for a long moment, then said, "I'm Twig."

Just then we heard the clack clack of a woman's footsteps coming down the hall. Twig's face went white. "Hide," she whispered and dove into the nearest door shutting it silently behind her.

"Why hide?" I asked. I turned to see who was coming.

The woman that rounded the corner and bore down on me was tall with pale, almost white hair swept up into a bun. She was dressed in a long white dress with a high neck and a white cape that billowed out behind her as she walked. Round her neck was a large medallion with a white dragon on it. Her face was so pale and bony that she looked like a walking skeleton, and she looked down at me past a sharp hooked nose. "You, girl!" she thundered. "What are you wearing?"

"This is my uniform," I said.

"Don't try to be smart with me," the woman snapped. "That color is forbidden and you know it. You'll be sent down below. What is your number?"

"Number?" I was confused. "I don't think I have a number."

"You must have a number. Are you from the latest batch?"

"Batch? I got here on Wednesday, but I was the only new one."

"And weren't given a number? Ridiculous. Come with me. We'll have to see the Regulator about this."

The woman grabbed my arm in a bony claw-like grip. Looking back as I was dragged off, I saw Twig's head peeking out of a door.

"Run!" Twig mouthed. I tried to pull myself away from the woman, but that only made her grip tighter. She put her other bony hand on the back of my neck and squeezed, forcing me to hunch my neck and look up at the ceiling.

"There'll be none of that. Now march!"

"Ow, you're hurting me!" I said indignantly but the woman didn't let go. As we walked into the next corridor I heard the sound of children chanting in singsong voices:

I am you and you are me,
We shall live in unity
With one mind in harmony.

I twisted my head away from the woman's grip long enough to see a classroom full of children about my age all in gray cloaks sitting in nice neat rows. In the front of the class the teacher wore a white cape and held a large stick.

Then my captor tightened her grip and I was marched on past the open door. Now I heard chanting coming from classrooms on all sides of me.

Our crops need no blessing,
They grow with our skill.
We work in the fields,
We hoe and we till.
First we dig the hole
Then we put a fish,
Then we plant a seed,
Then we make a wish.

'It's all nonsense,' I thought. 'Am I dreaming?' But the woman's grip on my arm was painful. Could you feel real pain in a dream? 'If I'm dreaming this would be a good time to wake up!' I told myself.

I GET RUN OVER

Then suddenly I heard the sound of raised voices, the crash of furniture being knocked over and a scream. A boy burst from a classroom, barreled into us, knocking us off our feet. I scrambled up as the woman pulled a whistle out of her cape. The boy was speeding off down the corridor.

"We have a runner!" the woman yelled. She blew the whistle, then took off down the hall after him. Teachers came out from all the nearby classrooms to run after the boy as well. Children in gray cloaks spilled out of the classroom to watch. Some of them dared to yell encouragement, though I couldn't tell if it was to the boy or to their teachers.

"Addy, come on." I looked around to see Twig tugging at my arm. "Quick. Now's your chance." She started pulling me away from the other kids, back down the hall. "You don't want to see the Regulator yet. Not dressed like that. He'll send you for conformation."

We ran down into an empty hallway and heard the footsteps getting farther away.

"Confirmation? I didn't know this was a church school. I don't go to church."

"Church?" Twig looked confused. "What's that? Where do you come from?"

"California."

"I meant what settlement. What's your settlement number?"

"My zip code, you mean? 92515."

"That's not near here."

"No, it's across the ocean."

"The ocean?" Again Twig looked horrified and delighted at the same time. "You must be really wicked to have been sent here from far away."

A noise down the hallway made Twig glance back and then drag me along at a greater pace. She opened a door and pushed me inside. "Stay here. I have to get back before I'm missed. I'll sneak back later and take you to the new arrivals mistress. That way you can get your uniform and your number without going to the Regulator." She looked terrified as she said the word. "But I'd cover up that forbidden color if I were you. Grab one of the old cloaks. And lock the door behind me when I go."

"Wait," I started to say. "What forbidden color. What's going on here?" But she was gone. I was alone in the small room.

It was more of a closet than a room. Gray cloaks clearly in need of mending hung on either side of me. It smelled dusty and musty and my nose wrinkled as if I wanted to sneeze. The room was lit by a single dim bulb hanging from the ceiling. At the back of the room was a full-length mirror.

I locked the door and leaned against the cloaks, my head spinning. What was this place? Was it another part of my school just for students who were being punished? Or, and my blood ran cold at the thought, was the mad house—the old loony bin—still operational on this side of the building? Was Twig here because she was somehow paranoid and crazy?

None of this made any sense. The problem was that I had felt that Twig was someone I could trust since I first met her in my dream. Wait. Things started to make sense. I had first met Twig in a dream. That dream had felt very real, too. Was I dreaming now and, if so, could I wake myself up? I caught sight of my reflection in the mirror. My face looked normal, except that there was something weird about my eyes. They were beginning to glow a soft green. 'Okay, I'm dreaming, I know I am. Wake up. Wake up.'

Behind me in the mirror I saw the door open. I jumped and shrank closer to the mirror hoping whoever it was would miss me in the dark. As I watched in the mirror I recognized Raj. He didn't seem to see me and started to close the door behind him.

"Raj, wait!" I almost shrieked. "I'm lost." The world flashed green around me. When I opened my eyes I was sitting on a cold tile floor. Raj opened the door and came out of a stall. He spun around to stare at me, looking horrified. "Addy," he said. "What are you doing in the boy's bathroom?"

I FIND THE BEASTS WE'RE LOOKING FOR

I scrambled to my feet, my face bright red. "I – I don't know." I stammered. "I was looking for Miss Neves's office and I got lost in a part of the castle I've never seen before. There was this horrible teacher running after me down this long creepy hallway. I barely escaped. There was ..." I stopped as I saw the expression on Raj's face.

"Addy – we're two doors down from the library." He grinned. "I think you fell asleep in front of the fire and sleep-walked in here or something."

"Yeah – I guess so," I said slowly.

A boy I didn't know walked into the bathroom and stopped short when he saw me.

"What ...?" he began.

"Sorry," I said hurriedly. "I'm just leaving. My mistake." And I pushed past him and raced out the door. Sure enough I could see the library just down the hall. This was beyond weird. It was creepy. Was it possible that I had dreamed the whole thing? After all, the first time I had seen Twig had been in a dream at Aunt Jean's apartment. But it all seemed so real. I could feel my heart still thumping in my chest. And that horrible woman in the white cloak. She must be a dream—no teachers in the school could really look and act like that? And the strange thing was that she reminded me of someone else I had dreamed about just last week – no wait – read about. A queen—a white queen ... That was it.

I walked back to the library with Raj, who snuck me a few funny looks but didn't say anything more.

"I hope the others are having better luck than me with the Seven Impossible Things," I said. "How did you get along?"

"Nothing much. I went through the library catalog," he said. "No books called that."

"I don't know how anyone finds anything in a library this size,"

I said, looking around at the towering walls. Many of the books seemed old and musty, with leather covers—just like Aunt Jean's bookshelves. I remembered how hard it had been to find a book I even wanted to read and I'd ended up with ... "That's it!" I said out loud, making other students look up from their work and frown at me.

"What is?" Raj looked at me as if I was about to do something else crazy.

"The White Queen – Seven Impossible Things before Breakfast. A mirror world. It was all in Alice Through the Looking Glass. They must have that book here. Where would I find Lewis Carroll, Raj? Fiction? Classics?"

"Over here, I think." He led me across to the far wall. "Lewis Carroll. Lewis Carroll ... Here it is." He pulled down a leather-bound copy of the book and handed it to me. "But I still don't see how..."

I was already thumbing through it to find that passage when we heard the others arrive. They entered talking loudly and one of the sixth formers had to remind them to be quiet. It seemed that no one had had much luck and they were all trying to make their own points as to where they should look next.

"Addy thinks she's onto something," Raj said.

They crowded around me. I held up the book. "I remember where I read that quote now. Alice Through the Looking Glass. The White Queen says that she has believed as many as Six Impossible Things before breakfast. I read it again a few days ago."

"I have read that book," Kobi said taking the book from my hands. "Please pay attention, everyone. Addy has discovered something."

The others grinned at Kobi's manner but they stopped talking and listened as Kobi read a few sentences from the book.

"That's the closest we've come," Sam said. " But it says six things and we're supposed to do or find or believe seven."

"Perhaps this represents six of the impossible things and we are supposed to find one more," Pippa suggested.

"Maybe we are supposed to do some of the things Alice does in this book." I started to flip through the pages. "What does she do? Meets Tweedledum and Tweedledee ..."

"Goes through a mirror," Pippa said.

I stopped and stared at her, my heart beating faster. I opened my mouth to say something. Did this have something to do with the haunted hallway and the strange school on the other side? But then it had been so weird and so horrible that there was no way I was going to expose the others to that white woman with the claw-like hands. And besides, it had only been a dream, hadn't it?

"Oh yeah, good idea," Sam said with a chuckle. "Let's go and bang our heads against a few mirrors and see which ones we can get through."

"And I do not wish to become bigger and smaller," Celeste said. "I like the size I am."

"Maybe there is a clue hidden in the book?" Raj took the book and shook out the pages but nothing dropped out.

We searched the shelves where the book had been found and the books around it and across from it. Then Gwylum cleared his throat. It wasn't until I heard him speak that I realized that he hadn't said a word the whole morning.

"There's no dragon in this one," he said.

Everyone looked at him. He turned bright red. "I meant there are no pictures. I used to have another copy that had pictures in it and one of them was of a dragon. I always liked that one because it looked just like the Welsh dragon."

"I've got the same book!" I yelled, making everyone else in the library look up and shhh us. "I remember now. It belongs to my Aunt Jean. I was reading it on the train and I must still have it. Come on."

We ran like crazy down the stairs, across the courtyard, past the fountain and up the other side, piling into the dormitory corridor.

"Here, what's going on?" Fern's shrill voice demanded. "What are you doing up here? No boys allowed in girls' dorms."

"We're just getting a book, Fern. For our class with Miss Rorrim," Pippa yelled over her shoulder as she ran past. "We won't be a moment."

"You boys wait outside the door," Fern said. "You know the rules. Otherwise I'll report you to the headmistress."

"It's okay. I'll go and get the book and meet you in the common room," I said.

It only took me a couple of seconds to find it. I didn't exactly have a lot of possessions these days. "Here it is!" I called, waving the book at them. "Lucky that Aunt Jean forgot to ask for it back."

I put the book down on the table and started turning the pages.

"There it is!" Celeste exclaimed as I turned to a page with a picture of a large woman wearing a white cloak and an impressive crown. Around her danced a bunch of mythical beasts: a lion, a unicorn, a fawn, a funny looking frog, a gryphon and, in the background, a dragon. The title of the picture was underneath. "Six Impossible Things Before Breakfast."

WE GO ON A TREASURE HUNT

"**I** know where I've seen all those creatures," Sam shouted. "The fountain in the courtyard. Come on."

"The Fountain!" everyone yelled almost in unison. We flew down the five floors to the courtyard, apologizing loudly as we almost knocked other students out of our way and ran by. The great fountain rose up in the middle of the courtyard with the statue of the dragon towering over the various mythical beasts while the water splashed out of mouths into the big carved basin below.

"What are we supposed to do now? Go for a swim?" Sam asked.

"I am not getting wet," Celeste said.

"I suppose we should search around it for a clue," Pippa suggested.

"Maybe it is like a treasure hunt after all. The next clue might be hidden somewhere."

"Hey, this is fun," Raj said. "A treasure hunt. That's cool."

We started working our way around the fountain, trying not to get too wet from the wind-blown spray coming from the spouts. I swept my hands over the statue of the griffin feeling in every crack and crevice for some clue.

"I've found something!" Raj yelled. In his hand was what looked like a lump of mud. He licked his thumb and ran it over the lump. Underneath the mud I saw a cut blue stone.

"It was in a hole at the base of the unicorn," he said and washed it off in the water.

"Do you think it's real?" Pippa asked.

"Don't be ridiculous," Celeste said. "No real sapphire is as big as that. It is only glass, I am sure."

I started poking around at the base of the griffin and dug out a green stone. I heard the whoops of joy from the others as they found stones under their statues. We washed them off in the fountain and compared what we had found. Six cut gems of different colors.

"There should be a seventh one somewhere," Sam said, counting the stones.

"Yes – the red one," I agreed.

"Why red?" Raj asked. "Because we need all the colors of the prism, I suppose."

I pulled out my necklace. "I was thinking of this. Look, the stones are the same colors as the ones in my necklace. I've had it since I was a baby and I guess it must be a Welsh symbol or something. Anyway the one in the middle is red."

"I don't think that is a Welsh symbol," Gwylum said looking closely at the necklace. "It looks like the Welsh red dragon in the middle but I have never seen it with stones around it like that in a necklace."

"It is a pretty little necklace," Celeste said appraisingly. "Of course it is a little small and I should prefer it in gold."

"I have seen that necklace," Kobi spoke up. "I had one like it at home when I was a little boy."

"In Ghana?" I was surprised. "It can't be Welsh then I guess. I thought maybe I was Welsh or something and that's why I had it."

"What are you doing?" Raj asked Sam. Sam was taking off his socks and rolling up his pants.

"Well, the seventh must be on the dragon somewhere, mustn't it? Someone's got to get it." He waded into the center of the fountain and started to climb until he could reach the dragon. He felt all around and below the statue of the dragon with no result. Finally he climbed up to stick his hand into the mouth of the dragon and yelped as the water that streamed out of it sprayed all over him. His yelp turned to a cry of delight.

"I've got something!" he yelled as he pulled out a small silvery metal tube.

"You better take it." He threw it down to Kobi. "I don't want to get it all wet."

Kobi caught it, opened it and pulled out a piece of paper. "It's a map." He held it up to show us. A small Red Dragon Academy was drawn on the map and in the mountains nearby an x marked 'The Heart of the Dragon.'

"That looks like it's miles away," Pippa said with a groan. "Are we supposed to go there?"

"How will we find a little stone miles away from the school?" Raj said. "This whole thing is a little ridiculous."

Kobi turned to him. "You think we have to find another stone?"

"Well," Raj said lifting up his stone for emphasis. "I think Addy's right. I don't see a red stone here and the heart of a Dragon would be red just like on her necklace. It would make sense that we are supposed the find the red stone."

"That's strange." Kobi was frowning. "I rather thought we were supposed to find the dragon itself."

"Find the dragon?" We looked at him and started laughing.

"Oh yeah," Sam said. "I've noticed lots of dragons in these parts. I expect the woods are full of them. Not to mention a few witches on broomsticks and a troll or two."

"Just a thought." Kobi frowned but didn't say any more.

"Well, let's follow the map anyway and see what we find," I said.

"It seems bloody impossible to me," Raj muttered. "Are we allowed to leave the school grounds on our own? It must be miles."

SAM HAS A CONVERSATION WITH A HORSE

We stood there trying to decide.

"I'm sure Miss Rorrim wouldn't have given us a challenge we couldn't do at all," I said at last ...

"Yeah – that's why she called it an impossible task," Sam said sarcastically. "Well – I guess we better get walking."

"Not walking," Pippa said with an excited look on her face. "Riding! Why don't we take horses? We can be there in an hour if we saddle up quickly."

"Are we allowed to do that?" I asked at the same time that Raj said, "Uh – I'm not a very good rider."

"You can ride behind me," Pippa said confidently. "I won't let you fall." She started walking toward the stables with such determination that we all turned to follow.

"Excuse me!" Celeste's loud voice made us stop and look back. She had not moved. "I am cold. I am starving and this drizzle is making my 'air frizz. I am not going anywhere without lunch and a warm jacket."

"Good point," Sam said. "I guess I'm a little wet, too." I saw that he was soaked to the skin. "I vote for warm jackets and lunch before we do anything more."

As I went into lunch with Pippa and Celeste I could hear parts of what Raj was saying to the other boys: "... right on the floor of the boy's bathroom ... Good thing she slept because she dreamed up the answer."

'Oh great,' I thought. 'Now everyone will think I am a weird sleepwalker as well as an idiot.'

As we entered the dining hall the other students looked up. I noticed Angela and her posse sitting by themselves, rather sour looks on their faces. 'I wonder if they got in trouble for missing Miss Rorrim's class.' I thought. 'It's strange that she didn't seem to mind that all the first years didn't show up. In fact she seemed pleased that there were only seven of us.' I stopped to think about this. 'Was that why she wrote seven impossible things? One for each of us? And what have impossible things to do with colored stones or my necklace? And what will we find if we go all that way?'

"Come one, eat up." Sam dug me in the ribs as he passed me a plate of pizza slices.

We studied the map as we ate. "There's a footpath that goes up into the hills this way." Gwylum traced a line on the map with his finger. "But I'm not sure what they expect us to find. There's not much up there – just fields and some cottages going up the mountain side."

As soon as we had finished eating, we raced up to the dorms to put on our riding clothes, then back down to put on our boots. We passed Fern's open door on our way in and out of the dorm and she just watched us in silence.

"Do you think we should have asked her permission?" I whispered.

"Her permission?" Pippa looked back scornfully. "She's not God. "

"Are first formers really allowed to check out horses when they want?"

"I am," Pippa said. "And this is an official school project so I don't see why I can't just sign you out, too. And I'd rather die than ask Fern for anything. You know she wouldn't allow us to do anything fun."

The stables were deserted when we arrived. The others looked around as nervously as I did, all except for Pippa who strode forward with confidence and started taking down a bridle from a hook.

"I'm not sure we should be doing this," Raj said. "I have a feeling we could get into serious trouble."

"Didn't they impress upon us that no student is to ride without a mentor?" Kobi asked.

"I'm the mentor," Pippa said. "I'm allowed to ride alone, so I'll be keeping an eye on you lot. Now come on, before someone comes and sees us. If we hurry we can be there and back and nobody will know."

"I think it is a stupid idea to go our riding in the rain," Celeste said.

"Then don't come." Pippa started saddling up the nearest horse.

Celeste gave a very French sort of shrug and took down a bridle from a hook. "Very well," she said. "I suppose I shall 'ave to suffer. You will probably need my 'elp."

Pippa, Celeste and Kobi were already experts at riding and got their horses saddled quickly. Raj climbed on behind Pippa who was riding a large bay horse.

"Don't hold on so tightly. I can't breathe," Pippa gasped. "I won't let you fall, I promise."

"I shall take Sultan," Celeste said. She tried to put a bridle on him but he threw up his head and danced nervously.

"I'd leave him if I were you," Pippa warned. "He's not the easiest horse."

"I am as good a rider as you are," Celeste said. She tried again but Sultan danced to the back of his stall.

"Celeste, leave him," Pippa said again.

Sam went up to the stall. The horse came and put its head over the gate. Sam stroked its nose then nodded. "I quite understand. I feel the same way, mate," he said. He looked up to see the others staring at him. "He don't like the rain, that's the problem," Sam said.

"Oh, he told you that, did he?" Raj asked, grinning.

"Well, yeah. It's easy enough to see, ain't it?"

"I don't understand how he came to you like that." Pippa was staring hard at Sam. "Where have you been around horses before?"

"The only horse I ever saw before I came here was a police horse in London," he said, "but animals take to me for some reason. I even had a pet mouse that used to come out of this hole in the floorboards at my last foster home. Cute little thing. Then the old witch caught it in a trap."

"Why do we stand here freezing?" Celeste demanded. "If Sultan does not like the rain, then I suppose I must choose one of these boring horses. And Sam, you may ride with me in case he says he is not happy and wishes to throw me off."

"If you ain't nice to me, I'll tell him to throw you off," Sam said.

That relaxed us all and we were laughing as we saddled up enough horses and set off. Kobi, Gwylum and I followed Pippa's direction and took three quiet-looking mares. My chestnut trotted willingly enough after the other horses and we set off up the pathway through the forest.

CELESTE GETS HER WAY

The drizzle had turned into a full-blown rain as we left the school grounds.

"See, Sultan was smart. He knew the rain would become worse," Celeste said. "Me, I do not like the rain either."

Gwylum rode in front. He and Kobi stopped once in a while to consult the map. The route lay along a pretty footpath up a green hillside then through some groves of oak trees. I was soaked to the skin and freezing after the first half hour but I realized I was still having fun. I was with other kids and we were doing something unusual and exciting. Unlike the tired old horse I had ridden yesterday this horse obeyed my every command almost as if it could read my mind. I only had to shift my body slightly to make the horse turn or speed up. A slight tug on the reins brought the mare to a gentle stop.

Gwylum stopped when we came to a place where the mountains began for real. Steep slopes rose ahead of us, crowned with rocky crags. On the slopes sheep were grazing and the sound of their baas floated down in the still air along with the pattering of the rain.

"We have arrived at the spot," Kobi said confidently.

"You're not expecting us to ride up there, are you?" Raj asked, staring upward to where the peaks disappeared into the cloud.

"No, it has to be around here, somewhere," Gwylum said. "See, the old Celtic cross is marked on the map and there it is, and the old copper mine shafts above it. It has to be here." Perched on the mountainside high above us was a small, ancient-looking cottage. We dismounted from our horses and stared around the rocky meadow. In front of us was an area of green grass, bordered by large stones and in the middle an old Celtic cross, so weathered that it was hard to see what it was.

"What exactly are we looking for?" asked Celeste. "A little red stone? In this wilderness?"

Kobi stared up the mountainside frowning.

"You still lookin' for your dragon, Kobi?" Sam asked, giving him a nudge in the side.

"It had come to me that this whole business had something to do with a dragon, yes."

"Of course it has. The stone to complete the dragon necklace," Raj said.

"Shall we go and ask at that cottage up there?" I suggested. "Maybe Miss Rorrim gave the owner a clue for us."

I thought I could see an old woman moving about in the garden behind the cottage.

"Why would Miss Rorrim give some stranger in a cottage a clue?" Pippa demanded. "I say we look around here first and see what turns up. We found the other stones easily enough."

"I don't know—I just wondered ..." I went on staring at that cottage. I could have sworn it was the same old woman I met in the school grounds that day when I was trying to run away. She wasn't wearing a red cloak today but an ordinary looking raincoat and hood and we were too far away to see her features. Maybe all old Welshwomen looked similar. And as I stared upward it seemed as if the old woman turned to me and into my head came a single word: Tentis. Tentis?

"Tents," I blurted out. "Maybe something to do with tents?"

The others looked at me as if I was crazy. "Tents? I don't see any tents," Pippa said.

"Maybe there's a tent up behind that cottage," I said.

"Who would be camping up on a mountain in this kind of weather in October?" Raj said.

"I do not wish to scramble up that rocky hillside for nothing," Celeste said.

"I agree with Pippa. Let's search around the cross first. It's a likely landmark," Raj said. "We can see if Kobi's dragon is lurking in the grass," Sam chuckled.

Kobi looked at him seriously. "I just had this feeling that we would be meeting some kind of powerful creature."

"That old ram over there doesn't look too friendly," Sam said. "He might well charge you."

"I do not wish to stay around in a field with dangerous sheep," Celeste said. "Can we not hurry up and go home?"

We began searching the field together, first around every inch of the Celtic cross, then walking slowly side by side in a line, turning over stones and rummaging through bushes. Soon I had a crook in my neck from staring at the ground. Now that I was not riding I felt even colder and more miserable. Only Pippa and Sam remained cheerful. Kobi kept glancing up at the cottage. "I really think I agree with Addy that we are supposed to go up there."

Celeste's steps got slower and slower. She seemed to have a new complaint with every step. "I am freezing. I shall catch a cold. My shoes are ruined. My skin will suffer in the wind. I shall be hideous for a week." I tried to tune her out and kept searching. Finally Celeste started sneezing and couldn't stop. I realized that she really did look miserable. Her eyes and nose were streaming. Her whole body shook with every sneeze.

"Are you all right?" Gwylum asked.

"I am very delicate. I catch cold very easily," she said. "And then I shall be in bed for a week and very ill."

"No, you won't. You'll be all right," Gwylum said. He put a hand on her shoulder awkwardly. "When my mum doesn't feel well I give her my special neck massage."

"What good will a massage do for my cold?" Celeste demanded. "I need hot lemon and honey. I need a hot bath. My voice will suffer." She stopped sneezing, however as Gwylum's hands touched her shoulders. "Listen. I am croaking already. Ruined. My beautiful voice is ruined."

"You'll be fine, Celeste," Pippa said. "It's not exactly pleasant for any of us, but you don't hear us complaining, do you?"

"It is different for you. You do not have a lovely voice," Celeste said. "This is hopeless and ridiculous. We shall all become sick if we stay out any longer. And the horses will suffer, too. Somebody needs to find it now."

"Find what, exactly?" Raj said. "That's the point, isn't it? We're not sure we're searching for a red stone."

"It could be a red stone. Me, I think it will be another necklace, like Addy's but bigger and more beautiful." Celeste gave her French shrug. "All I know is that I want to go back and I wish someone to find this thing now. It has to be here somewhere." She opened her arms wide and sang, "I wish to find the necklace. I command that somebody find it now." Her lovely voice echoed out from the mountains above. But then she coughed. "You see.

My voice, it is ruined. Never shall I be a great opera singer like my mother."

As cold as I was I had to laugh.

"Celeste, you're a bloody drama queen," Sam said.

Suddenly Gwylum dropped to his knees. "What's this?" he exclaimed. "Look!" He stood up holding out something shiny. It was exactly as Celeste had described—a larger golden copy of my necklace. In the middle of the golden dragon was a ruby that sparkled against the dismal darkness of the day. He handed it to Celeste and bowed with a most un-Gwylumish bow. "As you commanded, my lady." Then he collapsed into embarrassed silence as she took the necklace.

"You see, I was right. I knew this was what we were searching for. It is beautiful, no? It is probably a long-lost treasure and we shall be rewarded for finding it. In the meantime I shall wear it." Celeste put it around her neck with a smile.

I realized that the others were still searching. "He found it! Gwylum found it! Celeste ordered him to and he found it." The others gathered around admiring the necklace, clapping Gwylum on the back.

"Celeste does always seem to get her way," Pippa said as we made our way back to the horses. "I could swear that we already searched this area really well and found nothing. But I can't see her conjuring necklaces out of thin air."

I felt confused as I swung myself onto my horse's back. I too was sure we had looked on the ground in the exact spot where Gwylum discovered the necklace. It was almost as if Celeste really had commanded it to appear and it did.

"Oh, Celeste," Pippa called as she helped Raj up on the big bay horse and then mounted in front of him. "Could you conjure up some warm dry clothes, please?"

Celeste just laughed. She had stopped her complaining and was quite pleased now that she had the golden necklace securely around her neck.

"I told you it must be a Welsh symbol," I said to Gwylum as we drew level. "I bet we can find it on lots of necklaces in Wales. What's the betting this was some long ago Welsh king's necklace and it will go in a museum or something?"

Gwylum shrugged. "I've never seen one like it before. Perhaps it's very old indeed."

"You were clever to find it," I said and he looked embarrassed and pleased at the same time.

We reached the stables and then Pippa made us rub down the horses and put away the tack before we could go and change out of our cold wet clothes. It was almost dark before the horses were dry and well fed. Then we made our way back to Miss Rorrim's tower.

"Do you think we need to go and see her tonight?" Raj said. "Will she be expecting us this late?"

"I am cold and uncomfortable and sick," Celeste said. "Why do we not wait until morning?"

"You're not sick, Celeste. You haven't coughed or sneezed once since Gwylum gave you that neck massage," Pippa said.

"And I'm not sure if Miss Rorrim was serious about us finishing before breakfast, but I'm not about to miss breakfast tomorrow," Sam said. "I say we go now and get it over with."

"And I don't think we can risk having a necklace like that in the dorms," Pippa agreed. "Fern might tell everyone about it, or help herself to it."

"All right. Let us go to Miss Rorrim then." Celeste gave her big French sigh. "But now that I 'ave this delightful necklace, I do not wish to be parted from it."

WHAT APPEARED AND WHAT DISAPPEARED

If Miss Rorrim was surprised to find seven dripping first formers in her study she didn't show it. She seemed as excited as we were, like a child at the end of a treasure hunt. "So what have you discovered?"

Celeste took the necklace off her neck and handed it to Miss Rorrim. She took it and examined it carefully. "Amazing," she said. "And you found this?"

"Gwylum found it," Celeste said.

"Celeste told me where to look," Gwylum said.

Miss Rorrim was examining it carefully. "Where have you seen a necklace like this before, Celeste?"

"Addy has one like it," Celeste answered. "I was sure that we'd be looking for a necklace like Addy's, only better, because we found all the stones except for the red one. Did you hide the necklace there for us to find?"

"I did not," Miss Rorrim said. "I hoped that you would find something today, but this is as much a surprise to me as it was to you."

"This necklace, is it a Welsh symbol?" I asked.

"It is a very ancient symbol but it's not Welsh exactly. It is a symbol of working together, which is what I imagine you had to do to find this today. Tell me all about it." She looked from one face to the next. "But first you need something to warm you up." She disappeared into a back room and returned with mugs of steaming hot chocolate and a tray of cookies. We sipped gratefully, our hands around the mugs to warm us up.

There was a fire in Miss Rorrim's study and we gathered around it, glad for the warmth, and told her about our adventures.

"But you didn't go to the cottage?" Miss Rorrim sounded puzzled. "And you didn't speak to anybody there?"

"We saw an old woman in the cottage garden but we didn't talk to her," I said. "Kobi and I thought we should go up and speak to her but the others didn't want to."

"Interesting." Miss Rorrim looked hard at each of them. "And you found this necklace just lying in the meadow?"

We nodded.

"Only after Celeste told us to find it," Gwylum said.

"Miss Rorrim, so if we found this necklace, did we accomplish the task?" Kobi asked.

"Oh, indeed you did."

"But what were the seven impossible things then?" Raj asked. "I mean, the stones were in the fountain and they were hard to find, but not impossible."

"And the clue came because I'd just read Alice Through the Looking Glass, and Gwylum remembered seeing the picture that was in the version of the book I had with me," I added.

Miss Rorrim looked from one face to the next. "The task was in the doing," she said. "We always put our new students through a challenge to observe how they handle it."

"So were there seven impossible things that we did?" Raj insisted.

"I don't know. Were there?" Miss Rorrim smiled at him. "The necklace gives you the clue to the seventh impossible thing." She paused and we all looked at her, curious. "It is a symbol of working together to achieve a task. Seven very different children like yourselves working together is more impossible than you think. Rich and poor, black and white, boys and girls, shy and bold coming together to achieve impossible things." She held up the necklace. "This is an expensive gold necklace. Not all of you are rich. How did you decide that Celeste should have it? Did you have to fight about it?"

We looked at each other. "Well, Celeste sort of ordered Gwylum to find it and he did. He gave it to her and we thought it might be some kind of important necklace, like something worn by a king or queen," I said. "We thought it might have to go to a museum or something, but Celeste wanted to wear it on the way home so we let her."

"The most important thing was the task to be accomplished," Kobi said in his polished tones. "The necklace was the accomplishment of the task, not an individual trophy."

"Sort of ordered?" Miss Rorrim asked quietly.

Celeste shrugged. "I was becoming so miserable I said that somebody had to find the necklace or I would go home and I pointed at my feet and Gwylum looked down and there it was."

"Actually it was weird," I said. "She sang loudly 'Find the necklace!' And then the necklace was there. Almost like magic."

"Quite remarkable. Some might say impossible," Miss Rorrim said looking around at us.

"But it must have been there all along," Raj said. "Things just can't appear out of thin air, can they?" and he laughed.

Miss Rorrim didn't answer but she handed the necklace back to Celeste. "I think this is yours, my dear."

"Really? It's mine? Isn't it terribly valuable? Didn't somebody lose it?"

"No, I think you'll find that nobody lost it and you have as good a claim on it as anybody."

"But Gwylum actually found it," Pippa pointed out. "Maybe it should go to him."

"Maybe we should sell it and split the proceeds," Sam suggested.

Miss Rorrim shook her head. "No, I am absolutely sure that this necklace belongs to Celeste. But my dear, I hope you will remember the generosity of classmates and try to get along with them better."

"I will, Madame." Celeste looked pleased as she put the necklace back around her neck.

"Now go and get warm. You have missed dinner but go down to the kitchen and Gwylum can ask his mother to heat something up for you. I am proud of your achievement. Well done."

"That was the strangest lesson ever," Pippa said as we climbed into bed that night. "But the riding was brilliant. I've never been allowed to ride so far from the school before."

"Yes, what a strange day," I said sleepily. "I liked all of it except being chased into a cloakroom."

"A cloakroom? You're asleep already, Addy. Good night."

I EAT CHOCOLATE CHIP COOKIES

I awoke to find a full moon shining right into my face. All around was a delicious baking smell and I could hear low voices somewhere near. I sat up and saw that Pippa and Celeste were sitting together on the window seat, a plate of chocolate chip cookies between them. Pippa looked up as she saw me.

"Come and join us while they are still warm," she said. "They are so yummy."

I climbed up onto the window seat beside them.

"Mmm, these are delicious." I licked the melted chocolate off my fingers. For a while we ate in silence.

"This is the best night I've had here so far," Pippa said. "I'm glad you're my roommate, Addy."

"Thanks." I smiled feeling happy inside. "I hope we become best friends. Just don't run away anytime soon."

"I think I may stay for a while," Pippa said.

"Why do you run away so much?" I asked. "Do they usually send you to horrible schools?"

"Not really. I suppose I do it to get my father's attention. To remind him that I still exist and to stop my stepmother from poisoning him against me."

"Does she do that?" Celeste asked, dipping her cookie in a glass of ice-cold milk.

"Oh yes. She'd like to get rid of me, so that she could have my father's money to herself."

"What happened to your real mom? Did they divorce?"

"No, she died in a hunting accident when I was two. She fell off her horse and broke her neck."

"How terrible," Celeste said.

"I really don't remember her," Pippa said. "I had a nice nanny and it was just my father and me and it was great. But then last year he married again—this awful woman. I call her the wicked witch of the west. And now I find that she's trying hard to get rid of me. She's been telling my father awful things…"

"I'm sure your dad still loves you," I said consolingly. "At least you still have parents. I never knew my father. I just found out last week that I was adopted. I feel like I lost my mother twice." I swallowed hard, afraid I might cry. Pippa hugged me. A tissue appeared out of nowhere in Celeste's hand.

"Here—wipe your eyes. And please both of you stop crying or I shall start, too."

"Thanks." I took the tissue.

"It's funny that you just found out that you were adopted," Pippa said, "because so did I. I never knew before. My father never told me. But I overheard my stepmother talking to him and she told him to find out about my birth mother, and that adoptions could be undone, especially if the child turned out bad."

"What an awful thing to say," I said hotly.

"It was a terrible shock," Pippa agreed. "So now I feel scared all the time. I don't know where I belong any more."

"You belong here, with us," I said.

"Thanks." Pippa got up and went back to bed.

"We should go back to sleep, or we won't wake up in the morning," I climbed into my own bed.

"I'm just going to write in my diary for a few minutes," Pippa said. "It's so bright in the moonlight, isn't it?"

I STAND UP FOR PIPPA

I loved Sunday morning. We finally got to sleep in and breakfast was not until 9:00. The tables were piled high with bacon, sausages, eggs and toast.

"Come on, you lot, dig in before I finish it all," Sam called, his mouth full of food.

"You're disgusting. Didn't anybody ever teach you to eat properly?" Pippa said disdainfully.

"I think he's got years worth of eating to do," I spoke for him. "He hasn't stopped eating since I got here and he's still totally skinny."

"The food is all bloody marvelous," Sam said with his mouth full. "I've gained at least a stone since I came here."

"Then you must have been a skeleton before," Pippa said distastefully. "Because you still look pretty shrimpy."

"Hey, don't knock it," Sam said, grinning. "That shrimpy look helped me stay alive. You won't believe how many people I conned into giving me lost bus fare home. Tidy little business I had there."

"Conning people out of money?" Pippa said with distaste. "That's stealing."

"And what would you do if you was skint and 'ungry?" Sam asked.

"Come on, Pippa. Give him a break. You don't know what foster care is like," I said, giving Sam a friendly grin.

"Neither do you," Pippa responded. "I'd try to earn some honest money."

"Oh, like my lovely foster mum was earning an honest livin'— taking money from the government and then not feeding me? Just because I wasn't born in some castle with a silver spoon in me mouth and a nanny to change me nappies, don't think you can judge me," Sam said.

"Well I think you're lucky you weren't caught and sent to

prison," Pippa snapped.

"He almost was." I remembered the strange episode I'd had with Sam.

"How did you know that?" Sam looked at me strangely. "But yeah. That's how I got here. I tried to con the same plainclothes policeman twice. My stupid mistake. They were going to send me to a YOI ..."

"A what?" I asked.

"Young Offenders Institute," Sam grimaced. "But apparently some do-gooder decided to fork out some money to send me 'ere instead. My lucky day for once."

"It's really strange," Pippa said, forgetting to be angry for once and looking around their table thoughtfully. "Raj is here on a science scholarship. Celeste is here for English and Addy for manners. My stepmother found a brochure for this place at her spa. Isn't it funny how we all arrived here almost by luck—or bad luck, maybe," she added, glancing up as Miss Neves marched into the dining hall.

Miss Neves stared at our table and raised an eyebrow as if she had overheard, which she couldn't possibly have done. Sam went back to eating as fast as he could, unfazed by the argument he and Pippa had just had. I glanced at Pippa and we exchanged a grin. I felt a little bit as if I was one of them, as if I might even belong here. It was a good feeling.

"So what do we do today?" I asked, as I piled bacon, sausage, tomatoes onto my own plate.

"Absolutely bloody nuffink," Sam said with his mouth half full.

"I'm going to go riding," Pippa said. "A lovely long ride. Brilliant!" She looked at me. "I wonder if you'd be allowed to come with me?"

"I'm just a beginner," I said. "I don't think they'd let me. And I wouldn't want to hold you up." I shifted uncomfortably in my seat. I didn't want to admit that my behind was really sore from that riding we did yesterday. "Don't worry, I'm sure I'll find plenty of things to do."

"Too bad we are not senior students or we could go into town and do some shopping," Celeste said.

Raj laughed. "On a Sunday? This is Wales, you know. Everything's shut, expect maybe Tesco's."

Celeste sighed. "I do not understand how my mama could have

sent me to such a primitive backward place where no shops open on Sundays."

We'd just finished eating when a Sixth Form boy stood up and banged on the table for silence. He was very tall and slim—and good looking too, I thought. He looked like the lead singer of a boy band. His dark hair fell across his eyes and he brushed it away.

"For anyone who's new, I'm Barry. I'm the head boy. This is Alice, the head girl." A studious-looking girl rose, waved briefly and sat back down.

"Welcome to our student council meeting. For the first formers who don't know—we hold a student council meeting on Sunday mornings. Anyone has a right to bring up complaints and we hold a student court to decide punishment for any breaking of the school rules. Miss Neves created this school to be a democracy. We get to set most of the rules and then we decide what should happen to someone who breaks them. It's the fairest way. We've all been first formers, and we've all broken our share of rules, except for maybe Alice here—" He paused for the laughter. "—So everyone gets a fair trial and we hand out fair punishments. Right. Let's get down to it."

As he spoke the sixth formers were efficiently clearing the tables and sitting down at the teachers' head table.

"If anyone is bullying or stealing or sneaking out of school it affects all of us so we talk it over and the whole council decides what the punishment should be." He called out, "Gregory Maguire." A large blond-haired boy stood up sheepishly. "Your dorm monitor reports that you have been sneaking out during prep time."

I listened curiously as Barry and Alice reported the misdeeds of various students and handed down punishments that ranged from grounding in the school for a week to no desserts for a month. The kids seemed to take the punishments good-naturedly and there was a lot of joking and laughing as the meeting went on. 'It's like kid's court,' I thought. I didn't know any of the students who were asked to stand up so after a while my mind drifted. I wondered if I'd be allowed to go to the art room and paint today, or perhaps take an easel outside and try to paint the castle. I snapped back to the present when I realized that Barry had turned his attention to my table.

"Philippa Masters-Johnson, could you stand up, please?" I felt

144

Pippa tense all over and watched her turn beet red as she got to her feet. Everyone in the dining room turned to look at her.

"Angela has come to us and said that you used physical violence against her. Is that true?"

Pippa stared at him as if she had lost the power of speech. Then finally she mumbled, "Yes."

Barry had a kind look on his face as he continued. "Well – I'm glad you admit it. That makes it easier. We don't allow any kind of hitting or shoving at this school. We need to solve our problems with words." He raised his eyes to take in the whole group. "What do you think Pippa's punishment should be?"

One of Angela's friends got up. "I think she should be made to do Angela's chores for a month. Oh, and to apologize in public."

I couldn't sit still a second longer. I stood up. "That's really not fair, you know. Angela was being horrible to Pippa. She insulted her and said nasty things about her family first. And she got right in Pippa's face."

Barry turned to look at us. "Did she push you first, Pippa?"

"No," Pippa mumbled. "But she did insult me."

"So what would your other option have been, do you think? If she was saying things you didn't like to hear?"

"To walk away," some kids muttered.

"Exactly," Barry said. "You don't have to stay and be abused, ever. If you turn your back and walk away, the other person can't talk to thin air, can they?"

"No, but..." Pippa began, then she stopped.

"Fighting is one of the things we really have to turn over to Miss Neves. People have been expelled before now for physical fights. But I reckon you're new here, so I'm going to propose that we give you another chance. Do you agree, prefects?" He looked around the head table and the heads nodded.

"So what do we think her punishment should be? Angela's chores for a month?"

Sam bounced to his feet as soon as she sat down. "I think it is punishment enough just having it mentioned in the council. I'm sure our Pepper – I mean Pippa – will keep 'er temper a bit after this."

Barry smiled. "I think you're right – Sam, is it? But I'm afraid Pippa has to be taught a lesson."

"I suggest she take over all Angela's chores for a week then,"

Alice said.

Barry looked around the assembly. "All those in favor?"

"Aye." Most of the students yelled and banged heartily on the table. Angela glanced at her friends and grinned. "You wait till you see what chores I'm going to think up for her," she said, loudly enough for us to hear.

Barry looked at Alice. "Your turn," he said sitting down. Alice looked much more serious and much less fun than Barry. "Would Addison Walker please stand up?"

I GET INTO TROUBLE

"And Raj and Celeste and Kobi and Gwylum," she continued staring over the top of her sheet of paper at our table. "I'm sorry to tell you this, Pippa," she said, "but you're included in another complaint as well. Fern has told me that seven first formers left the grounds without a fifth or six former and took horses without a teacher's permission."

Kobi stood immediately. "Excuse me, please. We were completing an assignment that had been given to us by Miss Rorrim. We believed that we could do whatever we needed to in order to successfully complete the assignment, and we were following a map that sent us off the school grounds. It was too far to walk so we thought that riding would be a good idea."

Pippa looked absolutely miserable to have been called out twice in one day.

"Did Miss Rorrim give you permission to take the horses then?" asked Alice.

"No," Raj spoke up, "But she didn't tell us we were wrong afterward either. And she definitely knew we were going to leave the castle because she gave us a map that led us miles away."

"The rule is that a member of the lower school must have a fifth or six former with them whenever they leave the school grounds."

Fern rose to her feet. "I saw them going out in riding gear. They could have asked my permission."

"So why didn't you ask Fern? She's your dorm monitor isn't she?" Alice said.

Pippa and I glanced at each other. We didn't want to say that Fern would never have given us permission in a million years and we didn't want to ask her.

I felt it was up to me to do something. "Alice," I said, taking a deep breath," please ask Miss Rorrim. I'm sure she approved of what we did."

"All right—uh?"

"Addy," I said.

"All right, Addy. I'll do that. If she says she gave you permission, that I will lift the punishment. But until then I have to give you one." She conferred briefly with the other six formers and then turned back to us. I found I was holding my breath, although none of the punishments had been too terrible so far. "It seems to me the most logical punishment would be that you are not to leave the school or ride the horses for a week. All in favor?"

"Aye," said the students in unison and banged the table. I noticed Fern banging extra hard and giving a self-satisfied smile. She really was horrible.

It seemed that we were the last students to come up before the council. Barry and Alice gave some announcements and then declared that we were all free for the rest of the day. They repeated the rules about going off the school grounds, but as we were grounded anyway it didn't exactly matter. The moment we were dismissed, Pippa jumped up and rushed ahead of us pushing past other kids to get out of the dining hall.

"Pippa, wait!" I fought my way through the crowd to catch up with her.

"It isn't fair," Pippa said angrily as she stalked ahead of me down the hallway. "Miss Rorrim gave us that assignment. She didn't mind that we took the horses. I know it!"

"I'm sure she'll tell that to Alice," I said, putting a hand on her arm to slow her down. "Anyway it's not too bad a punishment. I was afraid they'd lock us in a dungeon or something. The worst part was everybody staring at us."

"Not too bad?" Pippa was incredulous. "Not to ride for a whole week? What if it had been not painting for a week? Then how would you feel?"

"Oh, Pippa – I'm sorry I forgot how much you love riding. And that stupid Angela telling on you for pushing her when she egged you on to do it."

"I'm not sorry I did that," Pippa said defiantly. "She deserved it."

"I didn't see that fight," Raj said. "What happened?"

"Angela tried to make me break my neck," I said. I told him exactly what had happened at the stables.

Raj nodded. "That girl is poison," he agreed, "but really you were bloody stupid to push her over, Pippa."

"She was really upset," I said quickly. "Saying that Pippa's family didn't want her. Well, you know how that must have made her feel, especially since she overheard those things about being adopted and her stepmother wanting to send her back to her birth mother."

"What did you say?" Pippa's face had gone deathly white. She spun to face me. "I thought you were my friend." She started to stalk ahead again. I glanced at Raj and Celeste, then ran after her.

"Wait, please wait," I shouted as Pippa kept running. "Pippa wait, what's wrong? What did I say?"

"How did you know I was adopted?" She spun around to face me, eyes blazing. "I have never told anyone that. Never! You must have read my diary. How could you do that?"

"I didn't read your diary. You told me about being adopted yourself. When we were eating the chocolate chip cookies last night."

"What are you talking about? What are chocolate chip cookies?" Pippa's face was still white with rage. "My diary is the only private thing I have. It's the only place I've ever written that I was adopted. You must have read it."

"But we sat and talked last night. On the window seat, remember?" I turned to Celeste. "You were there. You ate cookies with us."

"What is this? I do not know cookies." Celeste shrugged.

"Biscuits," Raj said. "They're called biscuits over here."

"I do not eat biscuits," Celeste waved a dismissive hand. "Zey are bad for my complexion. Too much sugar. Not good."

"You see!" Pippa was yelling now. "Celeste isn't going to cover up for you. You're a horrible snoop and I'll never trust anyone again." She pushed past me and ran down the hall. The others gave me strange looks and melted away.

I just stood there, staring after them, feeling sick and scared. It had happened in our dorm room just like I said. Why had Pippa denied it? We had sat together on the window seat and… Even as I thought it, I realized something. There was no window seat in our dorm room. And nowhere to bake cookies. The window seat and the cookies had been at home in California. I must have dreamed the whole thing.

ON THE OTHER SIDE

I spent an absolutely miserable Sunday all alone. The day seemed to drag on forever. It started to rain soon after breakfast so there wasn't even the chance of a walk through the grounds. Pippa had avoided me all day and deliberately ignored me all through Sunday supper, which was slices of ham and salad and french fries that I now knew were called chips. It was followed by ice cream, apparently the usual Sunday night treat. All through the meal Pippa had looked away when I glanced in her direction and instead talked to Kobi who was sitting on her right as if I simply didn't exist. I tried to chat with Sam and Raj while we ate, but I was feeling too sick inside to swallow properly.

At the end of the meal everyone got up to leave.

"Entertainment night," Raj said. "Are you coming?"

"Entertainment night?" I asked.

Raj nodded. "We have something every Sunday in the theater. Sometimes it's a concert, sometimes the sixth formers put on little skits and sometimes they show films. It's always good."

Pippa turned back to look at me. "I'm not going if she is," she said coldly.

"Don't worry," I said. "I'm feeling kind of tired. I'm going to go and read in the common room. I feel like being alone."

I deliberately turned in the other direction and walked away trying to look natural but feeling like I was going to cry. I felt terrible that I had blown my one chance at making a friend, but at the same time I felt confused. That discussion on the window seat had seemed so real—not like a dream at all. I remembered every detail of it, and I could still taste the cookies. Dreams were—well, just dreams, weren't they? Full of weird things that didn't happen in real life and they melted away when you woke up. I tried to remember whether Pippa had given away any hint about being adopted in our real conversations.... Something strange was definitely going on in this school. Strange things had started happening since the day I got here. Was it a school for troubled children? Had I cracked up after my mom died? What was real and what was in my brain?

And if this was that kind of school, were the children in the old wing, the ones who wore the gray robes and had the horrible teachers, were they the ones who were considered beyond help? Or was it some kind of punishment wing? If it wasn't a punishment wing, then why were those kids shut away? Why did the entrance to that wing appear to be a mirror, and why did Miss Neves let everyone think that the hallway was haunted?

Wait, I thought suddenly. Strange things started happening to me before I came to this school. I dreamed I met Twig and then I did meet her. Or was she just another dream? I stood alone in the deserted hallway and came to a decision.

"I'm going to find out the truth," I said firmly. "I'm wide awake now. I'm going to prove once and for all whether that other school is a dream or it's real."

I retraced my steps from the dining room, up the stairs and found the way to the haunted hallway without too much trouble. There wasn't a sound in the whole building. Night had fallen outside and a cold star shone in through a high window. I stopped as I approached the hallway. In daylight it was okay to make jokes about being haunted. At night it wasn't so funny. The hallway stretched before me, disappearing into complete blackness. A cold draft blew into my face, as if a door was open to the outside. I swallowed hard and looked back.

"Come on. You can do it," I said to myself. "It's now or never. Mom always said it was better to know the truth than not to know."

'Only I'm going to be careful this time,' I thought. 'I'm going to make sure I'm not caught. And if it is some kind of punishment wing, maybe I can do something to help Twig.'

I made up my mind, and took a deep breath to keep my nervousness down. Then I walked forward without stopping until I could see some kind of figure moving in front of me. I stopped. The figure stopped. I breathed a sigh of relief. It was only my own reflection in the mirror. Apart from me the hallway was empty. As I went toward the mirror I saw strange green lights dancing in front of me. It seemed as if my eyes were glowing green again. Just as before there was a strange crackling sound and an explosion of green light around me.

'Electricity,' I thought. 'Maybe they've electrified the entrance and maybe some kids get a shock if they try to get back this way.'

The crackling sound died away and I found myself standing alone in the hallway on the other side. The mirror was gone and the horrible portrait in its place. I put my hand on the portrait to see if I could go right back to the mirrored hallway but nothing happened. 'Okay – somehow I'll come up with a logical explanation for this one,' I told myself as I turned and looked down the hallway.

This time it was completely quiet and deserted. No chanting coming from classrooms, no harsh-voiced teachers. Of course, I realized. There would be no classes in the evening. These students were also relaxing on a Sunday evening. I tiptoed cautiously forward. All the classroom doors were shut. I continued down the hallway, peeping into rooms full of rows of old-fashioned desks.

Do you have one of the enemy in your dormitory? was written on one blackboard.

Things to report to the teachers.
Dreams.
Singing
Makes plants grow well
Wounds heal quickly
Can make objects move.
Failure to report: Punishment Level 3.

Then underneath another hand had written in big letters:
IS THERE A SPY OR A TRAITOR AT THE SCHOOL?
REPORT THE SPY AND YOU'LL GO HOME.

At last I heard sounds floating up from down below—children's voices. At the end of the hallway I found a narrow spiral staircase to my right, going down into darkness. I touched the cold stone of the wall and started to step carefully. Down and down, several levels until it ended in a door. I opened the door and stepped into bright sunlight.

For a moment I stood there blinking, my heart beating very fast. It had been night on the other side of the castle. I remembered seeing the star. So how could the sun be shining here?

I stood blinking for a few minutes until my eyes got used to the light. Then I saw that I was in an old and overgrown garden. Gnarled apple trees were surrounded by brambles and ivy and high grass. I started to walk along a narrow path through the apple trees. The castle building rose up, bleak and forbidding, to my right. Where was this part of the grounds, I wondered. I hadn't passed it at all before. And why was it so badly cared for when most of the grounds had been well-kept lawns and neat garden beds?

Suddenly I heard a noise ahead of me. Thumping sounds, then a raised voice, a cry, and more thumping. I dodged behind an overgrown bush and looked out. Beyond the buildings rows of children were working in a field, some swinging pick axes, some digging, some planting. And a white-robed teacher walked behind them, carrying a whip.

"You know what happens to slackers, don't you?" I heard the woman yell. "Do you want to go Down Below? Then put your backs into it or there will be no roots to eat next harvest. You don't expect the settlement to grow enough to feed us here, do you?"

I looked among the children but I couldn't see Twig. 'Maybe she's still inside,' I thought. This might be a good time to go and find her, when everyone else is safely working.

As I turned to creep back to the building I heard voices behind me and two white-clad teachers came out of the door. They looked almost as unfriendly as the first woman, but were younger. They stood in the doorway, arms folded.

"So Bush says the Regulator has called in Rancurs," one said.

"That's what I heard. Is it safe? I mean some of our children are quite young. You don't think they'll see them as a tasty snack, do you?"

"They will have their Fallon Gwyn handlers with them."

"Very reassuring," the other teacher said and laughed. "Those creatures give me the shivers. And I don't particularly want everything I say reported straight back to The One."

"Apparently it's our fault because we haven't caught a phantom child," the first teacher said in a whisper.

"We've searched every inch of the school and if a child with special powers is here right now, then she is mind blocking with a skill beyond anything I've seen."

They started to walk down the path toward me. I looked around wildly. There was nowhere to hide if they came any closer. Low bushes and brambles edged the garden plot all the way to the castle wall, but they weren't big enough to hide under. I dropped to my knees and started to crawl toward the castle wall, shielded by the bushes from the working children. With any luck I could slip out of the back gate into the forest and then make my way around the building to the safety of my part of the school. Sharp stones dug into my hands and knees. Brambles scratched at my face. I gritted my teeth and kept going. At last I could see the castle wall ahead of me and the thick forest beyond. I looked for the gate in the wall, but I couldn't find it. The wall towered, high and solid in both directions. I could hear the two teachers chatting behind me as they came closer. I was trapped.

TWIG IN A TREE

I stared at the castle and then at the wall. Wasn't this the same way I had come when I had gone into the forest and tried to run away that time? In which case why hadn't I seen the old orchard or the fountain? Suddenly a shrill whistle sounded, making my heart leap. I was sure that someone had spotted me. But then I saw the children picking up their tools.

"Back to the building. Quick march," the teacher commanded. One of the older boys started beating on a small drum. Boom. Boom. Boom. The students began to walk back in long rows, their tools over their shoulders. The teacher lingered behind them.

"Make sure there are no stragglers," she said to two large boys. "And make sure we haven't lost any." The boys turned and started to patrol along the perimeter of the wall

I wasn't about to be caught. I looked around, searching for somewhere to hide. But there were only low bushes and brambles between me and the wall. It was only a matter of time before one of the boys came in my direction…

"Up here," a voice hissed. Above the wall was a large oak tree with a branch extending over my head. I looked up to see a hand reaching down to me. I didn't hesitate but climbed up the rough brick of the wall, scraping my hands, grabbed the hand and was hauled onto the branch.

"Around the other side of the trunk where they can't see us," the voice whispered and I eased myself around the tree and onto another branch. It was only then that I looked up to see that the speaker was Twig. I went to say something but Twig put a finger to her lips and pointed downwards.

We held our breath as one of the boys lumbered past us. We let out a sigh of relief as the boy disappeared and there was silence all around. Through the branches I caught a glimpse of the countryside, stretching down to the sea. It seemed to be nothing but forest. I couldn't make out Conwy Castle or the town. Maybe we were facing another direction.

"Thank heavens you were up here," I whispered. "You totally saved me. What were you doing up here? Goofing off?"

"I—uh, had a message to deliver for someone," Twig said uneasily. "You came back, I hoped you'd got away. Did they find you and bring you back here?"

"No, I came through the secret doorway by myself," I said. "Nobody knows I'm here."

"Secret doorway?"

"Yes. It's kind of weird. It looks like a mirror. I'll take you if you like."

"If you know a way out of here that's not guarded, you should escape while you can. I think they're looking for you."

"For me?"

Twig nodded. "They've been searching the school like crazy and they asked if we'd seen anyone wearing the forbidden color. Of course I didn't say anything but there are some kids who will do anything to get out of here and go home."

I swallowed hard. "I think I heard some teachers talking about that. Thanks for not saying anything," I said.

"You were crazy to come back if you didn't have to." Twig shook her head so that her bright red hair danced wildly.

"I didn't know I wasn't supposed to. Why are they so mean on this side of the school? Are you guys in trouble for something?"

"Not exactly," Twig said. "They say it's to re-educate us into being good citizens, but really it's to see if any of us have evil powers."

"You're not evil. You've been really nice to me. Come with me if you hate it here."

"I can't."

"I'm sure Miss Neves would understand that you don't belong here."

"Miss Neves? Who's she?"

"The headmistress. You must know Miss Neves."

"I don't know a headmistress. We have Miss Bush but she just does what the Regulator tells her."

"The Regulator?"

Twig nodded. "He's in charge. He's sent here by The One."

"Why don't you run away?"

Twig shook her head sadly. "I couldn't. I don't want them to punish my family. Sometimes they conform whole families and I've got two little sisters." She turned a hopeless face to me. "I just have to get through this somehow and then maybe they'll let me go home, if I'm lucky."

"Why did your parents send you to a school like this if it's so horrible?" I asked. "Can't you tell them you hate it and they'll bring you home?"

Twig looked at me as if I was really strange, or stupid. "They didn't send me here. Of course they didn't want me to come here. No one comes here if they don't have to. That's why I don't understand why you came back to this place."

"This is going to sound really weird," I hesitated, "but I came back to see you and to find out if you were real or not."

"What?" Twig's face looked puzzled and amused. "Why would you think I wasn't real?"

"Well – I think the first time I met you was in a dream. Please don't think I'm crazy but – did you dream it, too?"

Twig's face turned white. She backed as far away from me as she could on the branch. "No – of course not. Where did you hear that? I have no evil powers, I never dream."

I MEET THE RANCURS!

Twig kept sliding away from me and started to climb down from the tree.

"Wait." I climbed down hurriedly after her. "Wait – what did I say? I'm sorry, Twig." I slithered down the last few feet and grabbed Twig's arm before she could run off. "Is dreaming so bad?"

Twig's face was blank. She looked straight ahead and said, "I would report any dreaming to a Watcher right away. Anyone dreaming might be a Fareeth."

"You've said that word before. What is a Fareeth?"

"You mean you really truly don't know?"

I shook my head. "I really truly don't."

"I can't imagine what sort of place you come from if you've never even heard of them."

I shrugged. "So tell me. What are they?"

Still staring straight ahead Twig said in a singsong voice:

The Fareeth were evil.
They made us their slaves.
The One overcame them.
He was so brave.
He drove them out
And now we are saved."

"... I must return to classes now." She turned away from me. But I wouldn't let her walk away.

"Wait a minute. I'm not going to lose another friend because I said the wrong thing. This isn't really you, Twig. You wouldn't report anyone. Twig, look at me." I spun Twig around to face me. "It's me, Addy. Tell me what's wrong."

Twig stared hard at me. Slowly she said, "Do you swear you're not a spy?"

I didn't take my eyes from Twig's. "A spy? What kind of spy? How can I be a spy—I'm twelve years old, for Pete's sake."

"Kids younger than us are conformed all the time. Do you swear you're not HIS spy?"

I still hadn't a clue what she was talking about or who HE was, but she was clearly upset. "Okay. I swear it."

"Do you swear it by the Power of Seven?"

I started to ask what that meant but I could tell that Twig was still about to run away from me if I asked any more questions. "I swear it by the Power of Seven."

Twig sighed and all the tension went out of her. "No spy of The One would take that Oath. You scared me, Addy. I thought you might have been sent here to trick me into admitting that I have dreams."

"Doesn't everyone dream?" I asked.

Twig looked serious at me. "Addy, where do you come from? Is The One really not in charge in your settlement? Dreaming is considered an evil power. It's why I was sent here."

"But you don't really think its evil, do you? I dream all the time."

"Well, that's how it's taught in school. The Fareeth were evil beings who had strange powers. They used to rule the land and made us slaves. The One saved us and made our life better." She lowered her voice and looked around. "But I don't think life could have been much worse before The One came. He has Watchers everywhere and they report everything to him, and if someone shows any hint of the powers, they get conformed."

"And what happened to the Fareeth?"

"Most of them were killed or conformed when The One came to power, but there are rumors that ..." From far off came the sound of a bell ringing. "I have to get back," Twig said. "I'll be in trouble if I'm late for roll call. Don't try to come back to the school, Addy. Now's your chance. The forest goes all the way up to the mountains and they say there are plenty of places to hide out up there. There may even be groups of, you know, Fareeth." She lowered her voice to a whisper. "They'll take you in. Especially if you can dream. Especially if you might be a real Dreamwalker."

I shook my head. "No, you don't understand. I don't need to run away. I'm in a different part of your school—but in the same building. We should be able to get around to my side of the castle from here, then I can go in the regular way."

"Your side of the castle?"

"Yes, it's much nicer than this. The teachers aren't mean and there's good food. Come on. I'll take you to Miss Neves. I'm sure she can make things better for you."

I led Twig through the forest in what I thought was the direction of the front of the school. "I'm very new here, but I think it's this way," I said half to myself as I pushed through tree branches. I looked around trying to spot one of the highest towers of the castle, but the forest was too thick. "I think I've gotten us lost," I admitted.

Suddenly Twig grabbed at me. "We need to get out of the forest right now," she whispered. "Look through the trees there. Over there."

I looked where she was pointing. A pair of yellow eyes was watching us.

"It's only a big dog, isn't it?" I whispered, trying to make out the shape.

"It's a Rancur."

"What's that?"

"You've never seen a Rancur before?" Twig's face was white and terrified.

I thought that Twig was over-reacting. It certainly looked like a large dog to me—a big, lanky grayish dog with yellow eyes and a long snout.

"It means they're nearby."

"Who are?"

"Fallon Gwyn."

"Fallon Gwyn? What's that?"

"You know. His special guards. They report to – *him*."

As if on cue the dog lifted its head and gave a blood-curdling howl. It was answered almost immediately by similar howls higher up the mountain.

Twig grabbed my hand. "Quick. Run."

Together we plunged through the forest. Brambles scratched our faces and we stumbled over tree roots. At last I saw light ahead and the great shape of the castle looming in the twilight. I had no idea whether the Rancur was still following us or how close behind it was. I just ran blindly, caught up in Twig's terror. We burst out of the last of the trees and stood gasping.

"They won't usually leave the forest," Twig said, looking back with terrified eyes. "Unless HE's sent them to track us. In which case we can never hide. They can smell us out anywhere."

I saw with relief the big towers at the front of the castle. "Come on," I said. "It's okay. This is the front entrance. We can go to Miss Neves here…"

I ran forward, then stopped. There were two guards standing on the front steps. Tall men with cruel faces and long white cloaks. In the setting sun I could see the glint of weapons.

I FALL INTO THE BOY'S BATHROOM

Twig was tugging at my arm. "We can't go in that way. That way leads straight to the Regulator. Come away, please, before they see us."

I allowed myself to be led away. A couple of times I looked back, puzzled. There was something different about the front of the castle, apart from those guards. Then I realized what it was. The round tower was on the left and the square one on the right.

"Come on." Twig tugged at me again. "We can't stay here. That place is crawling with guards and the Regulator is there."

From outside the gates came another howl.

"The Rancur. It's left the forest. Addy, please come on." She started to drag me into the shadow of the wall. "And you've lost your chance to make it safely to the mountains now, with Rancurs in the forest. So your only hope is that secret door you told me about."

I kept glancing back, trying to figure out what I was seeing, but I allowed myself to be led in the shadow of the wall around the building.

"It looks like there's a door in the castle wall over there," Twig gasped at last. "Let's make a quick dash for it. Come on. We have to get inside where they can't smell us."

She sprinted across to the castle building, her gray robes flying out as she ran. I glanced back at the castle gates. How could soldiers be standing where the entrance to the school should be?

Twig had already wrenched open a small rounded door in the rough stone wall. I sprinted after her and we stepped inside to complete darkness. A smell came to meet us that made me gag. "Where are we?" I whispered. "What's that awful smell?"

Twig was shaking all over now. "We're Down Below. It's where they send us for punishment. We have to get out of here somehow."

We crept forward along a narrow stone passage. The roof was rounded and so low it almost brushed the top of my head. Water dripped onto us. At last we saw the slightest glimmer of light ahead and heard sounds. A rhythmic creaking and rumbling. Twig froze. "I know what that is," she whispered. "We don't want to go that way. It's the Go-Around."

"Like a Merry-Go-Round, you mean?"

"This one isn't merry, trust me," Twig hissed back. "But we have to get past it somehow or we'll never find our way upstairs. This passage might work." She turned off to the left, down an even narrower passage. Suddenly another way opened up to our right, lit with what looked like flickering lamps along the walls that cast a red glow. I looked down it and stood staring in horror. I was looking at what seemed to be a giant wheel, like an old fashioned merry-go-round. A gray-robed child was strapped to every spoke and they were running around as fast as they could. Their robes were hitched up to reveal pale legs. Their faces were covered with sweat and grime. One coughed and stumbled and was dragged around by the others until he could stagger to his feet again.

"Come on. Come away." Twig dragged me past the creaking wheel until we found a stairway going up.

"What were they doing?" I whispered as we climbed. I found I was shaking. My voice echoed louder than I expected from the stone walls.

"They've done something wrong. They are being punished," Twig whispered back.

"But why the wheel? It looks awful."

"It has to be worked day and night," Twig said, "Otherwise there is no way to heat and light the building."

"You don't have electricity in your part of the building?"

"Electricity? You mean power? We have no power any more. They say that the evil ones took all power with them."

"Evil ones?"

"The Fareeth," Twig whispered. "They used to be able to make power and do all kinds of magic, so I've heard."

At that moment came the drumming sound of feet running above them. Twig grabbed at me and we shrank back against the wall.

"We must get you out of here quickly," she whispered. "They're getting ready for evening roll call. They'll have people patrolling the whole castle to see if anyone's missing. Let's see whether we're out of the punishment levels yet." She inched open a wooden door in the wall and looked out. Then she sniffed. A gaggingly horrible smell of cooked cabbage floated toward us. I know, I know, I'm worried about cabbage at a time like this? But I really hate cabbage. Twig didn't seem to mind, she heaved a sigh of relief. "Yes, this smells like the kitchens. Now I know where we are. You have to go up two more levels to your secret door. I'll try to take you."

We had just started up the next staircase when bells clanged, echoing so loudly that the noise hurt my ears. Twig jumped as if she was being burned.

"I have to go. That's the second roll call bell. I'll be sent down below if I don't show up on time." She crept along the hall and then opened a door. "Here, wait in this classroom until everyone's at roll call then go down this hallway to the end and turn left. That will bring you back to the place where we first met. Bye, Addy. Please don't come back again if you have the chance to get away. Promise me?"

"Come with me, Twig. I'll take you back through my secret door," I said, grabbing at her arm. "You don't have to stay in this horrible place. Miss Neves will make it right, I know."

"I can't. I wish I could, but I love my family and I want to go home. It's not long now until the harvest is in and there is the sending forth. If I can just make it a few more days…"

The whole castle echoed to the drumming of running feet. Twig pushed me into the darkened classroom and slammed the door behind me. Only just in time. I ducked behind a desk as the hallway echoed to marching feet. At last, everything was quiet. I hoped Twig had made it back in time. I certainly wouldn't want her to be sentenced to that awful wheel.

I opened the door, peered around and then crept out. At last I came to the familiar hallway where I had met the white-robed teacher. I moved along it silently until I came to the painting at the end of the hall. This was where I had come through, I was sure. Maybe if I gave it one more try. I pushed at the wall, but it was solid and didn't move. I looked behind the portrait of the man with green eyes, but only solid stone was behind it.

Last time, I remembered that I had come back through a cloakroom. I started opening doors along the small side hall until I found it. This was right. I had looked into the dusty mirror on the back of the door and…

Again the green glow, my eyes glowing, the crackling and I was kneeling on the floor of the boy's bathroom again.

"Totally weird," I muttered as I got to my feet.

I stood touching the cold porcelain of the sinks and tried to clear my head and think. "I was just in another place. It can't be part of the school because it was daytime there. But Twig was real. Everything was real."

The last time I had been in this bathroom Raj had told me that I had been dreaming. Could this possibly have been just another dream? That was the only thing that made sense. That was the only way I could believe I had just been in a scary place where it was day in the middle of the night. A sense of relief washed over me. I had dozed off and I was sleepwalking and dreaming strange dreams. I should go to Miss Neves or maybe Miss Rorrim and ask for some help. "I'll be OK," I said out loud to myself. The words echoed from the tiled walls. I stood to go and automatically checked my image in the mirror. My face was covered with small scratches. "What!" I put my hands up to my face. There were scratches on my hands as well. From the brambles when we had been running through the forest. The brambles had been real which must mean that the rest was real, too.

I came out of the bathroom, looking around cautiously. A picture of that wheel came back to me. What kind of school would allow children to be treated like that? Did Aunt Jean know she'd sent me to such an awful place? Would Miss Neves really allow such an awful punishment?

I started to run, hopefully in the right direction for my dorm. As I made my way back to a part of the castle I recognized I saw a tall boy coming toward me.

"Hey," he called to me. "You'd better hurry up. The film is about to start."

"About to start?"

"Yes, come on. Hurry up," he said. "Good film tonight."

"Thanks. I'll be there in a minute," I said and let him walk away. How could the movie be about to start when I must have been away an hour or more? Nothing made any sense any more.

PIPPA CALLS FOR HELP

I opened my eyes to complete darkness. I sensed that I was somewhere enclosed, some kind of tunnel, maybe, but I stood still, petrified, hardly daring to breathe. Where was I? What had I been doing? Was it day or night? Then off to one side I noticed a pinpoint of light. I turned and started to walk toward it. It was cold and damp underfoot and I realized that my feet were bare. I shivered and moved cautiously toward the light. As I came closer I saw that it was almost unbearably bright and I had to stand for a while, blinking. Then I went forward again. Much closer now. Soon I'd be out of this horrible place. I could make out some kind of large room with the sun streaming in through glass and reflecting from the marble floor. Any minute now I'd be out. I had a strong sense of excitement, that I was about to discover something important and that someone was waiting for me....

Then I became aware of a sound—a strange rhythmic clanking, creaking, groaning. It touched off a memory but I couldn't quite pin it down. Something bad though. Definitely something I wouldn't want to encounter again. I began to hurry toward the light room. Then I heard the voice, "Somebody, help me. Come and rescue me. Addy, please..."

The voice was Pippa's. I turned from the light and started running in the direction of the voice.

"I'm coming!" I sat bolt upright in bed. The light was streaming in the window. It was a rare perfect sunny day. I looked over at Pippa's bed. It was already made. I felt sick remembering how angry she'd been with me and how she had accused me of reading her diary. No wonder I had dreamed of Pippa in trouble.

Celeste was cheerfully pulling her clothes on, obviously delighted at the sun's appearance. She was singing a French song to herself in her beautiful voice. "Bonjour!" she said turning a rare smile on me.

"You're in a good mood today," I said a little resentfully.

"Mais oui. The sun is out. We will have special lessons today. Perhaps archery or fencing and a half day free."

"Half a day free?"

"A sun day."

"I've heard of snow days before but not sun days. Did you talk to Pippa this morning?"

"No – she was gone before I woke up. She is very upset." Celeste sat down on my bed. "Addy – you must not be so indiscreet. Of course I have read Pippa's diary. It would drive me crazy to see her scribbling in there every night and not know what she was saying – especially about me. But – do I tell her I have read it? Of course not. That is very rude. You must apologize. It will be most uncomfortable for me if my roommates are fighting."

"But – I didn't read it." I insisted and then stopped when I saw Celeste's face. How could I explain to Celeste that I had dreamed that conversation when I didn't understand it myself? I got up and reached for my uniform. "Thanks, Celeste. I'll find her and apologize."

I looked for Pippa all through breakfast but didn't see her anywhere.

"Archery today." Raj sat down next to me. "Of course we still have our Maths with Miss Neves. But we have archery before and a choice between a treasure hunt hike and riding after."

"You're kidding!" I looked at him surprised. "Celeste said something about it being a special day because of the sun but I thought she was just being Celeste. It has been raining since I got here. Does it really rain so much here that a sunny day is a holiday?"

Gwylum who was sitting opposite overheard me. "No – there's usually a sunny week in October. November'll be bad though. I don't think the other schools get sunny days off. You may have noticed that our school is a little unusual."

"You can say that again!" I said.

"Our school is a little unusual," Raj repeated with a straight face just like he had the first night we had met. Then he smiled and I laughed. The knot in my stomach eased a little. Raj seemed so nice and easy going… and kind. Maybe I could actually talk to him.

"Listen Raj. I need to tell you. I need to ask your advice. Can you walk over to archery with me? I just need to find Pippa and apologize first. Have you seen her?"

"I haven't seen her all morning. Gwylum, Sam," he called down the table, "have you seen the dreaded Ms. Pepper?"

"Pippa was quite peppery last night I'll tell you," Sam called back. "But I haven't seen her today."

"Yes – where is Pippa?" A nasty voice said right behind me. I turned to see a scowling Angela. "She is meant to be doing my washing up. Just like her to run and hide to get out of doing my chores. I'm going to find Alice and tell her about this."

"Oh no," Penelope said behind her. "Why don't you go and tell Barry. I'll come with you."

"Me, too," another one of Angela's hangers-on said. They walked off giggling together but not until Angela had given me a hard stare as if she suspected me of knowing where Pippa was hiding out.

RAJ IS ON TARGET

The first years had to assemble and then walk together to the large field outside the school. I tried to get Raj alone but Sam and Kobi came to join him. Everyone was all smiles to be out in the sunshine and away from regular lessons. Everyone else was joking around as if they hadn't a care in the world. I was the only one who felt as if my stomach was in knots and I was carrying a great load of worry.

Mr. Thomas greeted us as we came on to the field.

"Hello, my young archers," he called. "Ready to join Robin Hood then?"

He led us over to a rack of bows and helped us choose a bow of the right size. Gwylum and Kobi each had bows that were very tall. I tried to pull the string on one like theirs but found that I couldn't get the string back more than a few inches. Raj seemed to be having the same problem. He grimaced at me, a little embarrassed, and we switched to smaller bows.

"Now the bigger the bow, the longer distance you will be able to shoot," Mr. Thomas was saying. "But accuracy is what really counts." He lined us up across the end of the field and instructed us on how to pull back the string, to take aim at the targets set up on hay bales. I aimed at the closest one – only 10 yards or so away. The bigger and stronger students were aiming in the middle distance at the targets 20 yards away. Most of them were missing by feet or hitting the targets of other students. Groans and laughs were coming from the whole class as we cheered each other on.

"Were you trying to make your arrow go 20 meters forward and 5 to the side?" Sam teased Kobi who frowned at him. "That's a good trick." The others laughed. Suddenly Raj's arrow shot from his bow and slammed into the center of the target at the far end of the field. The other kids gaped at him in surprise and then cheered.

"I thought you said you hadn't a clue about archery," I said in

169

surprise.

"I could have sworn his eyes were closed," Celeste chimed in.

"Beginner's luck." Raj looked as surprised as anyone. "I was aiming for this close one here but then I thought I wanted to see your faces if I shot the far target."

"Bet you can't do it again, mate," Sam said.

"I probably can't – but what would you wager?"

"Winner eats loser's desserts for a week."

"There's no point in that as we can eat as much dessert as we want."

"Okay, then winner treats loser to ice cream the first time we're allowed into town."

"You're on." Raj walked back to the table to get an arrow. "I think I did close my eyes the first time," he muttered to me.

"Why did you take the bet then?" I asked.

"I dunno really. I just have a feeling – like arrows and me go together or something. I'm probably bonkers."

He stepped forward and pulled back the string of the bow. I noticed that even with the smaller bow he couldn't pull it back all the way. Then once again the arrow shot away from the bow at great speed. It flew so high that I thought it was going to go over the far target. Then at the last second I could have sworn that the target gave a little jump. It came down with the second arrow right beside the first in the bull's-eye. I blinked my eyes and looked around. Surely the hay bale couldn't have jumped. Had anyone else seen it? They were all crowding around Raj slapping him on the back and congratulating him.

"Yeah. Beginner's luck, mate," Sam said, laughing a little ruefully.

The rest of archery practice was both fun and frustrating. The closest I got to any target was to slam the side of the arrow into the closest bale of hay as the bow got away from me and clattered to the ground. The target ground was close to Miss Rorrim's tower and I could see her watching out of her study window. Every arrow that Raj shot hit the mark.

"I can see we'll be signing you up for competitions, Mr. Puri, bach." Mr. Thomas slapped Raj on the back as we walked back from practice. "You're sure you never took lessons before?"

"No – never."

"Well you will now, my boy. That's for sure."

I wanted more than ever to talk to Raj but I had to wait until he had gone over his triumphs with every boy present and been congratulated by each one in turn. I was beginning to think that they were going to follow us all the way to Miss Neves's office. But as we reached the school the other students followed Mr. Thomas to math class and Raj and I went towards Miss Neves's office.

"Nice shots, Raj," I said when we were alone. "I seriously think you were teasing me about your eyes being closed."

"No, really," Raj protested. "I have no idea how I did it."

"Did you notice anything weird about that second shot?" I asked hesitantly. "About the target?"

"Only that the arrow hit it!" He gave me a sideways glance that made me think perhaps he had seen something strange himself.

"So you didn't—uh—see the target move?"

Again he hesitated and frowned, then shook his head fiercely. "That's not possible. Inanimate objects just don't move on their own."

"And if you'd sort of made it move with your mind?"

Again he considered this, went to say something, then shook his head. "The mind can't move things."

"You're not making this any easier," I said with frustration. "Raj, I want to tell you something and I want you to promise you won't think I'm crazy."

MISS NEVES WRITES A NOTE

Raj laughed. "That depends what it is."

"Raj – do you remember that day that you found me in the boy's bathroom?" I began tentatively as we crossed the courtyard to Miss Neves's office.

"It was hard to forget, Addy! It's not every day I find a girl sleeping on the floor of the bathroom."

"Well that's just it. I wasn't sleeping. I think I was in another place. I got there through a mirror in the haunted hallway. I came back through a cloakroom and ended up in that bathroom. I know how crazy it sounds but it happened." Once I started speaking the words just came tumbling out.

"What kind of other place?" Raj wasn't grinning or anything. In fact he was looking concerned.

"Well – kind of a backwards place. It looks like our school but the teachers are really mean. They have horrible punishments and guards outside the school. I tried to get to Miss Neves's office but even the towers were backward. I know you think I was dreaming, but last night I went through again and I came back with these." I held up my hands to show the scratches. "The brambles in the forest outside the school. How do you explain that?"

Raj was silent a moment thinking. "Addy, you know me. I believe there is a scientific explanation for everything. The mind can play strange tricks on you. I have even heard of cases where crazy ... I mean really stressed-out people hurt themselves and forgot they had done it. I think you need to talk to a teacher about it. Think about it – a backwards school where everything is bad. Doesn't that sound like just the sort of thing your unconscious would make up if you were feeling really stressed about a new school?"

"You mean it's all in my head?"

"Well, that's a logical explanation, isn't it?"

"I know it does but it feels so real. So tell me. There's not another part of the school is there – for crazy kids? With children chanting strange things and teachers in long white cloaks." I felt my face turning red with embarrassment, but I was so desperate to get to the truth that I had to go on. "I wasn't sent there because I was cracking up?"

"Addy – I've been all over the school. It may be big but it's not that big. There is no section with chanting kids or teachers in long white cloaks. It's just a normal – I mean a weird but nice –English boarding school. Look – I'll go back to my dorm and you tell Miss Neves I forgot my prep. That way you can talk to her by yourself. I'm sure she'll know what to do. I know that it must be hard being in a new school and ... your mum dying and all. I think maybe you need some help."

'He thinks I'm crazy.' I thought. 'Maybe I am.'

We were almost outside the door to Miss Neves's office. Raj gave me one more concerned look. "Tell her, Addy. She will know where to send you for help, I'm sure," he said and then ran back the way he had come.

I stood outside the door for a moment and took a deep breath. Grownups were supposed to help you. I would tell a grownup what was happening to me and I would get some help. It was all in my imagination. I felt better just thinking that – it was all in my imagination.

As I was about to knock on Miss Neves's door I heard Miss Rorrim's voice, saying loud and clear, "But there are seven of them. What do you think we should do?"

And Miss Neves answered, "You know the rules. We watch and wait and do nothing."

"But one of them is clearly a Dreamwalker. If you had seen the archery lesson today you would know we have a Traveler. And I'm pretty sure we've got a Singer and maybe even a Whisperer. I'm not sure about the others yet, but we can't afford to let one of them get away, not now. Can we?"

"No," Miss Neves said. "We certainly can't afford to let one of them get away. Don't worry. We'll find her and bring her back."

There was a pause and then Miss Rorrim said, "You don't think there's a chance that she's gone through, do you?"

"There's always a chance, Rorrim. If she has, then there's nothing you or I can do about it. She'll be punished dreadfully or worse."

"It's much too soon!" Miss Rorrim's voice trembled, with what emotion I couldn't tell. "We have not prepared her."

"Then let's hope that she has simply tried to run away again. We will have to begin the search ... Wait – I think someone is listening."

Before I could move a muscle the door in front of me was flung open and Miss Neves stood there glaring down at me. "Yes, Miss Walker?"

"We have Math class now, Miss Neves," I said, trying to sound brave. "Raj went ..."

"I'm afraid Maths will be canceled today. Philippa is nowhere to be found. It seems she has run away. We must get everyone in the school looking for her at once." She paused. "Come in a moment." She beckoned me into the office. Her eyes bored into me and she seemed to consider what to do next.

Miss Neves went over to her desk and scribbled a short note. She carefully folded it several times, put it into an envelope and handed it to me. "Please take this to Miss Rorrim's study. You remember how to get to her tower? I need her help with this immediately. She may also have some questions for you."

"But Miss Rorrim is ..." My voice trailed off as I looked around the office. Miss Rorrim was nowhere to be seen. "Yes, Miss Neves." My brain was reeling. All thought of asking Miss Neves for help was gone. What had Miss Neves said? She was worried that Pippa had gone through the mirror? But who could Miss Neves have been talking to when Miss Rorrim was nowhere to be seen?

I took the note and walked slowly back through the hallways. Should I tell Raj what I had overheard? Would he believe me now? Maybe he would say that I was hearing voices – that I really was crazy. Or maybe there was just a well-hidden speakerphone and all this crazy stuff could be easily explained.

'Of course,' I thought. 'That must be it. And the note is just something that Miss Neves forgot to tell Miss Rorrim when she was on the phone to her.' I got an overwhelming desire to open that envelope. I had to prove to myself that this was just an ordinary communication between teachers, perhaps suggesting what they should do to look for Pippa.

I could hardly believe what I was doing as I fiddled with the envelope and found it wasn't properly sealed. Carefully I pried it open and unfolded the note:

It said, "She is the Dreamwalker. She can hear us. Communicate by note only. Watch her like a hawk. Don't let her get away."

I WALK THROUGH A MIRROR

I gasped and stared at the note for a second. Then looking around to make sure no one had seen me, I carefully folded it up again. I certainly couldn't take this note to Miss Rorrim. What did that mean, "Don't let her get away?" All the worrying, confusing thoughts and experiences of the last few days came flooding back into my head. It was almost as if I had been tricked into coming to this school, and so had Raj and the others. Why were we here? And exactly who were Miss Neves and Miss Rorrim? They seemed nice enough, but what did they want with us? And why was there that horrible part of the school with the teachers in white cloaks? And what exactly was a Dreamwalker? Twig had said that people who had dreams were punished.

I stepped out into the sunshine of the courtyard and stopped by the fountain. Was it only two days ago that they had had the fun treasure hunt? Everything had seemed like a big game then, but now everything was turning into a nightmare. As the word passed through my brain I thought of the horse with the skull face, the woman with the white cloak, Twig, Rancurs and Pippa's voice calling for help. "Help me. Where am I?"

Then suddenly I knew what I had to do. I knew how to find out if Pippa had run away. Her diary. I had to take a peek at her diary. I hurried up to the dorm room. The school was quiet. All the students were still in class. No hunt for Pippa had begun yet. I reached the room and lifted Pippa's mattress. The diary was there. So there was my proof. Pippa had not run away. She would never have left school without the diary. So where was she?

'I'm not dreaming now,' I thought. 'Pippa has really gone and I bet I know where.'

I rushed down the stairs from the dorm. I flew across the courtyard and through the twists and turns of the other building. Students were coming out of classes and I pushed my way through a tide of them, making some of them yell after me. "The haunted hallway," I repeated over and over. "Got to find the haunted hallway."

Then at last I came around a corner and there it was. I could see no movement at the end of the hallway this time. I could see the reflection of the sunlight outside on the mirror at the end of the hall but no figure moved in it. Except for that reflection the hallway was dark. I groped for a light but couldn't find any. I walked down the long hallway deeper into the darkness. I stopped when I reached the mirror and held out my hands to touch it. The smooth glass was cold under my hands. I pressed them against the glass. Just an ordinary mirror, after all. Then suddenly my eyes seemed to glow with a green light as I looked at my face in the mirror. But nothing else happened.

'How did I get through last time?' I thought desperately. 'Was it only in my dream?' Then I remembered that the other times I had passed through the mirror I had wanted something very badly. I had seen Twig and wanted to catch up with her, and then I had wanted to prove to myself that I hadn't dreamed that other part of the school.

"Pippa," I called in my mind. "Are you there? Do you need help?"

The mirror seemed to light up with a green glow. A voice thundered with urgency in my mind. Miss Neves's voice. "Rorrim, Thomas, Tiery. She's at the mirror. Don't let her get through."

"We're coming." Answering voices shouted inside my head. I heard a door open in the building and footsteps running toward me.

"Pippa. I'm coming," I called and stepped through the mirror.

I was in the familiar other corridor again. The same horrible portrait stared down at me with the bright green eyes in that white face staring right at me. I looked back longingly at the door to the cloakroom that led to the boy's bathroom on the other side. I still had time to change my mind and go back before it was too late. Then I shook my head. I had to find Pippa. I had to save her and get her away from this awful place. At least I now knew where kids were punished, and I was pretty sure that Pippa would be the kind of person who would get into trouble right away. I found the twisty staircase that I had come up with Twig and started downward. If only I knew where to find Twig. She'd help us and she knew her way around so well. I would just be blundering in darkness.

Down and down the staircase went. It was completely dark and I felt my way with my hand on the cold stone wall. As I went deeper the stone felt damp and slimy. A couple of times I almost stumbled as my foot met a broken step. Then suddenly I came out to a low, arched passageway. It was dimly lit with some kind of flickering torchlight. I went forward cautiously. Yes, we had come this way, past those doors with bars on them. I could hear sounds coming from behind those doors, sounds of heavy breathing as if someone was sleeping behind those bars.

A voice cried out suddenly, making my heart leap into my mouth. The cry was followed by a whimper and another voice saying, "Shut up and go back to sleep. If they find you dreaming, they'll take you up to the searchery."

'Surgery?' I thought, my heart now beating very fast. I didn't ever remember being more scared. "Got to save Pippa," I whispered to myself.

Then at the far end of the hallway I heard a creaking sound and the slap of bare feet on stone. The Go-Around. It had to be.

I crept closer and there it was. The kids were still moving around, but walking now, instead of running. They were staggering as if they were so tired they could hardly stand. Their faces were ashen gray. And I recognized one of them. Pippa was now wearing a gray robe and she was walking like a robot, her eyes staring straight ahead of her as if she couldn't believe what was happening.

I didn't wait a second longer. I dashed out. "Pippa," I called.

Pippa started as if waking from a dream and blinked a couple of times as if she couldn't believe I was real. The kids didn't stop moving as I ran up to Pippa and tried to undo the straps that held Pippa to the wooden wheel. They stared at me. I had to run beside the wheel, fumbling with the stiff leather.

"Stop moving," Pippa said to the other kids. "Addy will get us all out of here."

"We can't leave," a boy whimpered. "We have to do our twelve hours or it will be worse next time."

"Best to do your punishment and get it over with," a lanky girl said as she staggered past.

"I'm not staying here to be punished," Pippa said. "I haven't done anything wrong. I'm getting out of here, and you could, too. You could go home and get away from this place."

"Are you crazy?" the girl said, "Do you think they don't know where to find us? They have our numbers, don't they? And then our families would be punished, too. You don't want your whole family to be sent for conformation, do you?"

"My family," Pippa sounded unsure. "How can they punish my family?"

"Of course they can. They know everything and everybody. You can't escape, you know."

"I'm jolly well going to try," Pippa said, "and that's rot about hurting my family. My father's an important man and he'll take me away immediately from this school when he finds out how horrible it is. Come on, Addy, get me out of this."

Suddenly a big hand came over my mouth and I was yanked backward into the darkness.

I GET KIDNAPPED

I tried to fight and squirm but my arms were pinned to my sides as I was half-dragged, half-carried at a great pace. At last a door was opened and I was shoved inside. The only light came from one small candle and I could see hooded figures standing around me. Also that I was in a small space, like a dungeon cell with a low vaulted ceiling. My captors had evidently come in with me because I was conscious of figures standing behind me, too.

"Well?" one of the figures whispered and I was surprised that it sounded like a young voice.

"She was trying to disrupt the Go-Around," a voice behind me said. "Trying to release one of the kids."

A candle was held up to my face.

"Who are you?" I asked in a shaky voice.

"More to the point, who are you?" the first figure demanded. "I don't recognize you."

"She can't have been sent from the mountains, not now, with only one day to go," someone else said in a low voice.

"I'm Addy. I wanted to rescue my friend," I said trying to sound defiant and brave. "So I came through the mirror. She got here by mistake."

"I know her," a voice from the back of the chamber said. "I've met her before." The figure threw back her hood and held out her arms to me. "It's me, Twig. Why did you come back?"

"Twig? Where are we? Who are these people?"

"Don't say anything, Twig," a deeper voice commanded. "Not until we know where she came from and why she's here."

"I told you," I insisted. "I came through to rescue my friend. I met Twig when I came through before."

"What do you mean, came through?" The tall one with a deep voice stood towering over me. He took my chin in his hand. "Look at me," he commanded.

I looked. What I noticed beneath the hood were a pair of bright green eyes that glowed in the darkness like a cat's. And I heard the words, "Are you one of us?"

"I don't know what you mean," I muttered.

"You're not from the mountains? They didn't send you down to us?"

"I don't understand," I said. "What mountains are you talking about?"

The tall one looked around. "Did the Watchers discover you and bring you in from a settlement then?"

"I tried to explain this to Twig before," I said. "I'm from the other side of the school."

"I'm not sure about this. She's definitely a Fareeth," the deep voice said. "Look at her eyes and she could hear my thoughts, but how can we make sure she's not a spy sent by Him?"

"I wasn't sent by anybody," I said.

"I'm sure she's safe," Twig added. "She tried to help me escape last time she was here. She swore by the Power of Seven."

I looked from one hooded face to the next. All I could see was the glow of green eyes. "What did you mean when you said that I was a Fareeth? I come from somewhere else. And I thought the Fareeth were people who lived long, long ago."

"They ruled long ago," the boy said. "But occasionally children are still born with one of the seven powers. That's what this school is all about—trying to find out who might have one of the powers and then conforming the children before they can grow up."

"So what exactly are these Fareeth?" I asked. "Are they good or bad?"

"You mean you really don't know?"

"She doesn't," Twig said. "She doesn't know a thing. Her settlement is far away over the ocean. Perhaps they don't teach the same things in their schools over there. Perhaps The One isn't even in control over there."

"That's right," I said. "I lived in a city, not a settlement, in America. I'd never heard of The One until I came through the mirror."

"How can you come though a mirror?" the boy asked.

"Maybe there is a portal nearby," a girl's voice said. "And she's come back through from the other side."

I MEET THE FAREETH

"**D**on't be ridiculous," the boy's deeper voice said. "How would she have the power to come through at her age? Do you mean you came through a secret door?"

I hesitated. "That's what I thought it was. I don't really understand myself. I stand at the mirror. Everything turns green, and here I am."

There was a slight gasp. "You came through."

"I said I did."

"She did come through." The words were repeated.

"So you are really not from here?" a boy asked. They crowded closer to me.

"I don't know where 'here' is," I said. "I'm from California and then my aunt brought me to England and then she sent me to school in Wales."

"These places are unknown to us," the boy said. "You are in Gallia. That's all I can tell you. We know so little more ourselves. Maybe the Fareeth in the mountains know more but…"

"I asked Twig about the Fareeth, but I'm still not sure who they are," I said.

"We are," the boy answered. "All of us, and you obviously are, too."

"How can I be?"

"You have our eyes, for one thing, and you could hear my thoughts. We communicate with our minds. We may be hiding now but long ago we ruled Gallia and we have heard that it was a beautiful and prosperous place, until Grymur wanted all the powers for himself."

"Grymur?"

"He who calls himself The One. He thought he had destroyed us all, but we know that some Fareeth resistance fighters still hide out in the mountains. They send us help when they can, and we try to get kids away to them before they can be conformed."

"Can you get me away?" I asked.

"She has a special secret doorway. Perhaps it's a portal back? I wondered how she escaped last time ... I know how to take her there," Twig said. "I can take her back, now, before anyone knows she's here. Addy – why did you come back? I warned you not to."

"My friend is here and I'm not leaving without her," I said.

"Your friend came through a portal from the other side, too?"

"Yes," I said. "I'll wait until they let her off that Go-Around if I have to."

"No, that would be too much of risk," the tall boy said. "If you know of a way to escape, you should go now, while you can. You've no number, you're wearing the forbidden color. You'd be first in line for the ceremony tomorrow."

I took a deep breath. "I'm not leaving Pippa."

"I appreciate your bravery," he said, "but you have no idea what will happen if they catch you. You, Sky, give her your robe to put over what she's wearing. And I need a volunteer to take the girl's place on the Go-Around..."

"I will," a girl's voice said. "I'll be off by dawn, which gives us a whole day to get away before the ceremony so I suppose I can face it one last time."

"Thank you." The tall boy put a hand on her shoulder. "Two of you go and help Vine take the girl's place." The girl named Vine and the two others left quickly.

I looked at the remaining hooded figures. "You're all willing to do this for me? Won't you get in bad trouble if you're caught helping me?"

"Of course," the boy said. "But it's a risk we are all prepared to take. We took the oath when we formed our secret group here. Fareeth are ready to die for each other."

"Then come with me," I said. "Come back to the other side. It's not bad there and you'll be safely away from The One and his punishments."

"We can't go through, and I don't know how you can," the boy said. "You must have awfully strong powers."

"Powers? Me?" I shook my head. "I don't have any powers. I'm just ordinary."

"Do you know how many Fareeth have tried to escape through

a portal and how many have failed or died trying?"

I shook my head. "But I can't go and leave you here."

"Don't worry about us. We do have a plan and in the morning there is the sending forth. With any luck we'll all be released, and if not—well, we'll do our best to escape."

Outside a bell tolled and the sound of marching feet came past our door. We all froze. I held my breath until the sound of the feet died away.

Then we waited what seemed like an eternity until the door was opened again and Pippa, her face wide-eyed with fear, was shoved in through the door.

THE DOOR WON'T OPEN!

"Addy!" Her eyes lit up as she recognized me, then she jumped as she saw the hooded figures in the shadows. "It's all right. They are friends. They're helping us escape," I said.

Pippa looked around and went to say more but the biggest boy signaled her to be quiet.

"We'd better get moving. That's the second watch. We don't have much time," the boy said. "Your robe, Sky."

There was the sound of shuffling in the rear of the cell and a gray robe came flying at me.

"Leave it before you go through and we'll pick it up," the boy said.

"Thank you," I stammered. "I usually get back through an old cloakroom on the floor with the classrooms—where there's that picture of the horrible man in white on the wall."

"I don't think The One would be pleased by such a description of himself," the boy chuckled. "We had better leave a few at a time." The other kids filed out quietly.

"Where exactly are we?" I whispered when the door was closed behind the departing hooded figures. Only the boy and Twig remained. I struggled to pull the robe over my own clothes.

"In one of the old dungeons, down a level from the punishment cells. Nobody comes down here any more, so we've sort of taken it over."

"I don't understand, Addy. Who are these people?" Pippa seemed to wake from her stupor. She was still panting from her time on the Go-Around and her white face looked like a ghost's in the light of the candle.

"There's no time for talking. Go while you can," the boy whispered. "Go with them, Twig. Take them back to where they came from."

He put his hands on our shoulders. "Good luck. And may the Power of Seven be with you."

He blew out his candle and we were plunged into darkness. I heard him slipping through the door and melting into the darkness.

"Quickly, this way." Twig grabbed my hand and dragged me forward. I reached for Pippa's hand and we tiptoed together through the dark hallway. When we reached some stairs we started upward.

"Watch your step," Twig whispered. "Some of the stairs are broken."

It was awfully dark. Up and up we went. I could hear Pippa breathing heavily behind me and stumbling with exhaustion. I felt sorry for her but we dared not stop. At last we came out into a wider hall, lined with doors.

"This is it," Twig said. "Down at the far end."

Suddenly a shrill whistle echoed, somewhere far below. Other whistles responded and then there were shouts and the sounds of running feet.

"Runners," someone shouted. "We have runners!"

"Go on, get out of here, Twig." I hissed. "We'll be okay now and we don't want you to get caught."

"If you're sure ..."

"I'm sure. Please, get away while you can. Go." I gave her a shove. "Come on, Pippa." I started to run, dragging Pippa with me. "The cloakroom is just down here."

We ran as fast as we could, our feet echoing back from the stone walls and high ceiling. The shouts and whistles sounded horribly close now.

"There they are. After them," a voice commanded.

"Just around the corner," I gasped. I flung myself at the cloakroom door and tried to turn the handle. It wouldn't budge.

WE'RE TRAPPED

"Quick, they're coming," Pippa shouted.

"It won't open. It's locked," I gasped.

The corridor echoed to the sound of running feet and before we could think sensibly, two of the women in white had come around the corner, accompanied by tall guards carrying sharp spears.

"There they are," someone shouted.

"It's the girl who got away the other day. Seize her. Don't let her escape." It was the severe-looking woman I had met on the first occasion I had come through the mirror. She leered into my face. "A fine dance you've led us, my girl. Just where have you been hiding out, I'd like to know. "

"And this one got loose from the Go-Around," the other woman in white said, grabbing Pippa by the shoulders and giving her a good shaking. "You'll be sorry for that, my girl. You wait until the Regulator hears of this."

"Run and tell the Fallon Gwyn to summon the Regulator. The girl that he was looking for is here."

"Yes, Miss Bush." One of the guards bowed and left. Curious children gathered at the end of the hall pointing and whispering at us.

"Regulator. You are summoned. The girl is found." A loud male voice boomed in my head. Pippa looked around as if she too heard it but the teachers completely ignored it.

"Return this girl to the Go-Around for the rest of her 12 hours." Miss Bush raised her voice so that the children down the hall could hear. "No one escapes from the Go-Around."

"I think that may not be a good idea, Miss Bush." I jumped. A tall thin man was standing right beside us in the hall. He was also dressed in white—a white cape over a white shirt. The cape was fastened with a clasp that looked like a curled white dragon. It sparkled in the light with what seemed like diamonds. Somehow its light reflected up to his face, making his eyes look like hollow sockets in a skull. And I realized that I had seen him before in my dream.

"This girl will have a long walk tomorrow," he said. "I think it would be best to send her upstairs to rest."

"Regulator." Miss Bush bowed low. "Of course. Whatever you say. Take her." She nodded at the guard.

"Addy!" Pippa shrieked as she was pulled away. I tried to follow her but I was held back by a heavy hand on my shoulder.

"Well, hello my little Dreamwalker. I have been looking for you." His voice was low and menacing.

"I never dream," I said quickly, remembering what I had been told. I kept staring at Pippa's disappearing back, afraid to turn and look at him.

"You never dream? Not once in your life?"

"No."

"I'm sure that's not right. Everyone dreams. Only some dreams are more exciting than others. Did you ever dream you were flying?"

"No," I said.

"Or visiting strange places? Or riding horses? Or maybe dragons?"

"No," I said bluntly. "I told you, I never dream."

"I don't think you're quite telling me the truth, are you, my dear?" he asked. "Because if you were—" He turned me around to look at him. His lips did not move but I heard his voice clearly. "If you never dreamed, then you and I wouldn't have been able to have this little talk."

I tried to pull away from him and the voice in my mind began to laugh.

He turned to the teacher in white. "You were right to bring her to my attention, Miss Bush. I think we have caught ourselves a Dreamwalker. The One is looking for her. Take her up to the tower and make sure she doesn't escape until I receive orders as to what is to be done with her. "

"Regulator, if she is that important will she be safe in the tower?" Miss Bush looked a little afraid of me.

"She's only a girl, Miss Bush. Just make sure she doesn't fall asleep."

As we left the room I heard the Regulator's voice, loud and clear, "Yes, Master. I believe we finally have the girl who rode the dragon. Yes, I'm sure she's a Dreamwalker. Should I bring her to you right away?"

And then another voice, cold and clear.

"I can wait until the ceremony. Watch over her well then bring her to me with the others."

"Very good then, Master. Tomorrow, at the ceremony. Most fitting."

And then the second voice, ice cold, said, "And don't lose her this time, Regulator."

FIRST A DUNGEON, NOW THE TOWER

Miss Bush escorted me down the hallway again, only this time she kept her distance – almost as if she was afraid to touch me – and shot me glances that seemed tinged with fear.

My brain was working overtime, wondering how I could put this new fear to good use. "You'd better let me go," I said, "or you have no idea what I could do to you with my Fareeth powers."

The teacher looked alarmed for a moment then laughed. "Oh no, my dear. It would be more than my life was worth to allow a genuine Fareeth to escape. My job is to keep you safe until you can be taken for conformation. And since you're not a Traveller, I don't think you'll find a way off the tower."

Miss Bush led me up and up. I thought I recognized some of the twists and turns. It seemed the same way I would have gone to my dorm at Red Dragon Academy. Only when we arrived at the top, instead of dorm rooms we came to what looked like a large drafty storeroom. I kept looking for a way to escape. I was sure I could run faster than Miss Bush but other teachers appeared to be following us. As we entered the storeroom Miss Bush took a large key out of her pocket and locked the door behind us. Then she led me forward down a narrow hallway. 'If this were our school we would be almost at my common room,' I thought. But instead of a fire in the grate and students sitting around studying, there was only a cold stone room with a primitive wooden ladder against the wall going up to a hole in the ceiling. Miss Bush pushed me in and locked that door, too.

"Wait," Miss Bush said glaring at me. She climbed the steep stairs and loosed a bolt on a trap door in the ceiling above her. I looked around desperately for some means of escape but Miss Bush had locked the only way out behind us. She came down the ladder.

"Up," she said, indicating the ladder. When I didn't move she grabbed my arm and twisted it behind my back. "Or would you rather spend the night on the Go-Around? That can easily be arranged, you know. But I tell you, we've seven miles to walk in the morning. I think you'll need all your strength."

"Walking to where?" I asked.

"When we go to the castle for the Ceremony," she said. "Now move it. I've other things to do."

I clambered up and looked anxiously around the room above.

Before I could climb the final steps into the room, Miss Bush sent me sprawling with a firm push, and disappeared back down the stairs, pulling the door down over her head. It was dark in the tower and at first I saw only shapes. As I heard the bolt shut below me a delighted voice exclaimed, "Addy. It's you!" And Pippa stood up from the floor where she had been sitting. There was a mark on her cheek where she had been slapped or punched.

I rushed to her and hugged her. "I'm so glad to see you."

A group of scared-looking children sat against one wall of the tower huddled together for warmth. They glanced up at me but there was little curiosity in their eyes.

Pippa turned to the children and raised her voice. "What did that woman mean? What is going to happen to us in the morning? Where are we going?"

"We're going to ..." one of the younger girls started to say but an older boy stopped her. "Spies," he mouthed at her and she stopped. From then on none of the children would even look at us, let alone speak with us.

"Addy, I don't know what's going on," Pippa whispered in my ear. "A man was just here. An awful man. He pretended to be nice and friendly but he really wasn't. He tried to trick me into admitting all kinds of stupid things—that I could make plants grow and I could talk to animals and goodness knows what else. Of course I told him I couldn't. But this is the strange part. I could hear him talking and his lips weren't moving. And I must be imagining it but I looked away and when I looked back he was gone. It was like he disappeared into thin air. How do you think he did that?"

"I don't know but I met him, too. That Bush lady called him the Regulator," I said. "I don't quite understand it, but I think we're somewhere else."

"What do you mean?"

"Not part of our school but somehow like it. Doesn't it seem like we should be in our own tower? But it's only storerooms down below."

"Do you think we've traveled through time?" Pippa asked. "It seems awfully old-fashioned here."

"Maybe," I said. "I think we're in a world on the other side of the mirror. And Miss Rorrim knows about it, which is why she gave us that assignment to find the impossible things. That saying comes from Alice Through the Looking Glass, remember."

Pippa nodded. "A looking-glass world? A mirror world? But it's totally crazy."

"I don't understand it either but we're here. I've been outside this school. It looks like the castle. It looks like Wales, but then it doesn't."

"And you say Miss Rorrim and Miss Neves know we're here?"

"I'm sure of it."

"But you don't think they'll come and rescue us?"

"I think they're part of the plot. You know what I think, Pippa. I think we were brought here. We were lured—tricked into coming to Red Dragon Academy. Remember how my aunt got those pop-ups on her computer that said the school stressed good manners and discipline because that was what was important to my aunt. Raj came here because of science. Celeste was told they specialized in English for foreigners and had a good music department."

"But why? Why would anyone want us?"

"I think that it's something to do with the people who used to rule here," I said carefully, shifting my uncomfortable position on the stone floor as I still tried to think things through. "They believe we're the last of those old people and they want to destroy us."

"That's silly. How can we be the last of the people if we're not even from here?"

"Maybe I am from here," I said as this fact hit me. "And maybe you are, too. We're both adopted, remember. We could have come from anywhere."

We sat looking at each other. "Well, I don't care," Pippa said suddenly. "I don't want to be part of this country or this time or this world or whatever it is."

"You're right," I agreed. "We have to get away from here, Pippa. We have to get back somehow. We'll find some way to escape."

"But how? Look out the window. There's no way we could get out of here." I got up and went over to the window. Then I realized why it was so freezing on the tower. Cold air poured in through open slits in the side of the stone wall. The openings in the stone were big enough that even a large man could have crawled through. But there was nowhere to crawl to. I looked out of one of the slits and felt dizzy at the drop on the other side. The sheer sides of the tower had no convenient footholds like towers do in all the movies. I realized that the only way to escape would be to fly.

WE WAIT FOR THE WORST

"We have to be ready if we get the slightest chance," I said with a determination that I didn't feel.

Pippa's face was bleak. "But even if we escape, if the door to your cloakroom is locked, what chance do we have?"

"Maybe we could find a mirror," I suggested.

Pippa shook her head. "But not all mirrors work, do they? I've looked at myself a hundred times in the mirror in our bathroom at school and nothing has happened."

"You're right. When I look in the mirror in the haunted hallway, my eyes turn green and the whole world sort of crackles with green light."

"Yes, that's exactly what happened to me. Well, I guess there really is something strange about us. Do you really think we're one of these whatever they are called?"

"Fareeth?" I saw the kids sitting closest to us flinch at the mention of the word. "Fareeth." I lowered my voice. "I don't know. It seems pretty improbable, doesn't it? But then it seems almost impossible that we're prisoners in another place called Gallia."

"But I don't have any psychic powers or anything. Do you, Addy?" Pippa said.

"No," I said. "I've always been very ordinary, except…" I paused, thinking— "Please don't get mad at me, because you're the only friend I've got right now, but something happens when I dream. I don't just dream about somebody. I visit them. Like when I talked to you and you told me you were adopted. It must have been in my dream. I never read your diary, I swear."

Pippa looked down at her hands. "I believe you didn't read it now. I'm really sorry I got so upset."

"So am I, because you wouldn't have run away and we'd still be safe." A sudden thought occurred to me. "Did you run away? How did you get here? Through the mirror in the hallway?"

"Well – I wasn't really going to run away. It seems really dumb now. I just wanted a place to be alone for a while and maybe they would call my father and he would worry and come down to look for me ... I found this place by accident my first day at the school."

"You got lost on your way to Miss Neves's office?" I asked. Pippa nodded. "Me, too. It's almost like she wanted us to find it."

We sat close together in silence.

"So you really have a power," she said at last.

"I guess so. They called me a Dreamwalker, so I guess that's one of their powers."

"But how can it be dangerous that someone has dreams? Dreams can't hurt anybody."

I thought about this for a moment. "Maybe it's because people tell me things in dreams they wouldn't say in real life? I mean like ... like you told me you were adopted and you wanted that kept a secret."

"I see," she said.

"And apparently we can both hear someone when they are not talking out loud, which makes us kind of strange, doesn't it?"

Pippa sighed. "If we have powers I wish we knew how to use them to get out of here. You don't think you could dream us out of here, do you?"

"I've no idea how to use my power, whatever it is. Sometimes I go somewhere in my dreams, but I've never made it happen." I thought hard. "Maybe I should try. The Regulator said I was safe as long as I wasn't asleep."

"If you think you can, it's worth a chance. I'll wake you up if anything happens."

Even huddled together with Pippa I was too cold to sleep. "I must fall asleep. I must fall asleep," I chanted to myself. If I could find my red dragon then Pippa and I could ride it away... I stopped in the middle of that thought. Wait a minute. The last time I hadn't ridden it to safety but into danger. I remembered that dream clearly now—the tall man in the white cloak... he must be Grymur, whom they called The One. And he was looking for me. If I fell asleep I'd probably go straight to him. There was no way I was going to do that. I sat up again, forcing my eyes to stay open. I watched the stars through the open tower walls. The night was silent except for the wind.

"This is so awful," I whispered, looking down at Pippa, who was now breathing deeply, her auburn hair falling over her cheek. How could she look so peaceful? How come she wasn't scared out of her wits like me? Of all the nightmares I'd had in my life this was the worst. I was trapped in a place where no one would ever find me. No escape. No way out. And nobody really in the world to care if I was gone. That was the worst feeling of all. "Mom," I whispered. "I need you. I wish you hadn't gone and left me. Mom—can you hear me?"

And then a strange thing happened. I thought I heard a sort of rustling, whispering noise and a voice said, "My darling child. Be brave. I'll find you."

Only it wasn't Mom's voice at all. It was sweet and melodious, almost like a song. I sat up abruptly. Did the voice belong to my birth mother? But I didn't want her. I wanted my real mom, the one who had snuggled in bed with me when I was scared of thunderstorms and made me laugh when I was sad. And she would never hear me again ... I felt a hot tear trickle down my cheek.

I must have dozed off briefly because I awoke to hear a dog howling in the distance.

Through that open window slit I could hear voices murmuring at the foot of the tower. I tiptoed across the cold floor and leaned out as far as I could. I could see shapes milling about down below and hear the occasional voices of children and teachers. Even through the darkness their activity seemed to have an expectant urgency. I heard giggles coming up from some of the girls. It was the first time I had heard any student here act like an actual child. As it got closer to the dawn the fuzzy shapes down below grew sharper until I could make out the white robed teachers and uniformed students. Just before the dawn the teachers went into frenzied action ordering the children into two straight lines stretching away from the school's massive wooden doors. Just as I was wondering if everyone was going to leave us alone in the castle, the wooden boards of the floor flew up and a scowling head poked through.

"Come on, Fareeth. You'll get what's coming to you today." A large woman pushed a wooden tray up onto the floor. She was dressed like a cook and she was biting hunks off a big piece of bread that she held in her hand.

"Was that supposed to be our breakfast?" Pippa asked

suspiciously. The cook grinned maliciously.

"I have to keep my strength up for the procession. Besides, after today you won't remember it anyway. If the Watchers remembered, we would all be in trouble."

I looked at Pippa to see if she had understood any of this speech but she looked just as confused as me. "Come on then." The woman motioned for us to go down. "Move it."

"We're not going anywhere with you," Pippa said defiantly, standing up to face the woman. "It's time someone told us what is going on!" The other children looked as if they knew all too well what was going on. They had already started toward the hole in the floor when Pippa's voice stopped them. Now they glanced at each other. Did we have a chance to defy this order?

"The only way down is through this hole or off the side of the tower, Fareeth," the woman said, completely unfazed by Pippa's defiance. "And you'll be going down one way or another. The Regulator will be sad if there are a couple less for Conformation, but," she shrugged, "accidents happen."

"There's only one of her," Pippa spoke to the other kids. "What can she do to all of us?"

WE MARCH TO A CASTLE

Then up through the hole in the floor came a chanting sound. The cook was not alone. The voices of teachers echoed through the tower. "Shame. Shame. Shame," they chanted. The children bowed their heads. No one met Pippa's eyes as one by one they climbed down the hole. Pippa and I went last. As we reached the bottom of the ladder we were each flanked on both sides by white-robed teachers who took our arms and marched us down the many staircases of the castle and out the high wooden doors. They didn't stop at the entrance to the school but continued down the steps and through the lines of students.

"Shame, shame, shame!" chanted all the students as we passed them. Few of them met our eyes. The sun was just rising and I saw Twig as her red hair flamed in the sunlight. Twig was not among the prisoners in the tower but among the happy ones, the ones who had been giggling earlier, and I felt happy for her that she was going to go home after all. Twig briefly met my gaze and I saw both fear and pity in her eyes. When we had reached the head of the line of children, the teachers on either side of me forced me to turn around and I saw that everyone had turned to face the school. The Regulator stood in the doorway with Miss Bush standing by his side. The rising sun was coming across the top of the castle straight into my eyes.

As I squinted to watch, the teachers pulled the heavy doors closed with an ominous clang.

"Our duty is done," the Regulator intoned. "Our duty is done," the teachers repeated.

"Our unity won," Miss Bush chanted in her harsh voice. "Our unity won," the students repeated.

Planting till harvest,
Weed and hoe.
In autumn rest

And home we go.

The whole crowd chanted. Some of the younger children squealed with joy on the last word and were given reproving looks from the teachers.

The Regulator walked ceremonially down the lines of students, until he reached us. As he came to us he paused and a satisfied smile spread across his face. Then he led the whole group down the road leading away from the school. The road was roughly cobbled for the first half mile and then it turned into a muddy dirt track and we walked beside muddy ruts on the green grass.

At first I alternated between fear at where we were being taken and relief that I was warming up slightly in the sunlight with the exertion of walking. But as the walking continued hour after hour through countryside that alternated between small cultivated fields and patches of dense woodland, I stopped thinking of anything except the step I was taking and how hungry I was. The teachers walked close by my side and roughly grabbed my arms when I stumbled.

Behind us the children kept on chanting with the rhythm of their steps:

Planting till harvest,
Weed and hoe.
In autumn rest
And home we go.

We kept walking all that day. The teachers didn't seem to be in a big hurry. We stopped several times and the other children were allowed to sit and picnic in green fields. We prisoners were offered some stale bread, which the others wolfed down hungrily. I was feeling so scared that I found it hard to swallow.

Occasionally we passed through an old-fashioned-looking village, like something out of the pages of a fairy tale, only not as nice. The village was little more than a line of stone cottages and the people who stopped to stare at us were all dressed in identical gray. No stores, no tearoom like the one where I had met Miss Neves. Nothing bright or fun at all. People came out of houses and stood staring. Children ran beside the procession yelling and some voices shouted, "Shame, shame, shame." But I saw some curtains twitch at windows and sympathetic faces watching us, too.

"Where do you think we're going?" Pippa asked when she had a chance to draw alongside me.

"No idea," I mumbled. "They said something about a castle."

"If this were Wales we'd be walking to Conwy. Perhaps that's the castle they're talking about." Pippa seemed a lot brighter than I felt. "That village was strange, wasn't it? Did you notice— no shops or pubs or anything? Just houses. Oh, and no church."

"You're right, and you know what else," I said. "No animals in the fields. And we saw those men pulling a cart. There are no animals here."

"I wonder why that is?" Pippa said.

"I don't really care."

"I do. If there was a horse I could ride it out of here," Pippa said.

At last, after what seemed an eternity of walking, I looked up and saw a castle. "It is Conwy Castle!" I exclaimed. "Or at least it looks just like it."

It loomed, giant and forbidding, outlined against the red sky and the setting sun, its walls of rough stone towering over the tiny houses and its turrets rising into the sky. It stood on the waterfront, with an open area of green grass in front of it. I remembered this area when we drove past in the taxi on the way to the school. It had been a parking lot. But now it was full of people and it looked as if it was set up for a fair. Around the edge were booths and strings of flags. Someone was playing a primitive sort of music—the same three or four notes over and over on a flute accompanied by the monotonous beat of a drum. People were dancing. Everyone seemed to be in a good mood. 'Like a carnival,' I thought.

But before I had time to investigate more, my attention was taken by a line of white horses with helmeted white-cloaked riders approaching us. The sun was setting and the white horses seemed almost to shine in the golden rays. They looked beautiful at first glance. But as they drew closer I cried out in horror. The horses' heads were skulls and their eyes glowed with a red fire. The word "Nightmare" flashed through my mind. I had seen a horse like this before, in my dream. I tried to pull away from my captors, but they held me tighter as the men and women on the horses rode slowly right up to us. "Greetings, Fallon Gwyn," the Regulator said bowing low. "We have come to do the will of The One."

AND NOW I'M IN A CAGE

The white-cloaked riders nodded to him and took their place on either side of us. It made my skin crawl just to be so close to those horses. No wonder Miss Rorrim had run out of the room when I had described the nightmare in my dream. I found myself thinking about Miss Rorrim, so kind, so gentle, so understanding. Had she really wanted to send us here? Was she really in the pay of the evil people here?

As we came onto the green, trumpets sounded. The Fallon Gwyn edged their white horses forward and the crowd fell back, afraid. They rode through the crowd toward the castle and the teachers propelled us after them.

Outside the castle entrance a rough wooden stage had been erected. We were led up onto it and the crowd grew quiet expectantly as the Regulator stepped up onto the stage. He cleared his throat. "Behold. The candidates for Conformation." A great roar went up and the crowd surged forward toward the stage waving their fists and shouting, "Shame, shame." From the stage I could see the other school children entering the green. The crowd turned away from the stage as parents rushed to hug their children. I could hear squeals of joy from reunited families. A few weeping parents stood nearby looking sorrowfully at the stage, afraid to approach their children who stood there because of the teachers and guards who surrounded them. But I noticed the lips of parents whispering silent messages of love to the children beside me on the stage. It had grown cold again as the sun set and my legs were stiff from standing still after such a long walk. It seemed to me that we stood there forever wondering what was going to happen to us now. I tried to see where Pippa was standing but I couldn't. I really, really wished she was beside me, even though there was nothing we could do to try and escape.

The crowd hushed and we turned around to see four white-robed Fallon Gwyn coming out under the big arch of the castle. "You are instructed to hold the prisoners until the coming of The One," one of the Fallon Gwyn said. "His arrival has been delayed." And he motioned us away. The other children were led away one by one and I couldn't see where they were being taken. Then my turn came. The helmeted guard grabbed me by the upper arm and forced me through the crowd. With the other arm he cracked his whip at those who came too close.

The music and dance had begun again and there were even good food smells. My stomach growled with hunger. How long had it been since I had eaten?

We came to a line of cages. Like everything else on the green the cages looked like something from a different century. They were made of wooden beams lashed together and set into the ground. I wondered if we'd finally see what kind of animals they had here. The cage door had an iron lock as if a lion or something was supposed to be inside. Then the guard opened that lock with a huge key and kicked me inside so violently that I went sprawling onto the floor. The crowd who had been following them laughed and clapped. Before I could stand up something landed on my back.

My first thought was that lion or ferocious animal I had expected. But then a voice said, "Ow." And I recognized it.

"Pippa? Is that you?"

We scrambled to our feet.

"I'm so glad it's you," I said.

"Me, too. This is awful, isn't it? What do you think is going to happen?"

"Everyone else seems happy enough," I said, "apart from the kids on the stage. But I have a bad feeling about this."

At that moment something came hurtling into our cage. "Shame!" a voice yelled. Pippa retrieved the object. "It's a potato," she said. "I don't know about you, but I'm starving." She took a bite then handed it to me. "I've never eaten raw potato before," she said, "but it's better than nothing."

"Isn't it supposed to be poisonous or bad for you?"

"Who cares," Pippa said between bites. "I'm starving."

We sat side by side on the floor of the cage. Occasional vegetables were pelted at us. These we ate hungrily, but soon we were forgotten. The crowd was now being entertained. Some kind of show was going on on the stage. Great roars of laughter came from the crowd so we guessed it was a comedian or a funny play.

"Now would be a good time to escape," Pippa whispered.

"Oh sure, if we could find a way to unlock the padlock," I whispered back. "All we need is a key."

"If Celeste was here, maybe she could make it appear for us," Pippa said.

"Do you think she has one of the powers and she made that necklace appear?" I asked.

"Well, I know I searched that particular piece of ground and then suddenly there it was," Pippa said. "I wouldn't mind any powers right now." She sighed. "If I have a power, I have no idea what it could be. I just want to get away from here. You don't suppose there's a weak bar on this cage, do you?"

We tried shaking every bar in turn but the cage was strongly built.

The play ended and the crowd began to drift away.

"It doesn't look as if anything is going to happen for a while," I said. "I suppose they have to wait for that awful person they call The One."

"What do you think he'll do to us?" Pippa asked, her voice shaking a little.

"I don't know. I don't want to think about it," I answered. "I don't know about you, but I am so tired. I need to lie down for a while. We'll need to be able to think clearly when we're let out. And don't forget, if either of us gets a chance to escape, just run. Run for all you're worth."

"I'm not leaving you behind," Pippa said.

"Don't be silly. If you get away then maybe you can find someone to help."

There wasn't enough room in the cage to stretch out and the floor was only the rough grass of the meadow but we huddled together like two puppies. A gray mist had come in from the sea making everything cold and damp. "Need to find help," I muttered to myself. But who could help us? Miss Neves had been able to read my thoughts, but then she had tricked us and sent us here. She was the enemy. I tried to sleep but sleep wouldn't come. Beside me I heard Pippa breathing regularly. At least she was asleep. Outside our cage the sounds of the fair were going on with music and laughter. "If only we could let somebody know where we are.

Somebody who would believe us. Raj would be good. He's smart. He might know what to do."

And suddenly I was standing beside Raj's bed. He was curled up, asleep.

"Raj!" I whispered.

He opened his eyes and sat up, startled. "Addy, what are you doing?" he asked. "You're not allowed in the boy's dorms."

"I need your help," I said. "I'm locked up. You have to help us escape. Please, Raj. Please don't leave us there."

"I have no idea what you're talking about," Raj said. "Now let me go back to sleep."

"But you are asleep," I said. "Listen to me. We're trapped on the other side. Tell somebody where we are. Let somebody know. Maybe Miss Rorrim. And if you can think of a way to unlock a cage with a great big lock…"

"You're having a bad dream," Raj muttered.

"No, it's real. It's horribly, awfully real. If someone doesn't help us soon, it will be too late. If you could only see it for yourself."

"All right, all right, I'm coming." Raj started to push his bedclothes aside and struggle sleepily out of bed.

Pippa screamed as a heavy weight landed on us.

RAJ HAS A THEORY

"Ow," a voice said, and sitting between us was a bleary-eyed Raj, dressed in striped pajamas.

"Raj. You came. You got here!" I said excitedly.

"How did you do that?" Pippa asked.

"Do what?" Raj asked, looking absolutely confused.

"Get here," Pippa said. "How did you get here?"

"I have absolutely no idea," Raj said looking around and rubbing his eyes in disbelief. "One moment I was in my own bed and then I thought Addy was calling for help and I thought 'I'd better go and see what's wrong' and suddenly I was flying. I mean really flying. And I landed here. Where are we?"

"We're on the other side," I said. "You know—the mirror world."

"Mirror world?"

"You remember the seven impossible things? From Alice through the Looking Glass? Remember how she stepped through the mirror?"

"Yes, but that's a children's story."

"But it's true," Pippa said. "That mirror at the end of the haunted hallway. It leads to this place. We stepped through it. We're not quite sure whether we're back in time or just somewhere else."

"Not possible," Raj said, shaking his head firmly. "At least I suppose time travel is theoretically possible but it would involve…"

"It's called Gallia," I said, before he got too scientific. "And it's ruled by a horrible person called The One. And in case you didn't notice, we're in a cage."

"Exactly why would that be?" Raj asked.

"Because we're dangerous. They think we're some of the old ones who used to rule here," I said. "They're called Fareeth and they had special powers. We—we seem to have those powers. I'm what they call a Dreamwalker and maybe you are, too. You came here because I visited you in my dream."

"Are you sure this isn't still your dream?"

"I'm positive," I said.

"So what are they planning to do to you? Keep you locked up on exhibition like a zoo?" Raj asked.

"No. We're scheduled for Conformation," Pippa said. "We're not sure exactly what happens, but it can't be good. But now you're here. That's brilliant. You can help us escape."

"In case you hadn't noticed," Raj said slowly, "I'm also inside the cage with you."

"But you traveled here. You said that you flew. You can make yourself leave the cage."

"Addy, I've told you. I have no idea how I got here. As far as I know I don't have any special powers, except for a good brain."

"Then for heaven's sake use that good brain now," Pippa said.

"A knife or some kind of tool would be more use than a brain at this moment," Raj said. "It looks like we're well and truly stuck."

"I'm sorry, Raj," Addy said. "I must have brought you here. I didn't mean to. I hoped—well, I hoped you could go and get help, or tell somebody where we were."

"Hey, look at that," Raj said suddenly, staring up through the bars on top of the cage.

"What?"

"It's daylight here and it was night at our school."

"Yes, I noticed that time isn't the same."

"Cool," Raj said. "I wonder how that is done… what kind of theory. And you know what else? The sun is setting in the East. It really is a mirror world."

"Yes, I noticed that," I said.

"So everything's backward here?"

"The bad people wear white," Pippa said. "And they ride these terrifying horses called Nightmares. They look like lovely white horses but they have faces like skulls and they have red fire coming from their nostrils."

"Are you sure that this isn't a joke." Raj looked around. "Sam – is this your idea of a joke?" he called, peering through the bars and rattling the door.

"Yeah, Raj," he imitated Sam's cockney accent. "We spent all day building cages on the front lawn and dressing everyone up as wacko villagers to play a joke on you." If I hadn't been so tired and hungry and scared I would have laughed.

"I can't believe this is real. I must be dreaming. Pinch me ... Ow!" he said as Pippa pinched him hard.

Raj looked out of the cage, studying the scene. "Some kind of fair, apparently. Are we like the entertainment?"

"We are scheduled for a ceremony of some kind. Conformation they call it but we don't know what it is. Anyway, it must be important because there are guards everywhere," Pippa said.

"It will be interesting to see their faces when they notice another person is in the cage with you," Raj commented.

"They'll immediately assume you're another Fareeth with powers and you'll be conformed with us," I said bleakly. "Maybe I could try to dream you out of the cage. But then you might go straight back to your bed so that's no good."

"If only we could get our hands on the key," Pippa said.

"Maybe someone will come around to bring us food and we could grab the key then," Raj suggested.

But no food appeared. A guard patrolled the cages, barely looking into each one. Raj was still looking around with interest. "Look at these people. It's like something out of a movie. And those blokes look so cool in those helmets. They belong in a video game."

"You can switch off video games," Pippa said crossly. "I'd love it if you could find a way to switch off these people."

"I wonder whether I really flew or I only thought I was flying," Raj said. "Can people fly here?"

"Not that I've seen," I said.

"Interesting because scientifically speaking it's not possible," he went on. "I mean I know I'm sort of thin, but aerodynamically I am not built for flying and the sort of propulsion mechanism needed to lift me off ..."

"Raj, shut up," Pippa said. "We're trapped in a cage. We're going to be conformed, whatever that is. For heaven's sake use that brain of yours to get us out of here."

A clear high trumpet sounded. The sound seemed to come from everywhere at once and went on for a minute at least. Everyone turned in the direction of the high arched entrance of the castle. As the rays of the sun illuminated the archway a white rosebush grew up the pillars on either side of the archway and made a shining white bower. The stonework on the castle glowed until the whole castle looked as if it was illuminated.

"The One!" the crowd murmured. "The One is coming."

THE ONE COMES

As one person the crowd knelt in the direction of the castle. A sudden brilliant light appeared in the sky. As it grew closer I saw that it was a white dragon, with a man on its back. Lower and lower it circled until it landed on the stage outside the castle. Its brightness was so dazzling that it made my eyes water and I had to close them. When I opened my eyes I saw that the dragon had vanished and a tall man in sparkling silver-white robes was now standing on the stage. Every face in the crowd was turned up to him. Seeing him standing there and feeling my heart thumping with fear brought back the forgotten memory clearly. I had met him before in his palace. "I've seen him before," I whispered to Pippa. "I dreamt about him my first night at school when I had that nightmare."

The man walked toward the edge of the stage and held up his hands up for silence. The teachers rose from kneeling and stood behind him, their white robes shining. Their faces seemed strangely blank to me as if they were carved marble statues without expression. The One scanned the crowd, then his eyes lit up and I realized that he was looking at me, even though he was really too far away to notice me in a cage. "Ah, so there you are, my little Fareeth." His mouth didn't move but the words echoed around my head so loudly that I cried out in pain.

"What's wrong?" Pippa asked.

"I look forward to meeting you in person. You will be a great asset to me. Soon you will be mine," The One's voice continued. "But first please feel free to enjoy the spectacle. And now you must excuse me. I have business to attend to."

I dropped to the ground, holding my ears.

"What is it, Addy, what happened?" Raj asked.

"He spoke to me. He knows I'm here. Didn't you hear his voice? It was so loud that I thought my head was going to explode."

"We didn't hear anything," Pippa said.

"We have to get out of here now," I gasped.

The silence among the crowd was now electric. At last Grymur spoke. "Brothers and Sisters, I have come," he said. His pale face smiled down at the crowd with a fatherly expression of pride. "I have come to thank you for your loyal work and your service to our great Gallia. These beautiful children that you have brought to me are surely our future." He raised his hands and the crowd began to chant, "The One. The One." Then he lowered his hands and there was instant silence. "I have come to perform a ceremony that saddens me greatly." He continued. "Not everyone is good, not everyone is obedient or helpful. Some people are even working to bring chaos to our orderly society. My dear people, there are still members of the Fareeth among us."

There was a gasp from the crowd. "Yes, my beloved people," he said. "Those hated wizards still exist and are still working to overthrow our orderly government and take us back to the days when everyone was a slave to them. Do you want those days to come back?"

A great resounding "No!" went up from the crowd.

"Such people must be rendered harmless so that they do not disrupt our orderly society. We are not a vengeful people. We are merciful."

I was watching the teachers intently. I had never seen them all together at the school. 'They're like puppets,' I thought. When the man they called The One smiled they smiled, when he gave the crowd a stern look so did they.

"I will now go into the castle where I will meet with the candidates and bestow my merciful forgiveness on them," he said.

Trumpets sounded again. The One walked under the arch and into the castle, followed by the teachers. Fallon Gwyn took up positions at the entrance. The Regulator stepped forward. "Summon the first candidate for Conformation," he proclaimed.

A herald stepped forward. "Bring up Holly of Settlement 25."

The first of the cages was opened. A teenage girl was led out. She fought against the two guards who dragged her up to the stage. "I won't!" she shouted. "You can't make me."

She was half-carried onto the stage. I saw a couple who must have been her parents push their way through the crowd to the front. "Holly, my child!" the mother called out. "Don't forget us."

"Shame, shame." The chant went up again from the crowd.

The guards half-carried the writhing girl in through the arch. An expectant hush fell upon the crowd, except for Holly's mother who was sobbing loudly. From inside came awful screams that stopped abruptly. Then the trumpet sounded again. The One appeared in the gateway, holding Holly by the hand. She was now robed in shining white robes. A white cap hid her hair.

"My people," The One announced, "I present to you the newest Watcher of Settlement 25."

He smiled. Holly smiled an identical smile.

"What was broken is now made pure and whole," the whole audience intoned.

Holly's mother let out a cry of despair and tried to climb up onto the stage. Guards rushed up and she was dragged away. I turned to look at Pippa. I felt sick.

WE REALLY NEED AN ESCAPE PLAN

"We have to get out of here now," I said. "We can't wind up like that."

"Oh, good idea," Pippa said with sarcasm. "I'll just use one of my powers to melt the bars then, shall I?"

"I wish you could," I said. "Let's go over how Raj got here and maybe we could go home the same way."

Raj shrugged. "All I know is you called me and suddenly I was flying." His face lit up for a moment. "I was really flying, going incredibly fast."

"Do you think you could fly back, holding us?" I suggested.

"Maybe if you think it or wish it hard enough, you can do it," Pippa added. "Go on. It's worth a try. Hold onto us and then wish yourself back in the dorm."

"Close your eyes," I said. Raj grabbed us. Nothing happened.

"Nope," he said. "We'll have to come up with another way."

"Summoning for Conformation candidate Rock of Settlement 208," the herald's voice boomed out. Another cage was opened. Another person was dragged up to the stage.

"Look," Pippa touched my arm. "That guard standing over there. He's got the key on his belt."

The tall guard was now standing a few yards in front of us, keeping the crowd away from the cages.

"Does one of your powers let arms grow terribly long?" Raj asked.

"I don't think so."

"Pity."

Just then I saw a face I recognized in the crowd. "Twig!" I shouted. "Twig, over here."

Twig saw me and glanced around nervously before creeping closer. "Addy, I'm so sorry," I said. "I hoped you'd got away. I wish there was something I could do for you, but I can't think what. The leaders of our group stay well away from things like this. The One is too good at reading thoughts. So it's just me and they're letting me go home to my family."

"I'm so glad for you," I said.

"Yes, it's wonderful. I never thought this day would come."

"Twig, there is something you could do…" I hesitated. Twig seemed so relieved that she had been released from the school and was going home. Did we have any right to put her in danger now?

Before I could do anything, Pippa beckoned her closer. "See that guard? He has the key to our cage on his belt. If you could just get it—when the person is actually being conformed and everybody's watching. We'll do the rest. You won't be involved."

Twig looked first at us and then at the guard.

"Please, Twig," I begged. "We're so scared. Don't let this awful thing happen to us. Then we'll never get home to our own world."

Twig hesitated then nodded at me and turned back toward the guard. She walked casually toward him, coming to a stop right behind him. The ceremony on stage was reaching its climax.

"What was broken is now made pure and whole," the crowd intoned.

Twig reached out her hand. Raj, Pippa and I strained forward in anticipation, willing her close enough to grasp the key. The key seemed to swing toward Twig's hand as if toward a magnet. The metal loop that the key was on broke with a snap and the key flew into Twig's hand. Twig stared at the key in her hand so startled and terrified that she didn't move when the guard spun round.

"What's going on? What do you think you're doing?" he bellowed, staring at the key in Twig's hand. "Another Fareeth, huh?" He snatched back the key, then grabbed Twig's arm, twisting so violently behind her back that she cried out. "How did we almost miss you?" He turned to the stage and two of the teachers immediately looked up as if called and started in their direction.

"I'm sorry, Twig, I'm so sorry," I yelled, not sure if Twig would be able to hear me through the noisy crowd.

But Twig did hear. "Addy, help me." She cried as she was dragged her away in the direction of the stage. I gave a despairing cry as Twig disappeared into the crowd. "Let her go. It's my fault. It's all my fault, I made her do it," I screamed after them. "Wait. Listen to me."

But it was no good. Twig had gone.

NOW WOULD BE A REALLY GOOD TIME
TO ESCAPE

"We have to get that key," I said, shaking the bars in frustration as the guard clipped the key back onto his belt. "We have to save her before she is conformed. I won't let anyone get conformed for trying to save me. If we started fighting among ourselves, do you think that would bring him over?"

"Did you see the key?" Pippa said. "It jumped into her hand. She must have Fareeth powers, too. "

"These powers we're supposed to have," Raj said. "Do you know what they are?"

"Well, you can fly, obviously," Pippa said. "Addy visits people in her dreams. I don't seem to have any powers at all, except that people can talk to me without moving their mouths."

Raj was staring thoughtfully. "I wonder if we combined our powers we might be able to get that key to come to us. Maybe we made it move before. Maybe it was us wanting it that made the key jump into Twig's hand. It's worth a shot. When I count to three, let's all close our eyes, focus on that key and command it to come to us."

"All right," Pippa said. "Let's hold hands."

We crouched together, holding hands.

"Close your eyes and concentrate," Raj said. "Ready? One. Two. Three."

We opened our eyes again.

"Too bad," Pippa said. "Oh well, it was worth a shot."

"But it worked," I whispered. "Look."

The key had now vanished from where it had been tucked into the guard's belt.

"Where is it?" Raj asked.

"It's in your pajama top pocket." I leaned over and

214

triumphantly produced the key. "You have that power, Raj. You can fly and you can make things fly to you. I wasn't imagining things when I saw the target move for you when we were doing archery."

"I actually thought that target moved, too," Raj confessed, "but it seemed so scientifically impossible that I didn't want to admit it."

"Brilliant," Pippa said impatiently. "Now let's get out of here. Let's see if we can use that power to save Twig. Maybe you could make something impressive move—lift up the cage and drop it on the stage…"

"Hey, let's not get too ambitious here," Raj said. "I moved a key. I have no idea how I did it or if I did it. Maybe it was all three of us together. Besides, that would draw attention to us and I think the idea is not to do that."

"Where did they take her?" Pippa asked.

"Oh no," I groaned. "Look, we're too late."

A guard was marching Twig up toward the castle. For a horrible moment I thought that she was about to be taken in to The One, but then I saw that they went in at a side door, at the left side of the stage. Then there was still a chance.

"Quick, Raj, open the cage. We have to get up to her before she can be conformed," I whispered.

The next candidate was just emerging from the castle and the crowd was all looking at the stage. Their faces were upturned in rapture as The One spoke.

"Have you noticed," Raj whispered, drawing us close together, "when they do this conformation thing, it's almost as if they are all possessed. Look at the faces on stage. They all smile when he smiles. They frown when he frowns. It's as if he controls them all."

"Great, so stop talking and start acting," Pippa said. "If we don't hurry up, that's going to happen to us."

"But I'm still thinking," Raj said. "When they are doing this chanting, and he's controlling their minds, I don't believe they'd even notice us. We need to time things perfectly. We'll wait until the trumpets announce that The One is about to present the new Watcher—whatever that is—and then we make a run for it."

"We could use those booths to hide us," Pippa said. "There are some of them pretty close to the stage."

I came to a decision and turned to the others. "Look, Twig isn't your problem," I said. "We have the key. You two can escape.

Make your way back to the school. It should be empty, I think, because everyone marched here. Go up to the hall with the horrible portrait and then break into that cloakroom around the corner in the little hall to the left. That's how you can get back."

"We're not going anywhere without you," Pippa said. "Don't be so silly."

"You're being silly," I said. "No sense in all of us being conformed. You two have a chance. Tell Miss Rorrim. She seemed really nice, didn't she? Maybe she can do something."

"We're coming with you, Addy," Raj said quietly. "It's all for one and one for all."

"Don't say that. It's what that stupid One person says," I said, but I had to smile.

"So this is the plan," Raj said. "Only move while the actual conformation is going on. If The One is busy taking over the thoughts of someone, as appears to be the case, although that kind of mind control is way above anything I've read of…"

"Raj! Get on with it," Pippa said in exasperated tones. "In case you hadn't noticed, they just took out the people from two cages ahead of us. We're almost next in line."

I GO FOR A SWIM

"Okay, so this is the plan," Raj repeated. "We get to the edge of the stage while the new Watcher is being presented. Then we find a way into the castle."

"Oh yes, brilliant. Absolutely simple," Pippa snapped.

"Hold on a second," Raj said. "It just happens that at the beginning of term, when I came with my dad to see the school, we also did a tour of Conwy castle. Now I'm actually a pretty observant sort of bloke and I can still visualize what it looks like."

"But this isn't Conwy castle. It looks like it from the outside. The inside might be quite different."

"Maybe not," Raj went on impatiently. "Only I have to remember that we're in a mirror world, so everything would be backward. And of course in our world Conway Castle is a ruin so there aren't many actual rooms."

"Great. That's helpful," Pippa snapped.

Raj was still staring at the castle, pointing. "Twig went in through that little door on the left, which would be a little door on the right back in our world and I think there were several small rooms off the great hall where she could be kept. So all we need is another way in."

"Are there other ways into castles?" I asked. "I thought the whole point was that you could only get in through one entrance."

"I believe I noticed a little door up a flight of steps from the harbor," Raj said. "Worth a try, anyway."

"And I've got a good idea," Pippa said. "We'd attract too much attention if all three of us went in. What we need is a means of getting away fast. I'm going to try and get my hands on one of those white horses. Then I can gallop up, hoist up both of you and off we go."

"Pippa they're called Nightmares for a good reason," I said.

"And perhaps I should remind you that I fell off Blackie last week and he's an old plodding riding-school horse," Raj said. "I don't actually see myself leaping onto a bloody giant horse with a face like a skull that breathes fire from its nostrils."

"I've never yet found a horse I couldn't ride," Pippa said. "You can sit in front of me and I'll hold you tight, Raj."

"I don't think they're real horses," I said. "I think they're controlled by the minds of those creepy white guys that ride them – the Fallon Gwyn - and probably won't obey anyone else."

"It's worth a try, isn't it?" Pippa said. "If it doesn't work I'll meet you where those flag poles are. That's the part of the field nearest to the town. Okay, let's get the lock opened right now so that we don't have to fiddle with it later."

Raj reached out of the cage and turned the key in the padlock. There was a loud click. The guard turned around. Addy, Raj and Pippa sat staring out innocently. The guard turned back again as a group of people pushed forward.

"Get back now. Not too close to the prisoners," he grunted and fingered his whip.

"When we get out, just blend into the crowd," Pippa said.

"Right, blend in," Raj nodded. "Have you noticed I'm wearing striped pajamas?"

Pippa suggested, "Maybe grab something from one of the stalls?"

"And get conformed twice for stealing as well as having powers?"

"Hurry up," I interrupted.

"Summoning for Conformation candidate Ivy from Settlement 153," the herald announced. The cage two away from us was opened. A small girl let out a frightened scream. "I'll be good," she wailed. "I'll do everything right, I promise. I won't dream anymore. I won't ever sing again."

I felt desperate. I wanted to do something to rescue her but couldn't think of anything. The crowd was particularly interested in this one, maybe because she was so small.

"She's a Fareeth, this one. A real Fareeth," the whisper went around.

"Now," Raj said, as the crowd surged toward the stage. We opened the door and crept out. "Go," he whispered.

One by one we slipped into the crowd, cautiously making our way to the edge of the meadow and then darting from one booth to the next. The little girl was crying loudly as she was led onto the stage and there were murmurs of pity as well as the chants of shame. Everyone in the crowd was straining to get a glimpse of the stage.

At last we came to the edge of the crowd. There on our right was the harbor wall, with water lapping at the castle. Raj appeared at my side. "Oh nuts," he muttered, "I didn't count on the tide being in. Look, see that little door. It's just above the waterline. I thought we could walk over the rocks to it, but now we can't get to it."

"Yes, we can," I said.

"We have no time to get down to the harbor and steal a boat," Raj said.

"I'm from California," I said. "I learned to swim before I could walk. And I swim really well underwater. If I dive off the wall, I think I can swim most of the way across underwater."

"Well, I happen to come from Birmingham and I can barely manage one lap of breast-stroke," Raj said, "So that won't work."

"Then I'll have to go alone," I said. "It's probably better that way. Less chance of being discovered."

"And what about The One talking inside your head?" Raj demanded. "You don't think he'd pick up vibes from you if you were that close to him?"

"I'll have to risk it, won't I?" I said. "I'll try not to think. I'll hum or something."

Raj looked like he was going to say something else and then thought better of it. "Okay. Then give me a sign when you're ready to come back with Twig and I'll cause a distraction," he said. "Don't put yourself in danger. Don't draw attention to yourself. You don't exactly blend in."

"I'll do something simple like saying I've just seen someone stealing from a booth. Then no one will be looking at the harbor when you climb back up the wall with Twig."

"That sounds like something that only works in the movies," I said doubtfully. "But we don't really have a choice. Good luck, Raj."

Trumpets sounded. The small girl was about to be led out, dressed as a new Watcher. Everyone crowded closer to the stage again.

"Here goes nothing," I said. "Good luck, you guys. And if you manage to get back and I don't, well..." I couldn't finish the sentence. I didn't really have anybody who cared about me anyway.

I tucked my long gray robe into my underpants, scrambled onto the wall, took a huge breath and dove into the water.

I SEE A CONFORMATION

My biggest fear was that the water would be too shallow and I'd hit a rock, but I was relieved as I plunged into icy greenness. It was the cold that startled me and I almost had to come to the surface as it took my breath away. But I forced myself to stay down, swimming with strong strokes toward the castle. The visibility wasn't good and I just prayed I was heading in the right direction. When something wrapped around my leg, my heart nearly leaped up into my throat, but I turned and saw that I had just swum into seaweed. I kicked myself free and swam on. When I felt as if my lungs were bursting, the darker shape of the rocks around the castle loomed ahead. I came to the surface and saw the castle towering over me with the steps leading to the little door only a few strokes away.

I gave a few final powerful kicks and hauled myself onto the lowest step. Nobody seemed to be looking in my direction. I scrambled up the steps and tried the little door. At first it wouldn't budge but the rusty handle gave as I yanked at it with all my strength. I dragged the door open and slipped into total darkness. It was damp and cold. Ahead of me I could see light at the top of a flight of stone steps. I stood and listened but couldn't hear anything. Then I took off the robe and wrung out as much moisture from it as I could. It wouldn't do to leave a trail of drips for anyone to see. When I had squeezed all I could, I put it on again. It clung to me, feeling cold and wet and horrible.

Cautiously I made my way up the steps. At the top a passageway turned to the right. I followed it and came out into a large hall, with a high arched ceiling, adorned with fluttering banners. In the middle of the room was a throne and on the throne… I swallowed back a gasp and jumped back into the shadows. There, a few feet away from me was Grymur. His back was to me and I was sure he'd sense my presence and spin around.

But he didn't. He stood suddenly and, as I watched, another young person was half-dragged into his presence by two tall Fallon Gwyn. "I hate you," the boy shouted. "I'll always hate you no matter what you try. You can't make me love you. You can't make me…"

The words stopped abruptly as Grymur stepped forward and placed his hands on the struggling boy's head. The boy went rigid, his eyes staring straight ahead.

"Ah, but I can make you, you poor weak Fareeth," he said softly, while the Fallon Gwyn grinned. "I now take your thoughts. Your mind is empty. And you are mine. Who are you?"

And a flat voice came out, "I am your Watcher, Master."

"And what is your task, Watcher?"

"To serve you and obey."

"Well said, Watcher." Grymur clapped his hands. "Come, array him in the robes of honor."

Two white-clad teachers appeared from a side room, bringing white robes, which they put over the boy's head, then arranged the white cape and the white cap. All the time the boy stood like a puppet, moving his arms compliantly.

"We are ready. Command the heralds," The One said in a powerful voice. He took the white-robed boy by the hand. "Come, my newest servant," he said.

Trumpets blared out. The One started toward the open front door, preceded by the tall Fallon Gwyn. The teachers followed. I didn't hesitate a second longer. I sprinted across the wide hall and into the passage on the other side. As soon as I allowed myself to breathe again, I started searching room after room. In the room closest to the hall were the white robes that the Watchers wore laid out and waiting for the newest Watchers. On impulse I grabbed one. 'Better to be seen to be on the right side,' I decided, and pulled the white robe over my head. The whole level seemed deserted except for the hall but I walked as close to the wall as I could, trying to keep myself in shadow as I searched room after room.

Twig wasn't in any of the rooms. I tried to think logically, which wasn't easy. I could hear the crowd applauding outside as the new Watcher was presented. 'Think, Addy,' I commanded myself, trying to picture how Twig had been taken into the castle. Okay, the door through which Twig had been brought to the castle was on a level with the bottom of the stage. Lower than where I was right now.

Down a level. I found a twisty stair in the wall and made my way down. There was a line of doors with barred windows in them, sort of like dungeons. I glanced inside each until I came to the one at the end of the hall. I let out a huge sigh of relief. There was Twig, sitting with her head in her hands. Carefully I slid back the bolt on the door. Twig looked up and shrank back fearfully as she saw the white robe. I put my finger to my lips.

"I've come to get you out," I whispered. "Come on."

"How did you get out of the cage? How did you get here?" Twig seemed completely stunned. She stared at me in disbelief.

"Come on Twig." I took her hand and pulled her to her feet. "Let's get out of here."

"I can't. We'll be caught," Twig whispered. She didn't move from the corner of the room. "You'll be conformed, too. Run, while you can."

"We're going together." I yanked her up and pulled her physically toward the door. "We wait until The One is actually performing the Conformation. At that moment all his power is being used, and it seems as if he's controlling everyone else, too. He didn't notice me when I was standing a few feet away and that's a good sign. Come on—we just have to go upstairs and cross the great hall and then there's a little door above the water and we can swim to safety."

Twig shook my hand free. "I can't do it. I don't know how to swim," she said. "I'm afraid of water. Just get out of here and save yourself."

I considered the options. I was strong enough a swimmer to drag Twig back to the sea-wall, but what if Twig panicked? If she screamed or cried out, or thrashed around? She'd attract attention and I couldn't risk that. So what was the other option?

"Do you remember how you came into the castle?" I asked.

"I don't know." Twig's voice was shrill with panic. "I don't know."

"It's okay, Twig," I said, trying to sound calm. 'I'll have to figure this out on my own,' I thought.

"We can't risk Watchers seeing us wandering around the castle," I said out loud. "Let's sneak out the front while everyone is watching The One."

"The front?" Twig was still in full panic mode.

I put my hands on her shoulders. "Look, Twig, you were so

brave when you helped me escape from school. Now I want to help you. What's the worst that can happen? They catch us, and we were going to be conformed anyway, so we're no worse off, are we? Come on, it's worth a try, isn't it?"

Twig managed a weak smile. We made our way back up the stairs and waited in shadow. We heard the trumpets. The teachers rushed past us bringing the white robes. Then the trumpets again.

"Now," I hissed, dragging a trembling Twig forward. We burst into the Great Hall to see The One and his followers still passing through the archway and out to the stage. We shrank back into the shadows, then the moment the last teacher had stepped outside, we sprinted across the hall and fled down the steps on the far right. The little door opened easily enough and we stepped through.

"See. We've made it," I said jubilantly. "I told you we would."

A shadow loomed over us and I looked up to see a guard of the Fallon Gwyn only a foot away. What's more he was not staring in rapt attention at the stage. He was looking straight at me.

WE GET CHASED BY MANIACS ON HORSES

"Where are you going, Watcher?" he asked in a deep rumbling voice, "and where is your cap?"

"My cap?" For a moment my brain refused to work. Think, I commanded myself. I forced myself to stare right back at him with an expressionless face. "I was instructed to take this prisoner to the cages so that she joins the line for Conformation," I said.

The Fallon Gwyn frowned. "Instructed. Who instructed you to do this?"

"The Master, of course. Who else instructs a Watcher?"

"This is a job for one of the guard, not a Watcher," he said, eyeing us suspiciously now. "Come with me. We will seek further instructions on this matter."

I hardly know how to explain what happened next. All I can say is that I was determined to get past him. I heard myself saying, "You dare to question my orders?" And in my mind I was trying to make my voice sound exactly like the voice of The One that had thundered inside my head. I didn't know if you could imitate someone's voice in your mind. If you couldn't I had just given myself away but I couldn't think of anything else to do.

I saw the guard's expression change to fear. "Forgive me, Master. What is your will?"

"Come to me at once," I went on, realizing with amazement that I was controlling this man's thought. "This Watcher has a special mission from me."

"This Watcher has a special mission," The Fallon Gwyn repeated, then turned from us and went quickly in the direction of The One.

I grabbed Twig and yanked her into the crowd, pulling her behind an unoccupied booth. We crawled under the bunting that surrounded the booth and sat there, hardly daring to breathe.

"I can't believe you did that. He went away."

"I told him to." I was so relieved that I wasn't sure whether to laugh or cry. "I used The One's voice and told him to and he did."

"I heard you tell him. But you didn't move your lips. "

"I told him in my mind," I said.

"You really must be a Dreamwalker like they said," Twig stammered. "Only Dreamwalkers can control minds like that."

I shrugged. "I guess I am a Fareeth, anyway. If you heard me you must be, too. If we have some powers, we might as well use them. Come on." We crawled rapidly to the next booth and then the next. We could hear raised voices and shouts coming from the crowd. "That way, they went that way!" I struggled to get out of the white robe. "It wouldn't do to see a Watcher running away," I said. "When we get a chance make your way to those flags on the far left of the field. That's where I said we'd meet Pippa and Raj."

Cautiously we crept out from under the canvas. We could see guards towering over the rest of the population, walking through the crowd, searching. I linked arms with Twig. "Pretend we're having a good time," I said. I forced a smile on my face. "Come on, let's go and find mom and dad and maybe they'll buy us something nice to eat."

Twig looked at me as if I was mad. I skipped ahead, smiling at everyone we passed. Gradually we came nearer and nearer to the flags. There was the edge of the meadow and nothing between us and the streets of the town. But there was no sign of either Pippa or Raj. I looked around hesitantly, wondering what to do. Had they been recaptured? Was Raj still waiting by the seawall? In which case he'd be a sitting target in those striped pajamas.

"You go on ahead," I said to Twig. "Try to make for the mountains."

"I'm staying with you," Twig said firmly.

"But I have to find my friends."

"Then I'll help."

Suddenly something struck me in the back. I almost cried out, but spun around instead. Another rock hit me in the chest. It seemed to have come from behind a low line of bushes that separated the closest houses from the meadow.

"Come on." I started to run. We reached the bushes. Hands grabbed me and dragged me down.

"Get down, they've been looking for us," Pippa's voice hissed.

I stared from Pippa to Raj. "You both made it." I felt tears of joy and relief welling up inside me.

"And so did you. Well done," Raj said.

"I was worried you were still waiting at the seawall."

Pippa shook her head. "We saw you come out of the other door and then that big guard bloke started talking to you and that looked like trouble, so we found another guard and pointed out our empty cage to him. Then I said I'd seen kids running in the other direction. I thought you'd have more chance of getting away if there was a little chaos."

"Brilliant thinking, Pippa." I looked at her with respect.

"Actually it was all Raj's idea," Pippa admitted, "but we thought he'd better lie low, given the striped pajamas do make him stand out a little."

I actually giggled.

"I wanted to ride one of those Nightmares in and rescue you," Pippa went on.

"I'm glad you didn't go near one of those," I said.

"Well – actually I did," Pippa said with a grimace, "and it turned and blew fire at me. I was lucky I wasn't badly burned. Then Raj found me."

"I didn't think that even you could tame one of those things, Pippa," I said. "Thank goodness Raj came up with a plan."

"And I'm so glad you made it too, Twig." Pippa smiled at her. "I'm sorry we got you in trouble."

Twig smiled shyly. "I thought it was all over for me in that castle."

"So what do we do now?" I whispered.

"I reckon that the town is completely unoccupied at the moment. Everyone's at the ceremony. We shouldn't have too much trouble walking through it. We'll act as if we're happy, jolly children coming back from the fair," Raj said.

"Come on, then, let's get moving. Remember— happy, jolly children."

"Ha, ha, ha," Pippa said.

We slipped into the nearest alleyway.

"Do you remember the way back to the school?" Raj asked.

I frowned. "I know the way we were marched here, but it was along the main road. That wouldn't be a good idea. Those Nightmares could gallop along it really fast. Let's cut across to the forest as soon as we can. See how it comes close to the city walls over there?"

The city streets were deserted. Everybody was indeed at the ceremony. Our footsteps echoed from high walls as we clattered through narrow streets.

"Ow," Raj exclaimed. "It's okay for you guys, but I was in bed, asleep. I've got bare feet and these cobbles are killing me and I've just stubbed my big toe."

"Keep going, Raj. We have to get to the forest," I encouraged.

The streets started going uphill. The city walls loomed ahead of us. Suddenly we heard a great roar somewhere down below and then the drumming of feet.

"They're coming after us," I gasped. "Come on. It's not far now.'"

Pippa was sprinting ahead with Twig hot on her heels. I hung back to wait for Raj. Ahead of us was one of the city gates. Two guards were standing at the gate. They were relaxed and staring down the road, not expecting four children to come bursting out of the gate. By the time they had sprung into action we were through. There were cultivated gardens and fields ahead of us and on the other side was the forest.

Horns were blowing now—that strange wail like hunting horns. Voices were shouting and then the noise I had dreaded—the sound of horses' hooves drumming.

"We can make it," Pippa yelled. We plunged across the fields, trampling plants and stubble, stumbling over mounds of earth. My still-wet robe wrapped itself around my legs and threatened to trip me up. My breath was coming in gasps and my side hurt me so much that breathing was almost impossible. Ahead of us were the first trees. Pippa, with her long legs, had reached them first and plunged into the undergrowth. I glanced back to see what was happening to Raj. He was still slithering and stumbling across the fields, and behind him, gaining quickly was a row of tall white horses, with figures in white and silver on their backs. The skull faces of the horses shone horribly bright in the setting sun and fire came from their nostrils. The Fallon Gwyn on their backs leaned forward in their saddles, whips flying.

... AND NOW RANCURS JOIN IN, TOO

"Oh, please hurry, Raj!" I screamed.

"Go ahead. Don't wait," Raj gasped, stumbling and slithering and obviously in a lot of pain as the rocky soil cut into his bare feet.

"Of course I'm waiting. Come on." I ran back, grabbed his hand and half-dragged him into the forest. We blundered through the thick undergrowth, through tall dead bracken and dying blackberry bushes. I wasn't even conscious of branches whipping my face and brambles scratching me. All I wanted to do was catch up with Pippa's disappearing back. Behind me I could hear thrashing and crashing as the undergrowth was trampled and I wasn't sure if it was Raj or the horsemen. Any second I expected to feel a hand grabbing my shoulder or one of those cruel whips cutting me down.

A horse neighed. A horn sounded. Pippa was leading us well, ducking under low branches and plunging into the thickest part of the undergrowth where no horse could possibly follow. At last we came to a little hollow surrounded by old oak trees. Raj collapsed against one of the trees, gasping for breath and rubbing at his cut and bleeding feet. We stood there, looking around nervously.

"I think we've lost them," Pippa said, panting but looking rather pleased with herself. "Now all we have to do is work out where the school is and head for it."

"Oh yeah, right," Raj said. "I don't like to be pessimistic here but it's going to be dark any moment and we have no way of knowing which direction the school is in."

"The school must have been due south or southwest of Conwy," Pippa said. "Remember when we marched yesterday, Addy, the sun was directly behind us."

"Do you know your way around here, Twig?" I asked.

Twig shook her head. "My settlement is miles away. I've never been in these woods before."

"So you're going to try and make it home then, are you?" Raj asked.

"She can't go home, Raj," I said, realizing as I said it how sad this would be for Twig. "The Watchers would report her."

"Maybe it would make more sense to find a good hiding place and wait until they lose interest or until it's dark," Raj said.

Just as he finished speaking a howl echoed through the forest.

"What was that?" Raj asked, looking around nervously.

"It just sounded like a dog," Pippa said,

Twig spun around nervously. "It's not a dog, it's a Rancur," I said. "We have to get out of here."

"A what?" Pippa and Raj asked in unison.

"It looks like a majorly evil big dog," I said. "The guards use them to track people."

"Worse than that." Twig was shaking now. "They are specially bred to sniff out Fareeth. They find all Fareeth babies and kill them right away. They'd probably tear us to pieces."

"Oh, that's cheerful," Raj said. "As if a man who steals your thoughts and warriors on horses that breathe fire aren't enough to worry about, now we've got children-eating dogs. Lovely place this. I must come here on my holidays sometime."

In spite of everything I had to laugh. Raj was looking around.

"Then let's get into that stream over there," Raj suggested, pointing at a mountain stream that rushed by swiftly to their right. "We'll put them off the scent."

"That won't work," Twig said. "They can smell human blood from miles away."

Another howl echoed, further away, then another.

"They're passing the message about us." I grabbed at Pippa's sleeve and dragged her forward, starting to run. "We have to get out of here now. We'll have the whole forest full of them looking for us."

"Oh great," Raj said, struggling to keep up with us. "Just what I wanted, to be eaten by wild dogs."

"I don't think they'll eat us," I said. "I think they'll let the Fallon Gwyn know where to find us so they can bring us back to Grymur to be conformed."

"I wonder why I don't find that reassuring," Raj said.

"Well, we're better off than we were an hour ago," Pippa said.

"At least now we have a chance. The only problem is where to go, if the woods are full of these Rancur things hunting for us."

"I have this feeling we should go upward," I said. "Up the mountainside."

"And why precisely would that be a good idea?" Raj asked.

"I don't know. I just have a feeling," I said. "I get the sense that somebody is telling me to go up."

"Probably that creepy One guy," Raj said. "He was speaking to you before in your head. He wants you to go where it will be easy to capture you."

"Then do you have a better idea?' I snapped. "They'll probably watch all the main roads."

"That dirt track was a main road?" Pippa demanded.

"I think it is for here. Besides – I think The One might know about the mirror. He'll know that the school is our only way back."

"But is it?" Raj looked at us. "You said you stepped through the mirror to get here. Is there only one mirror that works that way?"

"No, we know there is at least one more—the mirror in the old cloakroom. I came through that into the boy's bathroom that time you found me, Raj."

"But we've looked in other mirrors at our school and nothing happened," Pippa said. "I look in the bathroom mirror in our dorm every day."

"So it must be just around a certain hot spot where the energy can transfer from one universe to another," Raj said as he ran. "An interesting phenomenon. I wonder what sort of scientific principle there is behind it. Maybe some distortion of string theory…"

"Raj, let's not get technical here," Pippa said impatiently. "Right now I don't care about any theories. I'm rather anxious to get away from those things."

"Then follow me," I said. "At least they won't be expecting us to go up to the mountain top, will they? Unless you can come up with a better suggestion? What do you think, Twig?"

"I know there are Fareeth still hiding out in the mountains," Twig said. "That's who I was passing a message from the day you found me. But I've no idea where, or whether they can help us."

We found a narrow path and began to follow it as it wound slowly upward through the woods. Oak forest turned into pine wood. We ran as fast as we could from shadow to shadow trying to use the trees for cover. It was now almost dark and the trees loomed as strange skeleton shapes, sending out bony arms to grab us.

"You know, they might not even realize that we've come through from somewhere else," Pippa panted as they hurried forward. "The teachers thought we were from one of their settlements, remember."

"That's right. The Regulator didn't seem to understand about California or airplanes."

"So they probably think we'll make our way back to our own villages," Pippa said. "They'll be watching the roads."

"And we should be able to cut around to the back of the school from this mountain," Raj agreed. "Not a bad idea."

A howl rang out nearby. "If we can avoid the Rancurs," Pippa muttered.

I turned to look back and saw yellow eyes below us in the undergrowth. "There's one behind us now. Come on, run, as fast as you can."

"Alright for you people. You're not stubbing your toes on rocks and stepping on thorns and sharp rocks all the time," Raj muttered but he ran. Behind us came a menacing snarl. We staggered forward onto green grass, up a grassy slope to where the mountain rose ahead of us in a steep cliff. Clouds raced across the sky, covering the summit above and blotting out the last of the twilight ...

"If we can just get into the cloud, maybe they won't see us," Pippa suggested.

"That will hardly matter if they can track us by smell," Raj said.

"Shut up," Pippa snapped.

We clambered up the steep grassy slope to the cliffs.

"Yes, but dogs can't climb straight up like this, can they?" I said. "Doesn't it look like a cave up there, halfway up the rock face? We can make it, come on."

"And your point in going into a cave halfway up a cliff would be what?" Raj gasped, fighting for breath. "Sitting and waiting until the Fallon Gwyn surround us or The One comes to get us?"

"Have you got a better suggestion right now?" I snapped.

"She may be right," Twig said. "I know that Nightmares see well in the darkness, but they can't climb cliffs. Neither can Rancurs. And maybe the cave leads somewhere."

"I hate caves. I'm horribly claustrophobic," Raj said.

"Claustrophobia or conformation, Raj. Which would I choose?" Pippa snapped back to him.

I reached the wall of rock and started to climb. My hands looked for cracks in the rock to grasp onto and I hauled myself up just as the first of the Rancurs appeared at the edge of the forest. "Come on, you guys. Hurry up," I screamed.

The others needed no second urging. Pippa and Twig went up the rock face like rockets, and Raj followed behind, groaning. Any moment I expected the Rancurs to be leaping and snapping at our heels, but they stayed at the edge of the forest. One of them gave a long howl.

'It's telling the Fallon Gwyn where to find us,' I thought. 'It really was silly to come up here. Now we're trapped.'

IS IT A TRAP?

We reached the entrance to the cave and fell gasping onto the stone floor. For a minute no one said anything as we just concentrated on breathing again.

"Maybe there is somewhere to hide inside the cave," I said, standing up cautiously and looking around.

"It doesn't look as if it goes anywhere to me," Raj said. "At least it's big enough not to give me the creeps."

"But I've got a good feeling about this place, haven't you?" I said. "I think we were meant to come here. Somehow I knew there was a cave here."

"Well, it's no use going into pitch darkness," Raj said.

"Look," I said. I pointed at the horizon. A big harvest moon was rising, full and golden. As we watched, it rose into the sky bathing the world below in silvery light.

A shaft of moonlight shone into the cave. Pippa jumped to her feet. "People have been here before," she said excitedly. "Look, here's the hearth where they must have had a fire. And look on the wall up there—someone has carved what looks like the badge of our school. Isn't that the six-sided figure with the dragon in it?"

We went over to examine it.

"That means Fareeth were here," Twig said. "That's the symbol of the Power of Seven."

"That's also the badge of Red Dragon Academy," Raj said. "But is that good or bad? Aren't those the people who got us here in the first place?"

"Let's go exploring," Pippa said. "It looks as if that fireplace was used fairly recently."

"I don't know if it is smart to go exploring in the dark," Raj said. "We could come across a hole in the floor of the cave and fall thousands of feet."

"We'll go carefully," I said. "I wish we had a flashlight."

"I didn't think to hide one in my pajamas," Raj said.

"Pity you can't make one appear," Pippa commented.

"Hey, Raj made the key come to us. He can't have every power, you know," I defended.

We set off, feeling our way along the cold rock wall. It was silent except for our footsteps and breathing and the occasional sound of water dripping into an unseen pool. We moved quickly, our ears tensed for the noise of followers. It was not pitch black as we had feared. The series of caves went upward. Every now and then there was a crack high in the wall and a shaft of moonlight shone down onto the floor. It was reassuring that we could see where we were going but also worrying that we might see a face suddenly peering down at us from one of the ledges high above.

"See, what did I tell you?" Raj said, grabbing at Pippa as she forged ahead. Moonlight was shining onto a pool of water. "You could have stepped into that."

"It's very pretty with the moon shining on it, isn't it?" Pippa said. "And you're right, Addy. This cave does have a good feel to it."

The cave branched off frequently. We had no time for long deliberations over which way to go and just followed the largest and lightest route. The floor and walls were smooth as if humans had worked them. The cave climbed as we went and as we reached what seemed like the top of the slope we suddenly saw a bright patch of moonlight ahead of us.

"We've made it. We're through to the other side. The cave led all the way through the mountain. Brilliant." Raj started to run.

"No, wait." I grabbed him. He turned back impatiently. "Raj. Don't go there. I have the strangest feeling that's not the way."

"But look down there—I see fields and isn't that the school?"

"But someone's telling me there's another way. Can't you hear it?"

"I only hear water trickling out of that little hole up near the ceiling," Pippa said.

"That's it!" I said emphatically. "That's the right way out."

"Oh definitely," Raj said. "It looks like a good way out to me— a tiny black hole to nowhere versus a path down to the school. I know which one I'd choose." He started forward again.

I managed to grab his pajama jacket this time. "No, Raj, I'm sure of it. We're meant to go up. It's the only safe way out. That way's a trap."

"Who's telling you this?" Raj asked suspiciously. "It's probably that One bloke. He's sending you straight to him."

"No." I shook my head violently. "I'm sure."

"I don't know, Addy," Pippa said. "I don't hear anyone telling me anything. And I rather agree with Raj. It does look like the school down below. If they are still guarding that cave at the other side of mountain maybe we'll have a good head start."

Twig stood there and said nothing. I couldn't even tell them what I was feeling. It wasn't exactly a voice, it was almost as if I was being dragged on an unseen rope. We stood facing each other, until finally I said, "Okay. Well, I'm going to climb up to that hole. You can do what you like."

I walked over to the cave wall, acting braver than I felt, and started to haul myself up. "Child, this way." I heard a whisper in my mind at exactly the same time as an image flashed into my brain: a large gray hound waiting in the woods below that exit from the cave.

"Come on," I hissed. "The Rancurs have found us."

"I'm following Addy," Twig said. "I reckon she knows what she's doing."

Raj and Pippa peeped out of the cave just in time to see the monstrously-elongated shadow of a huge dog thrown by the moonlight across the grass. I heard Pippa gasp and run over to me, scrambling like crazy to climb up the rock wall to reach me.

"Sorry, Addy. I guess you were right," Raj said.

"Okay, here goes nothing." I took a big breath as I readied myself to climb into the hole. I hadn't told Raj but I really hated small spaces, too, and I hated darkness. I would have said that this was my nightmare scenario, if I hadn't been living through a lot of nightmares recently. But we had no choice. The Rancurs had found the entrance to the cave. I got down on my knees and went into the hole. It was cold, wet and slippery and completely dark and I could feel the ceiling scraping the back of my head, sending icy drips down my back. Even worse, it got narrower rather than larger in the first few feet and there was no way I could have made myself go forward if the others hadn't been behind me.

"Go faster," came Pippa's panicked voice. "I think they've come into the cave."

"I can't," I hissed back. There was no longer space to crawl. I had to inch forward on my belly into the pitch blackness. As I went on, the thought formed itself in my mind that it would be impossible to go backward if we had to. I began to wonder whether Raj was right and it was The One who had led us into a trap.

Then I froze as a howl echoed very close by. A Rancur was in the cave. Panic made me wiggle and claw my way forward with renewed effort, not noticing how the stone scratched my arms and legs. How much longer can I keep this up, I wondered. How much further do we have to go?

At that moment hands grabbed at my outstretched arms and I was yanked out of the hole like a cork from a bottle.

THE PEOPLE OF THE CAVE

A hand came over my mouth, as I tried to scream and a voice whispered in my head, "You're safe here. Don't speak. And we can't use our minds or The One will hear us."

I heard the sounds of Raj and Pippa and Twig also being pulled out of the narrow passage. I heard the soft footsteps of other people in the cave. They must have whispered to the others because neither Raj, Twig nor Pippa made a sound.

Then we were running through complete darkness. A person held my arms on each side. They didn't have to tell me why we were running. I would have run twice as fast to get away from those Rancurs. A woman's hair whipped against my face. It had a sweet smell. 'Who are you?' I thought.

But the woman didn't answer. She put a finger to my lips.

Suddenly I was bundled onto what felt like a wooden platform. "Don't worry, we've got you," came the soft voice in my ear and then I was hurtling downward, so fast that my breath was taken away. Was I falling? The sensation went on and on until I realized—I was on a long slide.

After what seemed like forever I came shooting onto a bed of soft rags at the bottom of the slide and tumbled over. More hands helped me to my feet. Behind me I heard Raj yelling "Whoohoo!" as he came hurtling down.

"We have four of them. They're safe," I heard the words in my head. The cave was dimly lit although I could see no torches and there were hooded figures all around us. We stood in front of a rock wall. Suddenly one of the group held up his hands and a huge boulder rolled to one side. Then hands took mine again and led me forward. A faint light glowed, showing us to be in a rock chamber. As the boulder rolled back into place the light grew and I stood blinking. Green robed figures surrounded us. "Welcome,

welcome." The words were said softly, gently. Hands touched us and I heard the words "Our children, our children" whispered around. But I hardly noticed this because I was standing and staring in awe. I knew that we were deep in a mountain but the immense chamber was bathed in soft daylight. There was the sound of running water and tall trees grew up to the ceiling. Some of them resembled the tree that grew in Miss Rorrim's tower. Vines twined and flowers bloomed.

"Is this place magic?" Raj asked.

The occupants laughed. "We have Whisperers among us," a soft voice said.

"Whisperers, what's that?"

"You don't know the seven powers?" The woman looked perplexed. "But you are surely Fareeth like us. You were going to be Conformed. You answered the call and came here."

"Addy answered the call. She was the only one who heard you," Raj said.

"But you all heard us speaking up above in the cave. We were mind-speaking and you heard us, apparently."

"I suppose we did," Raj said. "Cool."

"Don't overwhelm them. Let them sit and recover. They have come from a great ordeal." An old man with long gray hair braided over his shoulders beckoned us over to him. "Come, my little ones. Sit down. You are safe and welcome here. Not even the mind of that creature who calls himself The One can probe through this much solid rock. Bring them something to eat and drink."

We were led to a stone bench, liberally piled with soft pillows. Raj grimaced as he walked.

"You are hurt," one of the men said.

"I had to run barefoot," Raj said. "I reckon I picked up a thorn or two."

The man examined his feet. "Not very pleasant," he said. "We must do something about that." He put his hands on Raj's feet.

"That tingles," Raj said, then he looked down. His cuts and thorns were gone. His feet looked perfect.

"How did you do that?" he asked.

"I'm a Healer. We have this skill."

"It that one of the powers?" I asked.

"It is," the old man said. "Now eat and drink. There will be time for talking later."

A tray was brought to us with fruits, fresh bread, honey and water.

"Our fare has been reduced to this, I'm afraid," the woman who carried the tray said. She looked hard at me as she handed me a cup. I felt a strange sense of recognition. I had seen this woman before.

"Which settlement did you come from?" the woman asked me.

"I didn't come from any settlement," I said.

"I did," Twig chimed in, now fully revived from her scare. "I came from settlement 125, up by the lake. But I suppose I'll never be able to go back there now."

"Not as long as Grymur and his henchmen rule the land," the old man said. "But you are safe with us now. We can help you. We can bring out your powers and who knows, one day things may change. Grymur can't live forever."

"He would like to," one of the men muttered. "Don't they say that the powers he takes during each Conformation make him stronger and prolong his life?"

"As long as he can't take the power of Tentis, he can never live forever," the old man said.

"Excuse me," Pippa interrupted. "Twig can stay here but we can't. We have to get back to the school as quickly as possible."

"You want to go back to the school?" the old man asked incredulously. "To that accursed place?"

"Not that horrible school. No – our normal lives – in the real world – in our time or place or whatever it is ... where there is no One –" Pippa struggled to explain.

"We came here through a mirror," I explained. "From our world."

There was a gasp from the people around them.

"They have come from the other side."

"Then a portal must have opened up again."

"You know who they must be, don't you?" The woman knelt beside me. Hands reached out from all sides to touch us.

I MEET THE GOOD GUYS

"You are our children," Someone dared to speak the words. Faces smiled down at us, looking at us with longing.

"Your children?" I asked.

"Every since Grymur took over our world and we had to go into hiding our children have not been safe," someone explained. "Those accursed Rancurs were trained to smell out the blood of children, and it didn't seem right for a child to grow up hidden in these caves, never seeing the light of day. So we put them through the portal and gave them a chance at a normal life in your world. Some of our folk had gone through and they received the babies on the other side and made sure they went to good homes. Until now none have returned. We didn't know if that was because the portals had all closed, or that nobody had strong enough powers to come through a portal."

"I don't understand," said Raj. "You have incredible powers. We would call it magic in our world. Why don't you fight against Grymur?"

"His are so much stronger than ours," the old man said. "He stole the powers from the whole council of seven, except for those of his sister. And he has surrounded himself with Fallon Gwyn who were once Fareeth like us, but have been taught to use their powers for evil. They would kill or conform all of us and then all hope would be lost. But you must have great powers if you have come here from the other side."

"Then how come babies could be put through?" Raj asked. He was clearly enjoying himself now that something beyond his scientific knowledge was involved.

"It seems to be different for babies. Their innocence means that they pass through with ease. But after that, the older you get the stronger the power you must have to come through," the old man said. "You may be the ones we have been waiting for. We have hoped and dreamed for a long time for ones like you. Why don't you stay? Your powers could one day help us to overthrow Grymur."

"They should go back. They'll be safer on the other side," one of the men said. "If Grymur knows they have come through, he'll surely want them captured."

"If you came through a portal you should be able to go back through it," a woman added. "You will need to go back to the same place. Where was the portal?"

"In the haunted hallway ... at our school." I said. "It came through to another hallway at the school here."

"Then we must get them back there." The woman turned to the old man. "We can't keep them here, Lord Madog."

"No, you're correct as usual, Eirwen. We don't have that right. And they have much to learn that we can't teach them. If they choose to come back later, it must be their own free choice." He turned to us. "This school of yours on the other side. Will it help you develop your powers?"

"I don't know," Raj said, looking at us. "It's run by two women, called Miss Neves and Miss Rorrim, but we don't know if they're on your side or not. They may be working for Grymur.'

"Miss Neves? Rorrim? These names are not known to us," Lord Madog said, looking around for confirmation. "Yet you still want to go back?"

I thought about this. I didn't really have anywhere that I belonged in my world so would I be happier among these kind and gentle people? But while I was still forming this thought Pippa said, "It's our world. Our whole lives are there. And our families. I don't want to live in a cave. I want to ride my horses and do all the things kids do. I want to grow up normal."

"Of course you do," one of the women said. "We'll make sure you get back."

"But the Rancurs know we're here," I said. "Aren't we pretty much trapped here?"

"There is a shortcut to the school," one of the men said. "Not for the fainthearted, but it may be your best chance. But you can't tackle it in the dark."

"They will rest here and leave at first light," the old man said. "They will need all their strength."

"This fruit is delicious," Twig said, eating greedily. "What is it called?"

"Apples," one of the women said, laughing. "Did you not have apple trees in your settlement?"

"We never see much fruit," Twig said, "Unless we find blackberries in the forest in summer. Usually it's mainly root vegetables and sometimes beans and peas in summer."

"Such a shame. Gallia used to be a land of plenty—rich orchards, fields of grain, cows and sheep ..."

"Why is that?" I asked. "Is the land no longer fertile?"

"There are no more Whisperers," the old man called Lord Madog said. "In the old days there were Fareeth in every village. There was someone to make the plants grow, to talk with the animals, to provide everything that was needed. The people with no powers grew lazy and relied on us for everything. When Grymur tried to kill all the Fareeth and drove us into hiding, our skills went with us. Gallia is now a sorry place, so I hear."

"What exactly are these powers you talk about?" Raj asked. "I've heard you mention whisperers and healers. What else?"

"Have you not been taught anything of your heritage?" Madog asked.

"Nothing at all. We just arrived at Red Dragon Academy and ...

"Your school is called 'Red Dragon Academy?'" Madog looked startled and pleased. "Then I think we do right to send you back there. The Red Dragon is the symbol of all who fight against Grymur."

"Good to know." Raj seemed impatient. "But the powers we might have are ...?

"There are seven powers of the Fareeth," Madog said. "Whisperers can communicate with plants and animals. They can make living things grow and flourish.

"Travelers can make themselves and objects travel."

Raj started to say something then shut up again.

"Singers can sing things into being."

Pippa and I looked at each other and said, "Celeste."

"Healers can heal by touch, Seers can look into the future and Dreamwalkers can communicate with others through their dreams."

"That's only six," Pippa said.

"Ah yes. The last power is secret and not possessed by many.

We do not speak of it."

He was silent for a moment.

"How was Grymur able to take over if you had all these powers?" Pippa asked.

Madog sighed. "We lived so long in peace. We had all we wanted. We had never used our powers to harm another creature. When Grymur turned on us we had no way to defend ourselves."

"So who was this Grymur then?" Raj asked.

"Grymur was young and ambitious and possessed exceptionally strong powers. He and his twin sister Tentis showed amazing ability from the day they were born. They were taken to Caer-Eira and trained by the best minds in Gallia. He was elected to the Council of Seven at a young age. It seems that even then he was plotting to destroy the rest of the council. He trapped them, one by one, tortured and killed them. And in the moment before dying, he stole their powers." He paused and looked up at us. "All but one. The Lady Tentis, his sister. Her body was never found and it has always been believed that she went through to the other side. We have not heard from her for many years. She may still live. So you see, he never got the last power. His domination over death will never be complete."

My eyes were nodding shut as he spoke. Lord Madog looked at me kindly. "You need to sleep. We will leave you in peace. Take them to the chamber of rest."

We were led through to a long chamber, lined with little stone beds cut into the rocks on which quilts and pillows were piled. The same woman took me. As she tucked me in she looked down at me. "I have dreamed of doing this for years," she said. "When I put my daughter through the portal I never dreamed I would see her again, but I never ceased to hope."

"Wait," I said. "Are you saying that you're my real mother?"

She was looking at me with soft gray eyes. "I would like to believe so. But of course I have no proof. You are about the right age for my daughter and you resemble my younger sister who was conformed by that evil person. And you heard my voice when you were in danger, didn't you? You called for me and I answered."

"Yes," I said slowly. "I heard you."

I sat there, looking at her with her gentle face and her long silky hair and all I could think was that my real mom had lived in California and run with me on the beach and made me chocolate chip cookies. After everything else I wasn't ready to have another mother. "My mom was the best," I said. "We had such good times together."

"You'll go back to her?" I heard the wistfulness in her voice.

"She died. A little while ago."

She nodded as if she understood. "Then you need time to grieve. It is enough for me to know you are safe back in your world. Maybe one day in the future you will choose to come back to us."

She wanted me to say something, but I couldn't think of any words. All I could think was that I wanted to go home, but I didn't know where home was any more. I felt tears welling up in my eyes.

"I'm sorry," I said. "This is all too much to take in. I guess I'm not ready for another mother yet."

"Don't cry. I do understand how hard it is for you. It's hard for me, too. But I'm so thrilled to see what a lovely young woman you are." She leaned over and kissed me gently on the forehead. I felt the sensation of the soft hair and savored its sweet smell. I tried to remember if I'd felt this before.

"My name is Eirlys. May I know yours?"

"Addy," I said. "Short for Addison."

"This name is unknown to me. Is it usual in your world?"

"No, not very usual. My mom was an artist. She liked unusual things."

"Ah. Then our people chose well for you." She smiled, such a sad smile. Part of me wanted to hug her, but part of me still found it hard to believe that I was from this place and that this woman had once held me in her arms.

She stroked my hair. "You're tired. Sleep well now," she whispered. Then she was gone.

I TRY NOT TO THINK TOO LOUDLY

I was flying. I was soaring up over the mountains again and I knew that I must make a choice. One direction led back to my own world and safety, the other led to the mountains over which storm clouds were gathering. But a sweet voice was singing to me in those mountains. Out beyond was an ocean and for a moment I thought I saw a figure walking along the beach. Her blonde hair blew out in the wind. "Mom!" I called and tried to fly down to her. "Mom, wait, I'm coming. Don't go."
Suddenly I was held in a beam of light.

"My little Dreamwalker," said a voice I recognized only too well. "A fine dance you have led me, but it was pointless to run and hide. Your power is no match for mine. Now you will come with me to the palace and you will belong to me."
Slowly I felt myself dragged downward into the storm clouds. I fought with all my being. "No!" I shouted and tried to wake myself up. "Help me, somebody help me."
Then suddenly I was standing in a cave. Beside me was a tall woman wearing a green robe. At her throat was a pin in the shape of a red dragon. And she held two little girls by the hand. Before them was a crystal clear pool. The woman smiled at me. "Come with us," she said. The older of the girls reached out her hand. I took it and we jumped into the water. I opened my eyes. I was lying in the dim light of the cave. Several of the Fareeth were standing around me.
"You cried out in your sleep," one of them said.
"He was coming after me again," I said, shuddering at the thought. "He had trapped me in a light beam. He would have gotten me this time, but a woman came to help me."
"What woman?"
"She was tall and beautiful. She wore a long green robe like

yours and she was holding two little girls by their hands. Then I held their hands and I stepped into a pool of water and I was safe."

"The Lady Tentis." The words were whispered among the Fareeth. "She went through."

Suddenly something struck me. "That pool we passed in the cave. Was that the pool?"

"It used to be a portal, yes," someone said, "but it closed long ago. If the portal is now at the school, it has moved there and that's where you must go."

I didn't want to go back to sleep. I went with the Fareeth to sit by the fire in another small chamber. Lord Madog joined us. "You met Grymur in your dream?" he asked.

I nodded. "I've met him before in my dream. He's been trying to capture me."

"He would. He didn't believe there were any more Dreamwalkers in our world. He's afraid of you."

"Of me? What can I do?"

"Dreamwalking is a strong power, young lady. When you've learned to harness it, you'll be a formidable foe. No other power can move so easily through place, through time, come and go across the universe. Other powers can make and heal. You can communicate, search the innermost thoughts of others, and when developed to full strength yours is the power to control lesser minds." I thought of that guard at the castle and how he had repeated what I had told him. Did I really have that power in me? Lord Madog looked up, as if he could see the sky and not the roof of a cave. "Dawn will be coming soon. If you are going, you must leave us."

The others were awakened and fed.

"If you're still sure you wish to go back, we will take our leave of you," Madog said.

I ran over to Twig and hugged her. "Stay safe," I whispered. "I'll miss you, but I'm glad you're here."

"I hope we meet again, Addy," Twig said.

"I hope so, too." I stood holding her hands, looking at her sad, funny face.

I turned to Lord Madog as a thought struck me. "How come Twig came from a settlement? Isn't Twig one of your children, too? Isn't she a Fareeth like us?'

"In the old days there was no such thing as Fareeth and non-

Fareeth," the old man said. "Children with powers were born to ordinary families, then they were taken to be educated in the Crystal City so they could go back to help their communities. Grymur can try to stamp out the Fareeth but new children will be born with powers, just as they always have been."

"Come. Dawn is breaking. We must go now. I am ready to lead you," one of the men called from the doorway.

I looked around for Eirlys, the woman who thought she might be my mother. I saw her standing in the shadows, watching with a wistful smile on her face. I went over to her and hugged her. "Don't worry about me. I'll be fine," I said. "And I will come back some day. I promise."

Eirlys hugged me fiercely. "May the Power of Seven be with you, my child," she whispered.

Then we left the great chamber behind and began to climb a long staircase.

"I'm sorry, there is no easy way up, unless you are all Travelers," the man said. "I hope you have strong legs."

"Did you make all these chambers and stairs in the mountain?" Pippa asked.

"This used to be a gold mine long ago," the man said. "Back in the days when our people still made things. We have merely adapted it to live in. We have other entrances but they would be watched. This one should be safe enough."

We climbed higher, our legs beginning to ache. "We must now be silent and try not think of anything other than climbing this staircase," the man said. "The One will be trying to pick up our thoughts."

"I'll try not to think too loudly," Raj said. We turned to glare at him and he grinned.

When we thought our legs wouldn't go another step, through the darkness we saw a sliver of light shining down on us from high above. Rocks were piled ahead of us as if there had been some kind of collapse. Above the rocks was an opening big enough for us to climb out.

"May the Power of Seven be with you," the man said, putting his hand onto each of our heads in turn. "I must leave you here. Grymur cannot know there are Fareeth in this mountain, so you must go on alone. You will see the school down below you." And he melted away into darkness. Then we were alone.

SURF'S UP

Raj was already beginning to scramble over the rocks toward the light. I climbed after him. Some of the rocks were loose and we slithered and stumbled as we went higher and higher. The patch of light had grown brighter. At last we squeezed through a narrow crack and found ourselves looking out over mountains and steep valleys, bathed in the soft gray light of dawn. We could see the towers of the school barely visible through the mist in the valley below.

"Oh great. This looks really inviting," Pippa said, clambering out to join us. Below us the mountainside had torn loose. An almost vertical sheet of loose rock plunged several hundred feet to the tree line.

"Would you two be quiet," I whispered. "We're not supposed to speak. There's the school right there."

"How do you plan to get down?" Raj said. "I know I flew once, but I'm not inclined to see whether I can repeat it here."

"I'm thinking all that stuff is loose," I said. "If we just sat on it, it would take us all the way down the mountain."

"Oh brilliant. And crash into trees if we didn't break out legs and arms first."

"I think we could do it," I said. "I used to surf all the time when I lived in Santa Cruz. This would be just like riding a wave."

"Only this is a little harder than water if we fall," Raj pointed out.

"And where do we find surf boards?" Pippa asked.

"We'll try and sit on a flattish rock," I said.

"Addy, I think you're totally mad," Raj said.

"No, you don't understand," I said. "I think this is what we're meant to do."

"The One wants us to do this, I'm sure," Raj said. "That way we break our bloody necks and he doesn't have to bother to kill us."

"I'm going to try it," I said defiantly. I lowered myself carefully down from the little ledge where we stood. The hillside started to move as soon as my feet touched it. "No, Addy!" Pippa yelled. But it was too late. I sat down heavily as the rocks started to slide, slowly at first and then gathering momentum. Soon I was flying down the mountain with small stones bouncing around me. The wind in my face made me gasp. I felt half-scared, half-excited, just as I had done when I rode a particularly big wave, or when I rode the dragon in my dreams.

The forest was rushing up to meet me and I realized I had no way of making myself stop. The others had been right. If I met a large rock or a tree trunk, I'd be done for. I stuck out my legs and tried to dig in my heels to slow myself down. The trees were way too close now.

Suddenly I was in a patch of tall grass and bushes. A large rhododendron bush loomed directly ahead of me and I was catapulted into it. I felt branches tearing at me but then miraculously I was held by the bush. As I pulled myself free Raj came hurtling toward me, his mouth open in what was either terror or excitement. I grabbed at his pajama top and was almost jerked off my feet as I dragged him to a stop.

"That was wicked," he said, scrambling to his feet. "I'd always wanted to fly and now I've tried it twice. Here comes Pepper." We moved to intercept Pippa as she came flying toward us.

"We made it. Nothing broken," Pippa said as she stood up. "Now all we have to do is get through the forest to the school without one of the Rancurs seeing or smelling us."

"Piece of cake," Raj said dryly. "Although after that ride down the mountain, I doubt that anything will seem too scary any more."

"You're right," Pippa said. "If we can survive that, we can survive anything."

A howl echoed somewhere far off to our right.

"Do you think they've spotted us?" Pippa whispered.

"Smelled us, more likely, if they can smell fear," Raj said. "Come on, let's get out of here quickly."

We plunged into the forest. At this level it was more open with oak and beech trees, the last of their leaves clinging brown and golden to their branches. Great carpets of dead leaves lay underfoot. We ran through these, glancing around nervously from time to time. Then we caught a glimpse of the towers of the school ahead of us.

"There it is," I called gleefully. "We made it!"

"And they shut up the school, didn't they? With any luck there will be nobody there," Pippa said.

"What do you mean, they shut the school?"

"It had something to do with the harvest. All the kids were either going to be conformed or going home," I said.

"So they open it when they get a new batch?" Raj asked.

"I've no idea," I said. "And what's more I don't want to know. I have no wish to visit this school ever again."

We came out of the forest. The huge building loomed up ahead of us, looking as gloomy and foreboding as the first time I'd seen it in our world with Aunt Jean. Nothing moved.

"Which entrance should we try, do you think?" Pippa asked.

"They locked the main gate, didn't they?" I said. "But there was that small doorway that led into the lower level near the Go-Around."

"What's a Go-Around?" Raj asked.

"Don't ask. You don't want to know," Pippa and I said in unison.

"But I do want to know, or I wouldn't have asked," Raj said.

I shot him a look and he shut up.

"All right. Let's try that door then," Pippa said. "We have to come out into the open whichever door we are going to try."

We were just about to leave the safety of the forest when the clouds parted and the first rays of the sun hit the castle. We said, "Oh," in unison and stepped back. The sun had glinted from the helmets of Fallon Gwyn who were stationed around the castle, guarding each of the doors.

BETWEEN A RANCUR AND A FALLON GWYN

"There's no way we could reach any of the doors without their seeing us," Raj said. "It's hopeless."

The sun disappeared again and we stood in the gloom of the trees, not sure what to do next.

"Well, we can't just stand here, waiting for the Rancurs to find us," Pippa said irritably.

"So we'll just walk out and give ourselves up then, shall we?" Raj countered.

"Don't be silly," Pippa said.

"Wait, I've got an idea," I said. "When I was here before once I went out through the courtyard where the students were gardening, and I found Twig had escaped by climbing up a tree. At least, she'd climbed the wall to get into the tree and she was hiding up there."

"So what you're saying," Raj said, "is if we could find that particular tree, then we might be able to climb down into the courtyard that way."

Pippa nodded. "They'd never look for us inside because the main gate is locked."

"It's worth a try," Raj agreed. "So where was this tree and what did it look like?"

"Like a big tree," I said.

"Oh, that's really helpful."

"An oak, I think. And it would have been at the back of the castle where there is a wall between the two wings—the way we go to the riding stables in our world."

"All right. Let's go," Pippa said.

We followed the wall around the castle grounds, looking up at the building from time to time and judging where we were. At last we came to the area between the two wings.

"Somewhere here," I said. "It grew close to the wall and one branch actually grew over the courtyard. We looked at one tree after another. Let me tell you, trees start to look all alike after a while. Then I saw it.

"This is it! I remember that big knothole as I was climbing down." I hauled myself up the trunk and onto the first big branch.

"It is the right one," I whispered down to them. "I can see into the courtyard and it's empty. Come on."

Raj climbed up after me and Pippa was just about to follow when there was a snarl and a huge shape leaped out of the forest. Pippa screamed and fought to climb higher. Raj and I reached down our hands to her. Pippa kicked wildly at the Rancur as its jaws snapped shut. Raj and I pulled frantically. There was a ripping sound and Pippa slithered up onto the branch, leaving the hound with part of her robe in its mouth.

"Come on, higher," Raj pleaded. "Quick."

We hauled ourselves up higher until we reached the branch that stuck out over the school wall. I was having trouble climbing, I was shaking so badly. The Rancur stood below the tree and began to howl. It was answered by other howls in the wood.

"Well, I guess there couldn't be a clearer way of advertising that we're here," I said, peering nervously through the dense woodland and expecting to see white horses at any second. "I wonder how long it will take those Fallon Gwyn to find us."

We crawled cautiously forward along the branch. The Rancur stood below, still howling. When we reached the point where we were directly over the wall, we lowered ourselves onto it, and then climbed down, hidden from the buildings by the big bush that grew there.

"If my dad could see me now," Raj said as he dropped to the ground. "He was always complaining that I spent too much time with books and computers and I didn't do enough outdoor stuff."

"Now all we have to do is find a way into one of the buildings," Pippa said.

"Before those guards get here," Raj reminded her. "Which involves a certain degree of haste, I suspect."

"No kidding." She gave him a withering look. "I was planning to do my hair first."

"This way," I said. "We can get to that wing of the castle hidden by that row of bushes. I did it once before." We moved forward, ducking low, until we reached the closest wing of the castle. The first door we tried was locked. So was the next door and the next. The windows were barred.

"There doesn't appear to be any way in," Raj said.

"You wouldn't like to try and make another key appear in your pocket, would you?" Pippa asked.

"I didn't make it appear," Raj said. "We just made it move somehow."

"If we could climb up to the second floor, maybe we could smash a window," I suggested. "There are windows without bars up there."

"Is one of your powers to turn into a fly?" Raj asked.

"No!"

"You'd have to be some climber to get up that wall," Raj said. "Those bricks are very well laid. It's completely smooth."

"Well, what do you suggest then?" I snapped, feeling close to tears.

Raj was staring at the dragon fountain in the middle of the courtyard. It was exactly the same as the one in our world, except that it had been neglected and was old and crumbling. Ivy grew up over it. You could no longer tell that the central figure had been a dragon and some of the mythical beasts were now headless.

"If all we have to do is see our reflections, then maybe we could see them in the water of the fountain," he suggested.

"The fountain is splashing," Pippa said. "The water wouldn't be still."

"If we could find a way to turn it off?"

"I don't see how it would work. We have to go through, like through a mirror."

"We can't get at the mirror, can we?" Raj said impatiently. "And if the portal is somehow a chink in the space/time continuum, then maybe anything reflective within its boundaries ... This fountain is quite close to the haunted hallway."

"Oh why not," Pippa snapped, the fear and frustration showing on her face. "It's worth a try. Anything's worth a try at this point."

"The fountain must turn off somewhere," Raj said. "Start looking. You take the right wing, Addy. Pippa take the left and I'll go along the wall."

We split up, moving along the walls and searching behind bushes and plants. At last Raj shouted, "I've found it, I think. But it's all rusted over. Come and help me turn it."

We ran over to a faucet that was brown with rust. Try as we might, we couldn't move it.

"Oh, this is so stupid," I exploded with frustration and fear. "It's hopeless."

"We can't give up," Pippa said. "When all else fails, try brute force." She picked up a rock that lay nearby and struck at the tap with all her might. The top of the tap came flying off. Water spurted out in a great jet.

"Oops," Pippa said. She looked up with a grin. "That was rather satisfying," she added.

"Look, I think you've done it. Good job, Pepper," Raj shouted.

He ran over to the fountain that was now just trickling down. We joined him as the last drops died away and peered down into the water.

"It's no use. The sun has to be shining to create a reflection," Raj said. "It's not high enough in the sky yet."

Suddenly the howling began again. There was a hissing, whooshing noise, like a jet plane flying past and white-cloaked figures appeared in the courtyard. The main gate burst open and ranks of Fallon Gwyn rushed in, their weapons drawn.

"There they are. Seize them," a voice shouted.

The sun blazed suddenly, making the robes and helmets dazzling white.

"Now!" Pippa shouted.

I looked into the water. My face, blurring a little as the breeze stirred the surface, looked back at me. 'It's not going to work,' I thought. 'It can't work.' Then the water was glowing, crackling green and I was falling forward, the water rushing up to meet me and …

Suddenly hands were grabbing me, hauling me out of the water.

SAFE AT LAST?

"**N**o!" I shouted, fighting to break free.

"It's all right. We've got you," a voice said.

I looked up into Sam's freckled face. "Out you come." He dragged me to my feet. Water was dripping from my hair and running down my face.

"I don't know what you lot thought you were doing," Sam said. "We've been looking all over for you."

"Why are you swimming in 'ze fountain? Have you lost your minds?" Celeste demanded, helping Pippa to clamber out of the water. "The whole school has been searching for you. I missed my music lesson and you are playing at mermaids?"

"It was Kobi 'ere who kept insisting that we look in the fountain," Sam said, glancing up at Kobi. His normally serious face was beaming with delight.

"And I was right. We found you," he said. "I knew we would. I just knew it."

I saw Gwylum standing shyly in the background. I caught his eye and he grinned with relief. "We couldn't think where you'd gone. Did you run away? Miss Neves thought you might be lost."

"What were you doing in that fountain anyway?" Sam asked. "Not looking for more jewels, surely?"

"It's a long story," Raj said. He looked up at the sound of running feet.

A group of students came into the courtyard, led by Barry, the head boy.

"Miss Neves," he shouted, "they're here. They came back. We've got them."

The courtyard was full of green uniforms. Miss Neves pushed her way through the crowd.

"Addy, Pippa, Raj. You came back. We were so worried."

"We pulled them out of the fountain," Sam said as the students crowded around.

"The old rumors must be true about the secret passageway from the fountain to the forest," Barry said. But he stared at us as if we had just appeared out of thin air.

"They must indeed," Miss Neves said, looking hard at us. "Is that what happened, Pippa? You ran away into the forest?"

I stared at Miss Neves's calm gray eyes. "Yes," I said. "That's exactly what happened."

"And I found Pippa was missing and went to look for her, and Raj found I was missing and went to look for me," I said.

"In your pajamas?" one of the boys said, bursting out laughing.

"I didn't stop to think," Raj said blushing.

"The main thing is that you came back and you're safe and sound," Miss Neves said. "I can't wait to tell Miss Rorrim. Everyone, go and get ready for dinner."

I looked at Pippa and we turned to go with the other kids.

"Not you three," Miss Neves said. "I want you to come with me. Alice, Barry, please help me escort them to my study."

Miss Neves's bony hand gripped my arm tightly as she led me back towards the castle.

I glanced across at Pippa who was being led by Alice. Wild thoughts ran through my head. Who was Miss Neves? None of the Fareeth had heard of her. So whose side was she on? Would she make sure we were sent back again and handed over to The One? A thought came into my head. I didn't have to stay here. I could call Aunt Jean and ask to go to another school, an ordinary school, far far away from Red Dragon Academy and Gallia, a place where The One could never find me. And I'd be safe forever. The closer we got to Miss Neves's office the more afraid I felt.

Miss Neves opened the door to her office and ushered us inside. It looked warm and friendly and safe enough but I found I was still shivering with cold and fear. There was a fire in the grate and three of us crowded around it, leaving a trail of drips across the carpet.

"Thank you, Barry. Thank you, Alice. You may go." As the head boy and girl left, Miss Neves looked at the three of us appraisingly and sat down behind her desk. "Now the truth. Nobody chooses to crawl around in a fountain on a cold night. Please tell me exactly what happened and where you were."

Pippa and I exchanged glances.

"I'm sorry, Miss Neves. I ran away and got lost in the woods. Addy and Raj came to find me," she said.

"And your clothes?" Miss Neves asked looking at our torn gray robes.

"Um ... some kids in the forest beat us up and took our uniforms and, uh ... we found these robes on a clothesline." I blushed as I saw the incredulous look that Raj gave me. "They didn't want Raj's pajamas."

"Clothesline?" he mouthed at me.

"That's how Pippa got her bruised face," I went on hurriedly, trying not to look at Raj.

"I see. And when you got back to the school you decided to jump into the fountain, did you?" Miss Neves's expression gave nothing away.

"We were really hot," Raj said, shivering as he spoke.

It was silent in the office for a whole minute. Then Miss Neves spoke. "I don't think this tale bears any resemblance to the truth, do you?"

FINALLY, SOME ANSWERS

There was a long silence. A log crackled and spat in the fireplace, sending up sparks.

"Let me offer an alternate explanation," Miss Neves said at last, looking at Pippa. "When you ran away you found yourself in a strange place, a place with a different sort of life from the one you are used to. Very different indeed. A different world you might call it. Addy and Raj followed you to that place – in quite a hurry," she added, looking at Raj's pajamas. "They did not treat you well." She looked at Pippa's bruised face. "And you found a way to come back. A way that glowed green – and that led you back into our fountain. Am I correct?"

We were silent, staring down at the floor.

"I can see that you do not trust me. I imagine that something very bad happened to you there to make you afraid."

"Who are you, really? How do we know that you don't want to send us back there—to him?" Pippa blurted out bravely.

A tired smile crossed Miss Neves's face. "Ah, so that's what you think?"

We looked at each other and nodded.

"We don't know what to think," I said at last. "It's all been so horrible and frightening and confusing. We still don't understand. And we don't know whose side you're on."

"Of course you don't," she said. "You were exposed to this long before you were ready. Brought on by your own headstrong behavior, I might add, Philippa. But if you need any proof of which side I am on, you might consider my name."

"Neves? What does it mean?" Pippa asked. "The other Fareeth didn't seem to know it."

"No, it is not a Gallian name, it was designed for this world, as a clue," Miss Neves said.

Raj looked up, his face lit up. "I've got it," he yelled out. "It's a mirror world, right? Your name is Seven. And Miss Rorrim is really Mirror."

Miss Neves smiled. "Very good, Raj. And you should know by now that followers of Grymur are not allowed to use the forbidden number." She paused and sighed. "We also fled from the one you fear. Miss Rorrim and I came to this world the same way you did. We were just small girls at the time, younger than you. We had to leave our homes, our families and everything we knew. We were brought through to this world by a wise woman. The most powerful woman of our time—the Lady Tentis."

Suddenly my dream flashed into my mind. "I saw you leaving. Two little girls holding a woman's hand and jumping into a green pool of water."

"You saw us? In a dream?" Miss Neves looked at me with an interested smile. "Yes – that was Miss Rorrim and I. Grymur had taken control. He was trying to wipe out the Fareeth, so that there was no more resistance to him. He was especially keen to kill all Fareeth children—any child with powers was either killed or conformed. We were chosen because we had powers that were deemed strong enough to make it through a portal."

"You need strong powers to go through a portal?" I knew I shouldn't be interrupting but I couldn't help it.

Miss Neves gave me one of those stares that seemed to look right through me. "Very few of the Fareeth have the power to go through a portal. Except for babies, of course. They have an openness of mind and lack of memory that makes it possible for them to travel easily between worlds. We came through as ten- and twelve-year-olds. It was a risk, of course."

"A risk?" Raj demanded.

"If someone is brought through unwillingly it can break the mind." She paused again. "As we grew up more Fareeth put their young children through to save them. Our task was to provide this link between the two worlds." She looked from one of our faces to the next. "We have had little contact recently. We can no longer go through and no messages have come to us for a while. So Grymur still rules with an iron hand?"

"Grymur," Raj said. "That's The One, right? Everyone there is in his power."

"I was afraid that would happen. He already had great power when we left. That's why we tried to keep you from the other side when we realized that a portal might have opened again. You were not ready to face his world yet."

"So is it true," I asked. "We were those babies, put through from the other side?"

Miss Neves nodded. "There are others like us whose job is to watch over our children until the time is right. You were found and placed with kind families. We have watched your progress your whole lives. All three of you were born in that world."

"And we all have powers?" Raj asked and I could hear excitement in his voice.

Miss Neves nodded. "You couldn't have passed through a portal unaided unless your powers were very strong indeed. But before I tell you our story I want to hear yours." Miss Neves's eyes sought out each of ours. "You can trust me." Her voice spoke in our minds and her mouth didn't move. "Addy – I believe that the first part of the story belongs to you," she said out loud.

Slowly at first but then gathering courage I told her how I had stumbled through the mirror. Miss Neves interrupted at points asking for more details. When I had finished telling of my encounters with Twig, Pippa took over the story and then Raj. We all three combined in the last stages of our escape. When we were finished the tower room was silent.

"You did very well," Miss Neves said. "There are few adult Fareeth who would have come through that trial unscathed. I'm sure there are questions you'd like to ask me."

"So – you're really from that place?" Pippa asked.

"Its name is Gallia."

"I think you were smart not to go back," Pippa said. "It is a horrible place."

"I can't go back if I wanted to," Miss Neves said sadly. "I don't have the power any more. And it wasn't always a horrible place. When I was small it was a beautiful place full of life and love. Then The One took all the powers to himself and we had to flee."

"Wait a minute. You call it a place." Raj was frowning. "But what do you mean by that? I've been trying to figure it out scientifically. It can't be a different planet because the only way we could have gotten there so fast would be to travel at the speed of light and then when we came back we would all be a hundred years old. Is it a parallel universe because I read something like that in a science magazine, but I can't see how it would work, unless it's some distortion of string theory and ..."

"Raj!" Pippa and I said at the same time.

Miss Neves smiled. "I'm afraid I don't have the answers to your questions. I haven't found a scientific answer for the two worlds although I have found plenty of evidence that they do touch and that people have gone back and forth throughout history."

"Magic?" Pippa said.

"Through the Looking Glass," Raj said, a thoughtful expression on his face.

"Dragons," I added. "Is it something to do with dragons?"

Then I thought of all the questions I wanted answered. "I'm still not quite clear about these powers we're supposed to have, Miss Neves. They said I was a Dreamwalker and they talked about Whisperers but I'm not really clear about any of them. We can speak with a kind of weird mind reading, can't we?"

"Telepathy is a basic power of all Fareeth. We could all read thoughts and speak with our minds when I was a child. But there are seven powers of our people that once made our world the most wonderful place." She stared out of the window.

"Long ago," she said softly, "Gallia was a beautiful peaceful place. I can't be sure but I think some of this world's legends – of King Arthur and even the Garden of Eden – were told by people who had visited our world. Many people had the power to communicate with plants to ask them to grow well and with animals who were our friends; others could foresee disasters and make sure of our people's safety, to cure diseases, to walk in dreams, to travel and to sing things into being. In every generation seven of us arose who had these powers very strongly. They were taught by our elders to use their powers wisely and well and became the council that guided us. The Council of Seven. When I was a small child Grymur was on the Council of Seven. He was not satisfied being one of Seven. He wanted to rule alone, to be The One. He discovered a way to take the powers of the others on the Council—through trickery and torture. From what you have told me – he is afraid of anyone else who shows any powers. This Conformation is truly terrifying. I had never heard of anything like that."

"And you knew we were from that place?" Raj asked. Miss Neves nodded. "So you tricked us into coming to this school."

"Not tricked. Invited. You all accepted the invitation."

"Then why didn't you just tell us all of this when we arrived?"

THE POWER OF SEVEN

"Would you have believed me?" Miss Neves looked at Raj inquiringly.

"If you did that 'talk in my head' thing then I would have had to."

"I'm not so sure." Miss Neves paused." But there are other reasons. The One has tried to send spies to this world before. There might even be some of them in this school at this moment."

"But now we know the truth – what do you want us to do?" Raj persisted. "What kind of powers do we have? What do you want us to do with them?"

Miss Neves didn't answer directly. "Let me tell you a story. I'll make it about a scientist for your benefit, Mr. Puri." She gave him a slight nod. "A biologist was studying Monarch butterflies. He had raised some from larvae and watched them make their cocoons. As the first one emerged it thrashed around trying to break free of its cocoon. The scientist who was watching was afraid that it would not break free on its own and he helped it by breaking open the cocoon. The butterfly came out and spread its beautiful wings. But it never flew. What that scientist didn't know was that the struggle to get out of the cocoon is what pushes enough blood into the wings for the butterfly to fly. Without the struggle it will remain flightless forever."

She rose and began pouring cups of tea from an electric kettle in the corner. "Please pull chairs up to fire. I am sorry to keep you in your wet things. I had to be sure what had really happened to you before anything else. "She handed us the hot cups of tea which we sipped gratefully and then continued.

"Your powers are a natural part of you – as natural as flight is for a butterfly. And they will come out naturally in their own time. To tell you what I think I see would be to limit their growth. I will tell you this." She looked at Pippa, "Follow your instincts." And to me," Write down your dreams." And to Raj, "Practice your archery." She walked over to a closet on the far side of the office. "I am going to ask you not to speak to any of your fellow students about this. Their own powers must also come out naturally. They must not know about our world until the time is right."

"Are all the students at this school from Gallia?" Pippa asked.

Miss Neves laughed. "Oh no, my dear. Most of the students are not. We have to pay the bills you know. We are in most ways an ordinary boarding school. And those students who do not have your history must never know. I need your solemn word on that." She reached up and unpinned the brooch she wore on her lapel. "I must ask you to swear that you will divulge nothing of what happened to you to anyone outside of this room, or you may risk the future of our entire world. Do I have your word?"

We nodded.

"Then place your hands on the symbol of the Fareeth and say, 'I swear to divulge nothing of what I now know and have seen.'"

We put our hands one over the other. I felt a huge jolt of electricity rush up my arms and through my entire body as Miss Neves put her hand over ours.

"Whoa, blimey," Raj said, almost trying to jerk his hand away.

Miss Neves smiled. "I sense your powers really are strong," she said. "You obviously do, too. Now please make the oath."

"We swear to divulge nothing," we repeated together.

Miss Neves pulled a cardboard box from the closet and began taking pairs of shoes out of it – all identical Prada shoes. "If I confiscate any more shoes from Celeste I may open a boutique."

"So – you weren't giving them back?" Pippa gasped. "They were all new? How did she get them?"

"She made them, I presume. She doesn't realize she has the power yet, but it's clear that she has it."

"And the comforter on her bed?" Pippa said.

"And the necklace!" I said. "So Celeste really can make things appear by magic?"

"Sing them into being, you mean? It would appear that way." Miss Neves smiled. "But remember that you are not to tell her."

"Wait a minute," Raj said. "The seven impossible things—there were seven of us who heard Miss Rorrim's summons. The rest of those seven were the ones who found us. Does that mean something?"

"It may well do," Miss Neves said. "But we must remember our butterfly. We can only hope and wait."

Raj looked at Pippa and then at me. "Why are we here, exactly?" he said. "What do you want from us? Apart from gathering all the Fareeth in one place, that is."

"As to that, Mr. Puri, I want nothing from you other than making sure you achieve your full potential."

"You want to send us back there, don't you?" I said as the truth dawned on me. "You're training us to go back and defeat Grymur."

"You can't be serious," Pippa said. "I never want to go back to that horrible place again."

"Let me make it quite clear, Philippa," Miss Neves said. "Your lives and futures are your own. I have no hold over you. If you choose to write to your parents and ask to leave this school tomorrow I should not stop you. I should be incredibly disappointed as there are indeed seven of you and your powers are so strong. But the choice is yours."

Raj sneezed violently.

"I have kept you in your wet clothes for long enough. I apologize. Please go and change into some dry ones and I will have the uniforms that you lost replaced. Pippa – you may receive some unpleasantness from your fellow students who spent all day looking for you. Try to keep your temper. And I don't need to remind you of your oath. Suffice it to say that you tried to run away again, which is the truth."

"As if they would believe me." Pippa looked suddenly worried. "Did you call my dad? Is he on his way?"

"I spoke to your stepmother. I'll call again and sort everything out. Now off with you. Go and get out of your wet clothes. Ask Gwylum to get you another cup of tea from his mother so you don't catch cold."

The three of us walked up to the fifth floor dormitory. I was cold again now and my dripping robe clung to me. Raj kept sneezing. I couldn't think of a single thing to say. I had so many questions that all of them seemed to crowd each other out. I realized that I could have asked Miss Neves to call my Aunt Jean to come and take me away, but I hadn't done so.

As we reached the entrance to the dorms and Raj went toward the boy's rooms Pippa suddenly blurted out, "Listen. I never really thanked you. I got you into that mess and you were nice enough to come and save me ... thank you."

"No problem," said Raj and sneezed again. "I'm going to change and get that cup of tea from Gwylum." He pushed open the door to the boy's dorm, leaving Pippa and me alone.

"You're welcome." I said and I gave her a hug.

"You know what," Pippa said confidentially, "I'm really glad to find out that not all the students are from Gallia. I bet Angela isn't a Fareeth."

"That's what I thought, too." I grinned.

"Just wait until we develop our powers. Maybe we can do something terrible to her."

"Pippa! Remember the powers were only used for peace."

"Just kidding," Pippa said.

We looked at each other and exchanged a grin.

"Pippa, you're not planning to run away any more, are you?" I asked as we came up to our dorm room. "It wouldn't be the same without you."

Pippa shook her head. "No, I think I'll stick around for a while. I'm dying to find out what power I have."

We opened our door and went in. I opened my closet and laughed out loud. A new uniform was already hanging there with my name on it.

ABOUT THE AUTHORS

Rhys Bowen and C.M. Broyles are a mother-daughter writing team who both love fantasy. Rhys Bowen is a *New York Times* bestselling author of two adult mystery series—The Molly Murphy Mysteries and The Royal Spyness Mysteries—and the winner of multiple awards, including the prestigious Macavity Award. She formerly wrote bestselling young adult novels under the name Janet Quin-Harkin. C.M. Broyles has degrees in music and literature and has written background music for plays (winning an Arizona Tony award), a children's opera and numerous songs. This is her first venture into prose.

Visit Rhys at www.rhysbowen.com and on her Facebook page at www.facebook.com/rhysbowenauthor

DREAMWALKER

48578379R00158

Made in the USA
San Bernardino, CA
29 April 2017